...ncey Novel

TOUCH AND GO

The sloop and corvette were converging at great speed and Delancey could not but admire the lines and the rig of his opponent. She was a fine craft and her white sails curved beautifully against the dark grey clouds behind her, a graceful vessel but temporarily in the wrong navy. Even as he watched, regretting what had to come, there was a flash from the corvette's forecastle, a puff of smoke quickly dispersed downwind, a distant jarring sound and a splash in the sea between the two opponents. It was a sighting shot and proved what Delancey knew, that the enemy was out of range. He made another quick tour of the port battery, having a word with the men as he passed. They were tense now, each at his post, each gun captain with the lanyard in his hand . . .

by the same author
in Magnum Books

DEVIL TO PAY
– the first Richard Delancey novel

THE FIRESHIP
– the second Richard Delancey novel

C. Northcote Parkinson

TOUCH and GO

MAGNUM BOOKS
Methuen Paperbacks Ltd

For Ann

A Magnum Book

TOUCH AND GO
ISBN 0 417 02460 6

First published 1977 by John Murray Ltd
Magnum edition published 1978

Magnum Books are published by Methuen Paperbacks Ltd
11 New Fetter Lane, London EC4P 4EE

Made and printed in Great Britain by
Richard Clay (The Chaucer Press) Ltd
Bungay, Suffolk

Contents

Maps showing Richard Delancey's exploits appear at the back of the book.

CHAPTER ONE

The Merlin

'And a damned good riddance!' exclaimed Rear-Admiral Fothergill. He was tall, grey, elderly and spectacled, a man now chained to his desk who would never go to sea again. He peered short-sightedly at Hoskins, his flag-lieutenant, who was red-faced, portly and short of breath. He frowned now, his blue eyes protuberant and plainly puzzled.

'Sir?'

'I mean, Simpson quitting the *Merlin*. I could never stand the fellow. Always asking for shore leave, always sick, the sloop always under repair.'

'His marriage was rather recent, sir.'

'Was that the chief trouble? I supposed that he had made some prize-money and wanted to spend it.'

'That too, sir. His successor is unmarried, I believe.'

Hoskins checked the fact, glancing at one document among the sheaf he carried. Yes, he had been right. Was he becoming fussy and old-maidish, he wondered, thinking of flag-lieutenants he had known over the years.

'Thank God for that. Is he here in Gibraltar?'

'Yes, sir. He landed yesterday evening from the *Birkenhead* storeship. Captain Delancey is waiting now in the outer office.'

'Delancey? Never heard of him. Hand me the List.'

'He is not listed, sir.'

'His first command, eh? He's damned lucky, in that case, to be given the *Merlin*; and lucky, for that matter, to serve in the Mediterranean. Send him in, Mr Fulmer, and let's hope that he is an improvement on Simpson.'

The flag-officer, Gibraltar, had his office on the first floor of an old house overlooking the sunlit harbour. Only the marine sentry at the entrance distinguished this flat-roofed building from others in the same street. The place was plainly furnished, almost bleak, the whitewashed walls relieved only by the blue and gold of the naval uniforms. There was a quiet bustle of activity with the scratching of quill pens as letters were copied in triplicate, each clerk's copperplate handwriting as characterless as if each document had been printed. The clerks stood at tall desks with candles fitted for use after dark, the scratch of their quills making a background noise like the sound of insects in a tropical garden.

A minute later the Rear-Admiral had the newcomer in his presence; a weatherbeaten officer of middling height, something under forty years of age, with dark hair and deep blue eyes, a self-possessed man who was giving nothing away. He was sturdily built with a strong face, deeply lined for his age, his expression that of a man who had known adversity and disappointment. His uniform was spotless, kept for just such an occasion as this. Fothergill guessed that he would rarely look as smart as he did today. He had been and was still most probably, a poor man; no aristocrat, despite his name, and no ornament to the social scene. His letter of appointment and an accompanying letter of recommendation had been handed beforehand to the flag-lieutenant and now lay, opened, on his desk. After making his bow, Delancey stood at attention, his cocked hat under his left arm.

'Welcome to the Mediterranean, Captain. You will have heard, no doubt, that the *Merlin* is taking the British Consul back to Tangier. She should be here again in a few days. Please be seated while I read the letters you have brought with you.'

A few minutes passed in silence and Delancey looked about him. The naval headquarters building was old but largely rebuilt. Delancey guessed that it must have been damaged during the previous war, the new plaster contrasting with the old. A cupboard behind the Admiral's chair contained leather-bound folio letter books, marked 'In' on one shelf and 'Out' on the shelf below. There was a ceremonial sword hung from a nail and the door was held open by a cannon-ball. There were several engravings on display, one a coloured etching of

Admiral Rooke and two of them scenes of the great siege, both very stiff and formal. Neither artist nor engraver had been in battle, Delancey concluded, and neither could portray the action. As an amateur artist he wondered whether he himself could have done any better. He might have put more life into it – and more death for that matter – but how could any painting or print suggest the *noise* or the smell of powder? There had been no comparable bombardment since 1783. The great siege had ended with the conclusion of the war itself and it was now 1799, over six years since this new war had begun. As a youngster, seventeen years ago, he had felt that he was making history here, small as his contribution had been. And Gibraltar had of course been the setting for drama with its stage and backcloth, its galleries and pit. To make the most of a battle one needed an audience! He smiled faintly at this idea, turning his head away from the engravings. He saw then that the Admiral was no longer looking at the letter. His eyes were now on Delancey with perhaps a hint of amusement.

'Not a very accurate picture, I agree. Have you been here before?'

'Yes, sir.'

'Then you need no advice from me. I gather that you were last on the Irish station?'

'Yes, sir.'

'The *Spitfire* being your last ship?'

'Yes, sir.'

'Lost, but with no discredit to you. It seems to me that you are fortunate, promoted into a very fine sloop of eighteen guns, copied from the French corvette *Amazon* and built as recently as 1794. You should by rights have been given the oldest sloop in the service, laid down under George II, taken from the Dutch or built under contract in Bermuda. My own first command was a sloop launched in 1767, ready to sink if anyone so much as sneezed. Indeed, she was lost at sea under my successor, poor fellow. The *Merlin* is a very different sort of ship and you are lucky to have her. You are unmarried, I have been told. Is that true?'

'Yes, sir.'

'I'm glad to hear it. Married officers are always in port with mysterious defects and broken spars. A bachelor myself, my preference is for more active officers, especially in trade protection. Tell me, however, about the situation in Ireland. There was a French landing, I recall, on the west coast. How did the story end?'

'Well, sir, General Humbert landed at Killala with hardly more than a thousand men. He was to have been reinforced but Bompart's squadron, with troops embarked, was intercepted by Sir John Borlase Warren. Humbert took Castlebar and drove off the Kilkenny Militia but then came face to face with Lord Cornwallis. He had no choice after that and surrendered at Ballinamuck – '

'He surrendered *where*?'

'At Ballinamuck, sir. Irish place names are often rather uncouth. Had all the French troops, four thousand of them, landed at the same place and at the same time, the Irish might have joined them. There will be no rising now, though. Lord Cornwallis has thirty thousand men and the coasts are well patrolled by our cruisers. We should have no more trouble in that quarter.'

'So General Humbert achieved nothing, eh?'

'I wouldn't say that, sir. He broke up the Bishop of Killala's diocesan conference.'

'Did he, though? I should like to hear your story. Perhaps you would care to dine with me today?'

'With pleasure, sir.'

After Delancey had gone the flag-lieutenant produced for the Rear-Admiral a copy of a recent *Gazette*, brought by the *Birkenhead* along with the newspapers and the mail.

The Rear-Admiral read the gazette letter slowly and with gaining interest. Written by Captain Ashley and dated September 14th 1798, it described how the *Hercule* came into Killala Bay after Humbert had landed and after Savary's squadron had gone and went on to describe an operation which resulted in the total destruction of the *Hercule* and the *Spitfire* and ended with Ashley's words of highest commendation, recommending Delancey for promotion.

'You have read this?' the Rear-Admiral asked.

'Yes, sir,' replied the flag-lieutenant.

'Don't you find it almost incredible?'

'I think there is much to be read between the lines.'

'So there is, by God. But I know Ashley and would believe him. So did their Lordships. My conclusion must be that Delancey is an outstanding officer.'

'No doubt of it, sir.'

'Well, we must make him tell us the whole story.'

No attempt was made to extract the story until the Rear-Admiral's guests had reached their dessert, nor was Delancey very forthcoming even then. It was a small party, held at the Admiral's house, the other guests being Captain Price of the frigate *Cynthia* who was going home on promotion to command a ship of the line, a Colonel of Artillery, a Major of the Royal Marines, two gentlemen from the Dockyard and a doctor. Sitting at the head of his mahogany table, with a portrait of George II behind him, the Rear-Admiral did the honours with practised ease. The usual toasts were drunk, the last to the new captain of the *Merlin*. This was the cue for Delancey to hold forth but he did so very briefly.

'But look, Delancey, the story outlined in Captain Ashley's letter to the Commander-in-Chief is not easily understood. It seems that you attacked a French seventy four almost single-handed, blowing her rudder off before anyone could say "Mon dieu!" If it is as easy as that, why don't we all do it?'

The question, posed by Captain Price, was fair enough, but Delancey seemed to hesitate over his answer.

'I was very fortunate', he admitted finally, 'in finding the perfect target for a fireship attack. The chances against it are overwhelmingly adverse and the chance of a fireship being there when wanted is surely remote. But if you ask how the trick was done I can say no more than this: study how the stage conjuror deceives his audience! His secret is a simple one. At each moment he does something, ensure that the audience is looking at something else. Should you still think me clever, sir, I must remind you of two important facts.

First, I owed my life to a couple of seamen who chose to disobey my orders. Second, I had to sacrifice the wounded from my own ship, blown up in the *Hercule*.'

There was a minute's silence after this, broken by the Rear-Admiral who said:

'And that is the worst thing of all, paying in lives for what has to be done. . . . And now I want to hear about the Bishop of Killala!'

The dinner party passed off pleasantly and Delancey learnt, informally, what work awaited him. The Rear-Admiral took him aside afterwards and made his role sufficiently clear. The *Merlin* would be employed in convoy protection and would operate between Gibraltar and the Levant. There was a French army cooped up in Egypt since the Battle of the Nile but this would be none of his concern. His task would be to protect trade and deal with enemy cruisers, especially in the western half of the Mediterranean. French corvettes and privateers were numerous and enterprising and British merchantmen had to proceed in convoy under naval escort.

It would be his fate, he gathered, to plod endlessly back and forth between Gibraltar, Port Mahon, Malta, Palermo and Cyprus, with little chance of gaining distinction and still less of making prize-money. He would wear out his signal flags in urging merchantmen to make more sail and expend his powder in warning them to keep in formation. He would also have to take the blame when they ignored him and were captured. He was fortunate in his ship, as the Rear-Admiral repeated, but he would gain no credit, it seemed, and make no prize-money. Nor could he complain for he had much to learn, as he realised, and this was almost his first command.

Two days later Delancey stood on the King's Bastion and watched the *Merlin* come into the anchorage. With him were David Stock, volunteer (first class), Luke Tanner, coxswain, and John Teesdale, captain's steward; the men he had been entitled to bring with him from his last ship.

Stock, the shock-headed and snub-nosed son of the Bishop of Killala, was tongue-tied and shy, an eager but ignorant boy. Tanner was burly, taciturn, devoted to his captain and utterly reliable. Teesdale was a dark, thin-faced man, intelligent, sensitive and inclined to talk out of turn. He could always sense the trend of opinion on the lower deck. As steward he was excellent, a good cook and valet and yet known to be fearless in action.

Behind Delancey the Rock of Gibraltar reared up, yellowish-grey in the sunlight, its lower slopes hidden by white buildings. To left and right, facing the sea, were the fortifications, massively built and bristling with artillery. In front of him, beyond the bay, was the coast of Spain and far to his left, the coast of Africa. In the middle distance, ending her passage from Tangier, was the sloop *Merlin* with all her sails set before a stiff breeze from the Atlantic. She was a lovely ship, no doubt of that, and Delancey, watching her lean to leeward, noting the foam around her bows, found there were tears in his eyes. It was an odd weakness and one of which he was ashamed but he was applying his handkerchief to the lens of his telescope and was able to wipe his eyes while nobody was looking. His own ship, his to make or ruin, no mere fireship but a proper sloop of war. . . . He remembered that his duties included the education of young David Stock. Handing his telescope to the boy, he told him how to adjust it and then went on to instruct him:

'That is our ship, Mr Stock, the *Merlin*, a sloop of war. She has three masts, as you can see, and so is ship-rigged, just like a frigate. Had she only two masts she would be a brig but might still be rated as a sloop, smaller than a frigate but bigger than a cutter, which has only the one mast. Now can you tell me how she compares in size with a frigate?'

'She is smaller, sir, with eighteen guns to a frigate's thirty-two or thirty-six.'

'That is almost right. She rates as an 18-gun sloop but actually mounts twenty-four, sixteen 6-pounders on her main deck, six 12-pounder carronades on the quarterdeck and two more on the forecastle. She was built at Frindsbury, measures 425 tons and is just over 108 feet long on the gun deck. What we call a sloop, by the way, the French call a corvette. And how many men should there be on board her?'

'A hundred, sir?'

'A hundred and twenty-one in theory and much the same, I believe, in fact. And for what work is she designed?'

'Fighting French corvettes, sir, and capturing enemy merchantmen.'

'If we are lucky, Mr Stock! More of our effort will go into protecting our own merchantmen, you'll find.'

Delancey watched from the King's Bastion until the *Merlin* dropped anchor and then, an hour later, went aboard, where he was greeted by the first lieutenant, Mr Waring, who, he knew, had once been master of a collier out of Sunderland. At a bellow from Waring the ship's company stood to attention and doffed hats as Delancey read his commission. Then they were dismissed and Delancey had time to meet the other officers; Will Langford, master's mate; Sam Bailey, the boatswain; Tom Helliwell, the gunner and Nathaniel Corbin, the carpenter.

There were two midshipmen, the senior being the Hon. Stephen Northmore, while the junior, Edward Topley, was generally regarded as more or less useless. Delancey was puzzled at first to find the son of a lord in a sloop rather than in a smart frigate of the larger (38-gun) class, with another aristocrat as captain. The boy, who could have been no more than eighteen, seemed bright, intelligent and pleasant, his personality as well as his birth clearly foreshadowed a quick promotion. It seemed, however, that the lad's father, Lord Bleasdale, was impoverished and apparently in disgrace, cashiered from his regiment and expelled from Brooks's following an incident at the card table. As merely the fourth son, young Northmore would inherit nothing but the breath of scandal, so that the *Merlin* offered him as good a berth, perhaps, as he could expect; one owed, apparently, to the fact that Delancey's predecessor was distantly related to the boy's mother.

The *Merlin*'s establishment provided for two lieutenants and the other one, filling a vacancy, reported for duty the following afternoon. He was a quiet young man called Nicholas Mather, slight and dark and had first gone to sea from

Whitehaven. He was of Cumberland stock, his father being employed in the management of Lord Lowther's estates. He was unmarried but a good brother to several sisters with whom he corresponded. He confessed to being a keen chess-player, a reader of poetry and a diarist. Within the next few days Delancey came to the conclusion that Mather was a very fine seaman and navigator, a perfectionist in his calling and a man to be relied upon in any weather.

The *Merlin* was in harbour for another ten days while her convoy assembled and Delancey had time to study his officers and men. Waring knew his trade as a seaman but his loud voice and blustering manner gave Delancey an odd impression of weakness. When stores were being shipped a barrel was lowered carelessly and was found to have started a leak following a bump on the hatch covering. 'Who did that?' bellowed the first lieutenant. 'Come here, that man – yes, you, Brown! – Didn't you hear me say "handsomely"? Do that again and you'll be flogged, sir! Don't argue with me, sir! I saw what happened, Brown, and I've seen your carelessness before.' Witnessing the incident, Delancey knew that the seaman's real name was Wilcox and that the delinquent had been another man called Withenshaw who was sniggering in the background. While he still had the deck, Waring went on to bawl at young Topley, calling him 'Mr Bottomley' and looking to the seamen for a laugh. That Waring was a good man in some ways might be true but he was unimpressive as a disciplinarian and leader. He should have known every man's name by now and he should have known better than to weaken what little authority Topley had. Looking back, Delancey could remember the difficulties of being a midshipman, ranking as a petty officer but seen as a potential lieutenant, knowing too little and yet responsible for much. Without some support from the commissioned officers the midshipman's life was impossible. He decided, then and there, to put Topley in the larboard watch, where Mather would train him properly.

Watching when Mather had the deck, Delancey realised that he had in Mather an officer who knew every man in the ship. He took endless trouble in teaching Northmore the elements of navigation. Mather was wonderfully patient with men who were doing their best. 'Better,' he would say quietly, 'but not good enough. Now, Ainsworth, show them again how to do it. We must do it quickly but we must also *do it right*.' He came to bc known as 'Do-it-right' and Delancey could see that the larboard watch was improving all the time. Waring might bellow and bully, being called 'Blaring' behind his back, but his men never seemed to improve. With Mather on board, Delancey began to have more confidence in the crew as a whole, knowing that any discontent or friction would be reported to him at once.

The *Merlin* left Gibraltar on February 20th with a convoy for Palermo. The thought had struck him, in the Admiral's office, that Gibraltar is a sort of theatre. The same idea crossed his mind as he gave orders to weigh anchor. In bright sunshine with a stiff breeze, the *Merlin*'s manoeuvres would be clearly visible from the ramparts and office windows, from the foreshore and the lower town, from the upper batteries and from the ships at anchor. He had a wonderful opportunity to make a good impression but there could be no more public place in which to make an error. Taking charge of the deck, he shouted the orders through the speaking trumpet: 'Man the capstan! . . . Bring to! . . . Heave taut! Unbit! Heave round!' The capstan revolved as the petty officers shouted 'Heave, my lads! Stamp and go!' They had been in shallow water and there soon came the cry from the forecastle 'Anchor's a-weigh!' – to which Delancey responded 'Pall the capstan!' Now came Waring's orders from forward: 'Hook the cat!' 'Haul taut!' 'Away with the cat!' 'Pass the stoppers!' At the right moment Delancey shouted 'Haul taut and bitt the cable!' and then 'All hands, make sail!' The sloop was alive with activity as Delancey called 'Away aloft!' – 'Man the topsail sheets!' – 'Let fall – sheet home!' 'Down from aloft!' – 'Man the topsail halliards!' – 'Haul taut!' and 'Tend the braces!' With a few turns of the wheel the sloop was heading out of the bay, leaning gently to the breeze, her sails golden in the sunlight, the foam white round her stern. 'Mr Northmore,' called Delancey, 'signal the convoy to up anchor and make sail.' Without a pause he added

'Mr Helliwell – one gun!' A quarterdeck carronade boomed out, the puff of smoke going downwind in the breeze and the sound re-echoed from the Rock. Slowly and clumsily the eight merchantmen put to sea and began to assume the formation which Delancey had explained to their skippers the evening before.

The convoy had formed line with the *Merlin* in station to windward. They would not be able to hold this formation for long, least of all after dark, but Delancey wanted to start the voyage with a flourish. He could not expect smart sail-drill from the merchantmen – they were undermanned for that sort of thing – but it was vital that they should be able to form line of battle. Seen from the Rock, the merchantmen looked like fat sheep being chevied by a well-trained collie. The trouble was that the ships were unequal to each other in speed, some clean and some foul below the waterline, some well manned and some with hardly a real seaman aboard. They began to straggle as the Rock fell astern and Delancey, who had gone below, could sense Waring's exasperation as light began to fail. Sails were being backed and filled, signals were being made and repeated and guns were being fired at short and shortening intervals. Another gun spoke as he came on deck, the smoke streaming away to leeward. 'Look at that damned floating haystack!' shouted Waring. 'Did anyone ever see such a parcel of lubbers? Can't they see? Can't they read a signal?' The first lieutenant was beside himself and Delancey knew that the moment had come to intervene. 'Mr Waring,' he said quietly, 'signal the convoy to shorten sail. Heave to now until that last brig catches up.' The necessary orders were issued and the tension relaxed.

It was during this first voyage, that Delancey found his feet as a naval captain. He had so far suffered from a feeling of unreality, as if he were a boy pretending to be a man. The captains under whom he had served had been godlike and remote, saying little but knowing exactly what to do. Now he was himself a captain, commanding a real man-of-war, not an anachronistic fireship, and he felt at first neither remote nor godlike. It was with a great effort that he assumed the role, becoming less human, more silent, less accessible, more decisive. He made one or two minor mistakes – being too lenient, for example, with certain offenders – but he tried to avoid making the same mistake twice. All the time, moreover, he was working his crew up to a higher standard of gunnery and seamanship. It was a matter, as he found, of continual effort and thought. He had to study the work of each gun captain, deciding in each case of apparent failure, whether the man should be retrained, reprimanded, encouraged or replaced. He had to time the topmen in making or shortening sail. He had to know the exact state of the ship in terms of spare sails and cordage, provisions and water. He had to work out a tentative pattern of possible promotion. Who would take the boatswain's place if he were killed? Who would be the next boatswain's mate? Who was there to replace the sailmaker or cooper? In these and a hundred other ways Delancey was learning the captain's art.

In the course of a gunnery exercise Mather reported to Delancey that Number Five Gun in the larboard battery was late again.

'How late?' asked Delancey.

'Forty seconds.'

'Any excuse?'

'No. They were thirty-seven seconds late last time.'

'So there is no improvement. I should say that Fuller has had his chance.'

'I could try again with him, sir.'

'No. You could improve their time up to twenty seconds. But forty? No. We need a new gun captain. Which crew is best? Number Three?'

'Yes, sir.'

'Very well, then. Shift Maclean to Number Five. Promote Samuelson as captain of Number Three and make Fuller his second.'

'Aye, aye, sir.'

As the weeks went by men were trained and tested, promoted or replaced, the results being measured with a standard of performance and a standard time. 'Do it right,' said Mather, 'Hewitt – you can do better than that.'

'Hey, you, sir, at the yard-arm – are you asleep?' bawled Waring and Delancey noted that his first lieutenant's coat seemed to be bursting at the seams. But how could he put on weight while at sea? It seemed that he could and did. Topley was putting on weight, too, but that was because he was happier in the larboard watch.

Delancey had his young gentlemen to dine with him in turn. Langford, the master's mate, was competent, stolid and dependable but would never rise higher than lieutenant. Mr Midshipman Northmore was hampered by laziness but was potentially a good officer. Topley was a different boy since he had come under Mather's influence. When Langford was asked to carve the joint Topley was now to be heard muttering 'Do it right,' or 'You, sir, at the yard-arm.' But the biggest change observable was in young David Stock, whose tongue-tied nervousness had disappeared and who had twice now been sent to the masthead for unheard-of insolence. David was in love with the sea and asked no more of life than canvas and hemp, knots and splices, blocks and tackle, sextant and log. But somewhere ahead lay a different test. The boy would some day have to kill the enemy. Langford would do that without the slightest hesitation, and so would Northmore; as ruthless as many another aristocrat, Topley had not even thought about it. As for David Stock, Delancey had his doubts. Boys grow into men but it was a hard fate which made Delancey teach youngsters what they had to be taught. Who was he to put cold steel into a mere child's hands and say 'Now, kill!' and yet that in the end was the message he had to convey among the commissioned officers. Waring might bawl and Mather might teach but his function, the captain's function, was to kill and to see that others did the same. War was his trade and he knew no other.

CHAPTER TWO

Escort

Delancey faced no crisis until a wild and wintry day in early April 1799. The *Merlin* was then escorting a convoy from Minorca to Leghorn, a motley collection of nine vessels, some quite small though a few of them might be regarded as valuable. The merchantmen were supposed to be in formation but had actually straggled in the approach to Corsica, the point of greatest danger since it was within easy reach of Toulon. The wind was southerly with low scudding cloud and gleams of sunshine alternating with heavy rain and the *Merlin* lay to windward of her convoy under shortened canvas. It was Mr Waring's watch and Delancey was below when the look-out reported a strange sail. Young Northmore knocked at the cabin door a minute later. The boy made his errand consciously dramatic, his hand raised in salute, his eyes a-scare for adventure.

'Beg pardon, sir, Mr Waring's compliments and there's a ship in sight.'

Delancey was on deck in an instant with his telescope focused in the direction to which Waring pointed. The vessel sighted was not a ship but a brig, so much he could see, but she was hidden soon afterwards in a rainstorm.

'Well, what do you make of her?' he asked Waring.

'Can't see very well but she's not one of ours, sir.' Waring's thoughts were very obvious. Here was a smaller opponent, offering a chance of promotion or prize-money.

'No, not one of ours. Send a good man to the mast-head and let me know when she is more nearly identified.'

An hour later came a new summons and this time with better information. Visibility had improved and the brig was near enough for careful study.

'She is French, sir,' said Waring eagerly. 'A national brig corvette under British colours and heading so as to close with us. Shall I clear for action, sir?' Waring was no coward, as Delancey had to admit, but he was too red-faced, noisy and overfed, he had no brains and, above all, no sense of *time.* He might be inwardly excited himself but this was no moment to show it.

'Not yet, Mr Waring. We'll pipe hands to dinner first; a little early if the cook can manage it. And please signal the convoy to close up on the leading ship.'

Delancey stared through his telescope again. Yes, a brig corvette of about fourteen guns, a smaller vessel than the *Merlin* with, obviously, a smaller crew. But what was her captain planning to do? He must have identified the *Merlin* as an 18-gun, ship-rigged sloop, too big an opponent for his corvette. Did he really mean to give battle? And if so, why? Even as Delancey watched, the corvette struck her red ensign and hoisted the tricolour. It would have made more sense if the Frenchman were steering so as to cut off the last straggler in the convoy but here, apparently, was a Frenchman spoiling for a fight. She would be within range in less than an hour, giving the *Merlin*'s crew time to finish their dinner, to which they now had been piped. Still mystified, Delancey paced the deck and stared at his opponent. What was the trick to be?

When dinner was finished, Delancey at last gave the order to clear for action and beat to quarters. The drum beat the rhythm of 'Hearts of Oak' and the ship was instantly alive with ordered activity, every man having a task to be done at breakneck speed. Partitions were demolished and furniture tossed into the hold. Guns were loaded and run out with ammunition to hand and weapons for boarding. The decks were sanded and buckets of water placed between the cannon. Small-arms men raced up to the fighting tops with muskets and bandoleers. The midshipman's berth was turned into an improvised hospital although the ship carried no surgeon. The sails were wetted with the fire engine to prevent them burning. The carpenter stood ready with plugs and stoppers, the gunner went to the magazine. There was no hint of confusion but only the scampering of feet and the continued throb of the drum which ended only when every man was at his battle station.

The French brig was just out of range, a sinister-looking craft as seen through the spray, evidently in very good order. Meanwhile, the wind was veering south-westerly, even westerly at times. The leading merchantman in the convoy had shortened sail and the laggards were crowding canvas to catch up. Moved by some instinct which he would have found it difficult to explain, Delancey came to a sudden decision. He decided not to accept the French challenge. His first lieutenant reached the opposite conclusion at the same instant.

'The wind is coming westerly, sir,' said Waring, 'the enemy is no longer to windward of us.'

'Thank you, Mr Waring.'

'We could close the range, sir.'

'So indeed we could.'

'That corvette could be our pup-pup-prize within the hour!'

Delancey knew exactly what Waring wanted. The first lieutenant was stuttering and red in the face, his fingers drumming on the quarterdeck rail. Delancey remembered that Waring had a wife and a large family in Sunderland, more than he could well maintain on lieutenant's pay. And now the man had seen his chance to better himself. After a successful action, the enemy brig captured, Delancey would be posted into a frigate and Waring would become captain of the *Merlin*. There would be a useful sum in prize-money and a useful paragraph in the *Gazette*: 'The corvette was taken by a boarding party led most gallantly by the first lieutenant, her colours being hauled down fifty minutes after the action began. I am more particularly indebted to . . . etc. etc.' Delancey was himself tempted, heaven knows, but his decision had been made.

'Heave to, please.' The order was quietly given and it seemed for a moment that the first lieutenant had failed to understand it.

'Heave to, sir?' he asked stupidly.

'If you please, Mr Waring.'

To heave to meant to back the foretopsail, making the sails

act against each other and so bring the ship to a standstill. In this instance it meant increasing the range and refusing battle, the correct movement for protecting the rear of the convoy.

'*Heave to*, sir?' Waring had now taken in the full extent of the disaster. He looked to heaven for inspiration, looked at the helmsman, looked at young Stock, Delancey's A.D.C., and finally, aghast, at his captain. His lips moved but he was lost for words.

'You heard me, Mr Waring, HEAVE TO!' The first words were uttered quietly, the last two fairly barked. Stung into action, Waring bawled the necessary orders. There was a flurry of activity as the foreyard was backed. There was a similar flurry on board the Frenchman, her crew just visible and her captain probably surprised. Both the French corvette and the convoy were still going ahead, the *Merlin* relatively losing ground.

The first lieutenant was plainly furious, muttering under his breath to the master's mate, Langford, who was commanding the quarterdeck guns and who made no response of any kind. Delancey took no notice, watching the corvette to see what her reaction would be. He half expected her to follow suit but she held her course. Three minutes later the look-out hailed the deck. Another sail had been sighted, almost in the same direction as the corvette but some miles further away.

'Mr Langford', called Delancey, 'take a spyglass and tell me what more you can see from the main topmasthead.' Stolid as he might be, the young man was up the rigging in a flash, quick as a cat. He reached the deck again in five minutes.

'Another Frenchman, sir – a ship-rigged corvette – bigger than the one near to us. I glimpsed her for a moment and then she was lost again.'

'Thank you, Mr Langford. Make sail, Mr Waring!'

The foretopsail filled again and the sloop was once more under way.

His face like a thundercloud, Waring went forward to the forecastle, his proper station in battle, ostensibly to check the gun crews, actually so as to splutter in disgust to anyone who would listen – in this case, the boatswain and young Topley.

Mather, who had been in the waist of the ship, came aft at this moment and touched his hat.

'Well, Mr Mather?' Delancey asked.

'Beg pardon, sir, a man in my watch believes that the nearer corvette is the *Malouine*, the other the *Mouche*. He says that they work together.'

'That I can well believe.'

'I should guess, sir, that the *Malouine*'s guns are loaded with chain-shot, bar-shot and canister.'

A ship normally engaged an opponent with round shot at close range, attempting to damage her hull, cause casualties and silence her guns. But when her captain had a different object, wanting to cripple his opponent and then break off the engagement, he would choose a longer range and would load with special ammunition designed to damage sails and rigging.

'No doubt of it,' replied Delancey, thinking that Mather was a man after his own heart – a man quick to understand the situation and draw the right conclusion. How he would shape in battle remained to be seen. It was clear, in the meanwhile, that he could use his brains.

Within the next hour or two the French corvettes fore-reached on the convoy and made off northwards while the crew of the *Merlin* stood down from their guns, put the ship to rights and resumed their ordinary routine. Delancey went below to write his report and Waring was free at last to express his disgust.

It was Mather's watch but Waring remained on deck, looking longingly towards the French corvettes, each no more than a blur on the horizon. He swore to himself and hit the gunwale with the palm of his hand.

'I thought at one time, Mr Mather, that the corvette was as good as taken. We've lost our chance now!'

Mather was pacing the quarterdeck, looking now at the binnacle, now at the sails and now at the men who were replacing a broken ratline on the main shrouds. He paused near Waring and replied in a tone of hardly veiled contempt (didn't the man understand even *now*?).

'There never was a chance. There was a trap, sir, and

our captain refused to fall into it.'

'A trap? What d'you mean?'

'The *Mouche* followed the *Malouine* but so kept behind her that she was always hidden. If we had engaged the *Malouine* she would have fired at our rigging until we were crippled. After she had broken off the engagement, the *Mouche* would have sailed into the convoy, taking half of them before nightfall.'

All this was so obvious to Mather that he wondered still that any explanation should have been necessary. It was like talking to a disappointed child. Waring had taken his hat off and was twisting it in his hand as if it had been an opponent's neck. When he spoke it was with a splutter of indignation.

'All very clever! The fact remains that we let the enemy escape. The crew must feel disgraced and those two corvettes will go on to play havoc somewhere else.'

'But our task is to protect this convoy.'

'Even if more valuable ships are afterwards taken in the Straits of Messina?'

'We are not responsible for what happens in the Straits of Messina. We have been ordered to bring these ships safely into Leghorn and that is what we are doing.'

'Obeying orders is all very well. There have been great admirals who could do better than that.'

'When we are admirals, sir, we may do the same.'

Alone in his cabin and alone with his thoughts, Delancey finished his report and signed it. There is a time to fight, he reflected, and a time to avoid fighting. He felt that he, personally, had passed a new test. Courage, he knew, is not enough. But what of his officers? So far from finding the answer, Waring had not even seen the problem. There still was this to be said for the man, that he had courage. He would have led the boarding party without thought of danger – all that was true. He had learnt his seamanship in a tough school, on board a collier out of the Tyne. He was a good man in some ways, but completely brainless.

Mather, by contrast, had instantly grasped the situation. He might not be a first-rate leader – Delancey rather doubted whether he was – but he certainly had brains. The pity was that Waring was the senior. Langford was a useful man, he thought, and Northmore a promising boy. He was uncertain as yet about Topley but gave him the benefit of the doubt. As for the crew as a whole, they were shaping very well. He asked Teesdale, very casually, what the crew thought of the recent encounter.

'Well, sir, there's no gainsaying that they were disappointed at first, clearing for action, seeing the enemy and no action after all. Some of the younger men talked of running away and that. But the older men – seamen like Mike Garley and Nathaniel Taylor – properly put them in their place. They knew what the French game was and the rest came to see it in the end.' So it was as it should be – the veterans were teaching the rest. Apart from that, hard work was showing results. There could be no doubt about it, the *Merlin* was becoming a smart ship.

When he took her into Gibraltar the following week, once more under the eyes of so many critics, he thought that there was nothing to be ashamed of. If the Rear-Admiral should be watching, so much the better. In point of fact he *had* been watching, as became apparent when Delancey reported to him.

It was to the same office he came, where the quills were still scratching and where the clerks, to all appearance, might not have moved from their desks since he saw them last. The same flag-lieutenant ushered him into the inner office from the window of which he could glimpse the *Merlin* at anchor.

'I observe, captain, from the way you entered harbour, that you have a sense of style. Any adventures?' Delancey told him about the French corvettes.

'*Malouine* and *Mouche*? Yes, I've heard of them. You did well to let them alone. The question is – where are they now?'

'I'm told, sir, that they often cruise between Palermo and Tunis.'

'That is probably correct and that is where you may well see them again. For the next eastward-bound convoy will be carrying supplies and stores to our squadron on the coast of Egypt, with some other vessels bound for Malta and Cyprus. The convoy will be under the command of Captain Doyle of the *Lapwing* and he will be glad to have the *Merlin* as whipper-in. I should send another sloop if I had another but I don't.'

'When do we sail, sir?'

'As soon as the last three storeships arrive from England; in two or three weeks' time.'

Delancey made haste to call on Captain Doyle. The *Lapwing* he knew by sight, an old 28-gun 6th Rate, the smallest class of ship to justify a commander of post-rank. He found, however, that Doyle was in lodgings ashore, an elderly man who looked far from well. He was bedridden in a room above an apothecary's shop, wearing a flannel nightgown and a nightcap, with a cup of tea at his elbow and an array of medicine bottles. Delancey repeated the instructions he had received.

'Glad to have your help, captain. I'll be happy, however, when this voyage is over. I think it will be my last. I began on the lower deck and it took me a lifetime to reach post rank. I haven't been very active of late and the chief physician here thinks that I should retire soon – or should indeed have retired already. These pains in my back give me trouble and I have headaches as well when at sea, with an occasional touch of fever. I'm like the *Lapwing* herself, almost worn out.'

Delancey expressed his sympathy and went on to tell Doyle about the two French corvettes. Captain Doyle had a fit of coughing and managed to upset his teacup. When set to rights he resumed the conversation.

'Yes, I sighted them once. But they would never come near a frigate. Let me once reach Gibraltar again, the convoy safe, and I'll take the next passage home. Can you guess where I mean to retire?

'In Ireland, sir?'

'Well, I come from there, true enough. But my plan is to settle down near Bristol. I never married, you know, but my sister lives there. I want no more than a cottage, you understand, with a woman to do the housework and another to cook. I first went to sea fifty-five years ago. I feel that I've done enough and maybe too much.'

Delancey expressed all the right sentiments and came away

rather depressed. Any hopes he had of trapping the two corvettes could now be forgotten. Old Doyle was not thirsting for battle but for a well-earned rest. He looked quite unfit for service and Holroyd, the *Lapwing*'s first lieutenant, was trying to persuade him to stay ashore. Holroyd he had met before, a blunt and competent seaman with a strong Yorkshire accent, who had been disfigured by a facial wound. He had been the *Lapwing*'s real commander for months past. There was an element of self-interest in Holroyd's advice but he was honestly worried about the old man, doubting whether he would survive another period at sea. Delancey thought that a bachelor's retirement must be a lonely and miserable experience, one he would rather avoid. He must himself marry before it was too late; as soon, perhaps, as the war was over. As things stood, however, he had little or nothing to offer and the ending of the war, whenever that should be, would leave him with, if anything, less.

Dining ashore at the gunner's mess, Delancey met with Holroyd again. There was talk about Gibraltar's strength as a fortress and its usefulness as a base. Its weakness lay in the fact that its harbour was all in view of the Spanish coast – whatever happened there was clearly seen and quickly reported. A gunner captain asked whether that really mattered.

'It matters in this way,' said Holroyd. 'Suppose we are assembling an eastward-bound convoy, as we are at this moment, the number of ships, the date of sailing, the value of the cargoes, and the strength of the escort is reported to the Spanish. The next ship bound eastwards from Malaga takes full information to Palermo, which lies right in the path of the convoy. Then the French cruisers decide whether to intercept it or let it alone.'

'How interesting!' said another gunner officer, 'I had supposed that they cruised near a usual landfall and merely hoped for luck.'

'No such thing, sir,' said Holroyd, 'they act on intelligence and there is no lack of it from Gibraltar.'

'But the convoy's destination can be secret, surely?' objected the Major.

'How can it be secret?' asked Holroyd. 'The crews of merchantmen know where they are going and were told, indeed, before they signed on. I mustn't tell you our route and am not supposed to know. But everyone along the waterfront can tell you, and your mess servants probably know already.'

Coming away together, Delancey and Holroyd discussed the matter again. 'A man-of-war's destination could be made the subject of a false rumour,' said Delancey finally, and Holroyd agreed that this was possible. What rumour had he in mind? 'Well, just by way of example, the *Lapwing*'s crew might think that their ship was going no further than Minorca.' There was a minute's silence as they paced the quayside and then Holroyd replied 'I see what you mean, sir.' Holroyd could take a hint and needed no reminder. That the *Lapwing* would go no further than Minorca was soon a matter of common knowledge, known to everyone before the convoy sailed.

After eight days at sea Delancey was surprised to see the *Lapwing* hove to while the convoy sailed on. When the *Merlin* thus came up with the frigate, Holroyd's voice could be heard hailing Delancey:

'Captain Doyle is sick, sir. I have taken over the command.'

'Is he dying?'

'Could be, sir. He should be in hospital, anyway.'

'Very well, then. I am now the senior officer. Alter course for Port Mahon.'

'Just this ship alone, sir?'

'No, the whole convoy. *Merlin* will now replace you as leading ship. You will take station astern.'

So the rumour turned out to be almost true. Captain Doyle was taken ashore at Port Mahon, Minorca, and Delancey sent for the masters of all the merchantmen.

Chairs were set out round the mahogany table in the after cabin. Young Topley had pinned some charts to the bulkhead and stood by them with a pointer. Northmore guarded the doorway and announced each master by name. Teesdale had placed decanters and glasses on the sideboard. Holroyd had been among the last to arrive, his boat having furthest to row, and he took his place on Delancey's right, Waring and Mather on his left. Delancey began by telling them that Captain Doyle had been sent to hospital.

'I am now in command and am fortunate to have Mr Holroyd as second. I think it possible, though not certain, that we may be intercepted off Sicily by two French corvettes. On a recent occasion their plan was to engage the escort sloop with one corvette while the other would thus be free to attack the convoy. If they do that again, we have a surprise for them: the presence of the *Lapwing*. To make this a complete surprise, we must hide the frigate behind three of the largest merchantmen, the *Cumberland*, the *Hopewell* and *Boyne*.

'On the cabin table before me I have arranged corks to represent the convoy. The three ships I have named are here in the centre with the *Merlin* here to windward of them and the *Lapwing* to leeward – *here*. Here are the French, ready to fall into our trap. But all depends upon masking the *Lapwing* until the last moment. Can I rely on you, gentlemen?' There was a murmur of agreement and one skipper spoke up:

'You might be interested to know, sir, that the story current in Gibraltar was that the *Lapwing* would go no further than here and would then turn back. So the frigate mayn't be expected, anyway.'

'That's right,' said another skipper. 'I heard that, too, strictly in confidence.'

'I'm glad to hear it,' said Delancey, glancing at Holroyd innocently. 'Odd how these stories come to circulate. Are there any questions?' The conference broke up, the skippers having a glass of wine before they left, and the remainder of that day was spent in a hurried repainting of both men-of-war, the *Lapwing* made to look more like a merchantman and the *Merlin* merely made to look different, like another sloop of the same class.

At daybreak the *Merlin* fired a gun and the convoy put to sea again, each ship gradually taking up her assigned position. The formation was far from perfect but Delancey realised that this was an advantage if the huddle in the centre was to look accidental.

Five days later, on a sunny but cold afternoon with foam-capped waves and a strengthening north-easterly wind, a sail to windward was reported from the mast-head. The stranger was a corvette and Delancey had the feeling that it had all happened before. There were, however to be differences, the first of which would be his own failure to sight the other corvette. This time he was going to fall innocently into the trap, engaging the nearer corvette and failing to suspect the presence of the other. The light this time was less favourable to the French but he was going to be as unobservant as Waring had been on the earlier occasion. Steadying his telescope against the mizen shrouds, he looked carefully at the distant corvette. Yes, she was the same brig, no doubt of that.

He ordered the helmsman to keep closer to the wind, lengthening the distance between the *Merlin* and the convoy. He noted with satisfaction that his ship lay between her opponent and the centre ships of the convoy, all rather bunched and overlapping. With perhaps half an hour to go, he gave the order to clear for action. The drum beat to quarters, the guns were run out, the decks were sanded and the gun crews numbered off. Waring took command of the port battery on this occasion and began to make estimates of the rapidly lessening range. Waring was at his best on such an occasion, his confidence an inspiration to his men, his crude jokes welcome to the older seamen, his fearlessness a good example to the young. 'Wait until we have the frogs within range,' he shouted. 'They'll be beaten before they've finished dirtying their breeches!'

Commanding the other battery was Mather whose manner was different and probably less effective. He talked to each gun captain in turn and had a word of encouragement for those who had not been in battle before. On the quarterdeck Langford was telling his gun crews they would have a good view of the battle, far better than men could have on the main deck. They were also more exposed but he said nothing about that. On the forecastle Northmore was extolling the virtues of cold steel: 'Soften them with gunfire, I say, and finish them off with the cutlass! They never dare stand up to us, man for man!'

As Delancey made his rounds, with Topley and Stock at his heels, he could sense that his men were spoiling for a fight. Stripped to the waist with kerchiefs tied over their ears, they hid their fears under a loud bantering of talk of prize-money, bets being taken on how long it would be before the French colours came down. Delancey talked little but said a word of reassurance to the youngsters, to the powder monkeys who had to fetch the cartridges from the magazine. 'Don't keep the gunners waiting, lads!' Topley, he noticed, had a useful air of nonchalance but David Stock was white-faced and frightened. 'It's the waiting you'll find hard, boy. You'll feel better when you hear the guns!' God knows whether that was true but the child managed to show a sickly grin in reply.

The sloop and corvette were converging at great speed and Delancey could not but admire the lines and the rig of his opponent. She was a fine craft and her white sails curved beautifully against the dark grey clouds behind her, a graceful vessel but temporarily in the wrong navy. Even as he watched, regretting what had to come, there was a flash from the corvette's forecastle, a puff of smoke quickly dispersed downwind, a distant jarring sound and a splash in the sea between the two opponents. It was a sighting shot and proved what Delancey knew, that the enemy was out of range. He made another quick tour of the port battery, having a word with the men as he passed. They were tense now, each at his post, each gun captain with the lanyard in his hand.

By the time he had regained the quarterdeck the moment for battle had come. He drew his sword and called out: 'You may open fire, Mr Waring.' The deck reeled under him as the guns thundered. A minute later, after the smoke had cleared, the corvette was hidden in her turn and the sound came of shot flying overhead. A hole appeared in the *Merlin*'s foretopsail and a jagged strip was torn from the main course. Just as he had expected, the French were firing high.

It was not until then that a look-out man slid down the rigging and reported a second sail beyond the enemy. Delancey thanked the man absently and sent him to join the forecastle gun to which he was stationed. Looking to windward when the smoke allowed, he glimpsed the other corvette, visible now from the deck and heading for the convoy. Meanwhile, the *Merlin*'s gunners were firing into the corvette's hull while the French continued to fire high, gradually reducing the *Merlin*'s sails to ribbons. As a result, she began to lose speed, falling astern of her opponent.

This was the moment for which Delancey had been waiting. Giving the order to tack, he put the helm hard over, crossing the corvette's wake and giving Mather the order to open fire. The starboard broadside crashed out with the guns at maximum elevation, loaded alternately with chain- and bar-shot. Raking the corvette, these whirling missiles played havoc with sails and cordage. Urged on by Mather the gunners reloaded and fired again, this time with grape-shot. Delancey tacked again, putting the *Merlin* on the same course as her opponent but now to windward of her. The corvette had lost speed through damage to her sails and the *Merlin* was able to keep level while Mather hurried from gun to gun, checking elevation and aim. After the third broadside, grape-shot again, he ordered all gun captains to concentrate on the corvette's mainmast shrouds, using the chain-shot only.

The enemy were firing back, aiming high as before but surprised perhaps to find that the British were doing the same. Grape-shot came tearing through the canvas above Delancey's head and there was a crash forward where the foreyard had come down in the slings. The mizen-mast was hit and splinters of wood wounded three men at one of the quarterdeck guns. Two more on the forecastle were wounded and one of the ship's boats was smashed by a stray shot. The two opponents were fighting at about two cables' distance and Delancey was careful not to close the range, partly to avoid heavy casualties and partly to give his grape-shot sufficient spread. With guns firing independently the noise was shattering and continuous.

At long last, however, and after what seemed hours of fighting, the expected result was achieved. The corvette's mainmast went over the side. When the last of the weather shrouds had parted the unsupported mast broke off about eight feet above the deck. Fire was now concentrated on the foremast shrouds, save that the quarterdeck guns fired grapeshot still at the enemy's mainmast stump, discouraging the efforts of the men sent to clear the wreckage. Five minutes later the *Merlin*'s foremast went, followed by her main topmast.

There was a frantic scene forward where Northmore was coping with chaos, half his men trapped under the fallen canvas and others entangled with the rigging. The boatswain went to his aid and axes whirled, severing the tangled shrouds and letting the foremast drift clear. Amidships there was a scene of similar confusion with Mather directing the efforts of his men. Delancey sent Langford to help him and Copley to assist Northmore. Stock he sent to ask the carpenter whether the ship was leaking. For the time being the action was over, the two vessels drifting apart, rolling and pitching in a choppy sea. All firing ceased and parties of seamen began to deal with the damage. The *Merlin* would not be under sail for another half hour at least.

Telescope to his eye, Delancey was trying to see what had happened to the other corvette. He could see that the merchantmen were hove to around a central cluster of ships. There was no gunfire and the *Lapwing* presently detached herself from the remainder and made sail, close-hauled, towards the *Merlin*.

Frantic efforts were being made on board that sloop and her opponent, knotting, splicing and fishing the wounded spars. Had they been alone the advantage would have gone to the first under sail. In fact, however, the frigate would arrive before either could be ready for action. While Delancey watched, the *Lapwing* took up a position athwart the corvette's stern and fired a single gun. The tricolour was hauled down instantly and the action was over. Young Stock made a gesture, pointing to Delancey's left forearm and his captain noticed, for the first time, that the sleeve was soaked in blood. Before he could do anything about it the *Merlin*'s first lieutenant came aft, red in the face, almost apoplectic with rage. He was hatless, with his coat torn and his sword missing.

'Look, sir,' Waring yelled, beside himself, 'that corvette should have been prize to us! We could have brought her to close action! We could have destroyed her at pistol-shot range! We could have fired a double-shotted broadside and boarded her in the smoke! Now all the credit will go to the *Lapwing* – yes, and all the prize-money too! I protest, sir! I beg leave to ask for a transfer. What sort of warfare is this? How will it read in the *Gazette*? I am ashamed, sir, to have taken part in such an action!' All this was bellowed in the hearing of half the men on deck. Delancey's thundered reply was just as audible:

'Silence, sir! Stand at attention when you address your superior officer! Where is your hat, sir? Fetch it and report back to me.'

Waring, who had been in the thick of the fray for over an hour, had every excuse for being hatless but Delancey used the point of etiquette to bring the man to his senses. On Waring's return, now able to salute properly, Delancey spoke as loudly as before.

'Now, Mr Waring, you are to take fifteen men on board that corvette, batten her crew below hatches, hoist our ensign over the tricolour and take station astern of the convoy. Is that understood?'

'But I submit, sir, that the corvette struck to the *Lapwing*.'

'So she did, but I had previously agreed with Mr Holroyd that she should be ours and that prize-money in respect of this and the other prize taken shall be equally shared between his ship and mine.'

Waring's mouth was agape, his finger to his mouth like an abashed schoolboy. His lips moved convulsively before any sound came, and then he stuttered:

'Very gug-good, sir. . . I'm sorry, sir.'

'Let me remind you of another circumstance. When you take command of that corvette, please ask yourself whether your task would have been made easier by our having riddled her with gunfire at point-blank range. I am giving you the temporary command of a jury-rigged corvette. Would you rather have had a blood-stained bundle of firewood?'

'No, sir.' He opened his mouth to say more but no words came.

'One other thing, Mr Waring. You are disappointed not to have captured that corvette by boarding. Why? Because a spectacular victory would have led, you think, to your promotion. I want you to realise that such a dramatic scene would have cost me twenty men killed or wounded. Why should I throw men's lives away to gain promotion for you; or for me either? We have captured a man-of-war fit for service, undamaged below the hammock nettings, and it has cost me five men wounded. That is a price I am ready to pay. Your idea was to pay a far heavier price for something which would by then have been worthless. I won't do it, Mr Waring. I won't do it. And nor will you if you value your future in the service.'

By the time that the crestfallen Waring had taken over the *Malouine* from the midshipman who had been sent to her from the *Lapwing*, Delancey had signalled for Holroyd to come aboard. A friendly meeting followed on board the *Merlin*.

'Congratulations, Captain Delancey! Two captured men-of-war and both of them fit for the service!'

'Thanks to your co-operation, Mr Holroyd. Did the *Mouche* give you any trouble?'

'Only in trying to escape but her attempt didn't answer. She was trapped among the merchantmen, who solidly blocked her way. So she hauled down her colours and I sent a prize crew on board.'

'My hope is that the *Mouche* will be taken into the service, with you as commander. I shall make the recommendation to Rear-Admiral Fothergill.'

'Thank you, sir. May I express my own hope that you should be made post into the *Lapwing*?'

'There is no vacancy, Mr Holroyd, while Captain Doyle is alive. I think, however, that Mr Waring might go to her as first lieutenant.'

'A good idea, sir, if I may say so. I am sorry to see, sir, that you are wounded.' Holroyd was looking at Delancey with real anxiety. 'You should see our surgeon, sir – I'll send him over. We can't afford to lose you, sir; we all think you have a big future in the service. This recent action did you credit, if I may say so.' Holroyd was a rough character and Delancey was touched to see his real concern.

'No surgeon needed, Mr Holroyd. This is a mere scratch – I never noticed it. Thank you, however, for your good wishes. You deserve to command your own ship and should do so with distinction.'

Teesdale appeared now at Delancey's side, carrying a basin, sponge and bandages. He helped his commander off with his coat and sponged the cut, applying a bandage to the forearm. He looked anxiously to see whether Delancey had any other hurt. His look of hero-worship was shared by David Stock, who was holding the coat with its tattered sleeve. But Delancey was still talking to Holroyd.

'I shall have to ask you to put up with Waring until you go to your first command. He is not without some useful qualities. . .' He paused for a moment, choosing his words, 'He might be a useful officer in some ship or other. . . but not, I think, in mine.'

CHAPTER THREE

The Siege of Valletta

'Captain Delancey is here,' murmured the flag-lieutenant.

'Show him in,' replied Rear-Admiral Fothergill. 'I only wish I had better news for him.' Delancey entered, bowed and stood at attention. He thought that Fothergill looked tired and old, perhaps disappointed over some expected appointment. Or was he disappointed on Delancey's behalf?

'Good-morning, Delancey. Do please be seated.'

Sitting down, Delancey looked round the sparsely furnished office and saw that a chart of Malta and Gozo had been pinned to a board behind the Admiral's chair.

'I regret to tell you that your very creditable action off Sicily has not gained you the promotion you deserve. As you know, Captain Doyle recovered sufficiently to take the *Lapwing* back to Plymouth. She was condemned after survey and broken up. Doyle retired and Mr Waring is now employed by the Transport Board. Their Lordships did not consider an action against an inferior force could justify more than one promotion, that of Mr Holroyd.'

'I quite understand, sir.' Delancey showed no emotion and had not, indeed, expected anything different.

'I dare say that they would have been more impressed had your losses been heavier.'

'It is more important to me that my men should trust me not to throw away their lives.'

'You are perfectly right. I remember, by the way, that you were yourself slightly wounded.'

'A mere scratch, sir. I never even noticed it until we had ceased fire. There's hardly a scar now.'

'I am glad to hear that it healed, anyway. Well, I couldn't

secure your promotion but I can give you a change from escort work. Your next convoy will be destined for Malta and I shall authorise Captain Ball to retain the *Merlin* for service there, at least for the time being. I don't think we have sent you there before?'

'No, sir.'

'So the time has come to look at the chart.' The Admiral rose and went to the board behind his chair:

'Here is Malta and here is Grand Harbour guarded by fortifications and overlooked by the city of Valletta – here. The adjacent island of Gozo has no harbour of comparable importance. But note the position of Malta, midway in the passage which connects the eastern with the western Mediterranean. Its strategic value is immense and Grand Harbour could be of great value to us.'

'Yes, sir.'

'You probably know what the situation is. Malta, you recall, was taken by General Bonaparte on his way to Egypt. After the destruction of the French fleet by Lord Nelson at Aboukir the isolated French garrison in Malta was in danger. The Maltese then rose against the French, raising some ten thousand men under the flag of Naples. Muskets and ammunition for about twelve hundred of these were landed by Sir James Saumarez. So the French, numbering some three thousand men under General Vaubois, withdrew to Valletta where they are still besieged. A small French force at M'dina (he pointed to the chart) was massacred and a yet smaller French garrison, in Gozo (he pointed again) capitulated to us. We now have a squadron blockading Valletta and Captain Ball is ashore, giving what help he can to the Maltese.'

'Why doesn't Vaubois surrender?'

'Well, you must remember that Malta was Bonaparte's own conquest. He has since become virtual ruler of France. So we may assume that Vaubois has been ordered to hold out.'

'Can't the Maltese storm Valletta?'

'The city is virtually impregnable. The fortifications built for the Knights of Malta are of gigantic size and fantastic strength. Something could be done by a regular army under an experienced general with heavy artillery and a corps of engineers. Come and look at the chart. . . . Here is Grand Harbour, one of the finest landlocked harbours in the world. Valletta occupies this headland, fortified across the neck.' The Admiral came away from the chart and sat down again.

'Who commands the Maltese, sir?'

'Some priests and notaries, one or two of their nobles; but none with any knowledge of war.'

'So the stalemate is likely to continue?'

'It would seem so. But the situation is damned awkward, made worse by the fact that the French have a squadron there – three sail of the line and three frigates with Rear-Admiral Decrès and Rear-Admiral Villeneuve. These are all safe under the guns of the fortress. We tie up as many ships to blockade the place. Apart from that, we want the harbour for ourselves.'

'But the French must be starving.'

'They are, more or less. But one or two ships have run the blockade with supplies and ammunition, the last being the frigate *Boudeuse,* in February.'

'Would you suppose, sir, that they will try again with a larger force?' Delancey's tone was optimistic.

'That is their only hope but it is a question what force they can collect. In the meanwhile, we have a small garrison in Gozo, a squadron on blockade duty and our Maltese friends ashore. Our next convoy in October will consist of storeships laden with all that is needed to sustain the siege. Having escorted these ships on their passage you will relieve the *Hornet*, which is due for overhaul, and thus come under the orders of the senior naval officer, probably Commodore Sir Thomas Troubridge. The storeships will return here escorted by the *Hornet*.'

'Aye, aye, sir. When shall we sail?'

'In about three weeks' time. I forgot to tell you, by the way, that Mather is confirmed as your first lieutenant and that another officer called Stirling has arrived and will join you as second.

'I'm glad to hear that, sir.'

Withdrawing at that point, Delancey met Mr Stirling in the

outer office and was favourable impressed. The young officer was of average height but broad and stocky in build and immensely strong. He was fair-haired, bronzed, tough and compact; not a man to quarrel with. Judging from this first impression, Delancey guessed that this was a man on whom he could rely.

Over the following weeks Delancey came to recognise that his first impression of Stirling had been correct. He was an excellent officer, recently discharged from hospital after being wounded in action. He was a lowland Scot by origin but had been brought up in Hampshire and sent to sea as a boy. He was complementary to Mather, more forceful than the first lieutenant but less intelligent. Where Stirling was ruthless and cheerful, Mather was sensitive and subtle. In the hard work of refitting the *Merlin* they gained good results by an alternation of method.

The crew had done well in action against the *Malouine*, a smaller ship with fewer guns, but some would need much further training before Delancey would be satisfied. It was not enough to be average; he wanted his ship to be exceptional. This was now possible, with Mather a better first lieutenant than he himself had ever been and Stirling in some ways a better officer than Mather.

What had he that they lacked? He came in the end to realise that it was imagination and detachment. He could see the situation from the enemy's point of view – it was this gift which ended the career of the *Malouine* and *Mouche* – and he could decide cold-bloodedly whether to fight or not. For one who had started life without much confidence, he had come to the surprising conclusion that he deserved to command. He was lucky, he decided, to have two outstanding officers and yet knew himself to be better than either. He felt confident as never before; and very lonely indeed.

There was a delay in collecting the necessary supplies and the convoy for Malta did not sail until November 24th. After calling at Port Mahon, Delancey was off Malta on December 19th, reporting on that day to the Commodore. The island looked bleak under low cloud with heavy seas breaking on its rocky shore. The *Merlin*, however, was looking her best and hove to with a flourish. In obedience to a signal Delancey had a boat lowered and was rowed over to the *Culloden*, flying the commodore's flag. She was cruising back and forth outside the entrance to Grand Harbour, keeping just out of range of the shore batteries and so placed as to prevent any French ship leaving harbour without being immediately engaged. Knowing about Troubridge from hearsay, Delancey looked at the *Culloden* as he boarded her, with something like awe. Looking back at his own ship, however, he could do so with pride. In less than a year he had brought her to something like perfection in appearance, smartness, sail-drill and gunnery. Her figure-head gleamed in gold leaf and his boat's crew were uniformed in black jackets and white trousers. Tanner brought the boat to the *Culloden*'s entry with a flourish and oars were tossed smartly and together. None of this was wasted on the bluff and burly Sir Thomas, to whom Delancey reported on the quarterdeck.

Troubridge was something of a legend, known as Lord Nelson's close friend and follower, a man with a great reputation as a seaman but not as a courtier when ashore. He was noted for a severity which was originally copied from Lord St. Vincent, the greatest disciplinarian of all. If the *Merlin* passed muster with Troubridge, Delancey had achieved something.

'Good-morning, captain. Your ship does you credit. You will, I fancy, have brought us the mail?'

'Yes, sir. I have also to hand you, in person, this letter from Rear-Admiral Fothergill. It is to place the sloop *Merlin* under your orders.'

'I can make good use of her,' replied the Commodore, taking the letter, 'and your first task will be to take your convoy over to Gozo, where the bulk of the supplies will be unloaded. You will guard the anchorage there until the unloading is completed. Report to my pennant when this has been done.'

'Aye, aye, sir.'

The purpose of this order was clear enough. Gozo was quite close to Malta and had a small port on the nearer side, with an outer anchorage sheltered to some extent by the larger island.

Gozo was in British hands and was serving as a base for the close blockade of Valletta. The port of Gozo was a narrow creek with white houses on either side and a small breakwater. Beyond it, inland, could be glimpsed in the distance the dome of the cathedral at Vittoria, the island's capital. Once the storeships were in this anchorage the *Merlin* dropped anchor to seawards of them. She was still there, as it happened, on the last day of the year, which was also the last day of the century.

Delancey marked the occasion by inviting all his officers and midshipmen to a late supper which would end after midnight. He had provided for the occasion a lamb, a small pig, some chicken and plenty of Maltese wine, with some captured brandy to finish with. The warrant and petty officers had planned a party under the boatswain's presidency, the two watches were celebrating and only the look-out men were on deck providing the anchor watch. It was a dark but windless night, still enough to catch the sounds of celebration on board the storeships, at anchor together nearer the shore.

The after cabin in the *Merlin* was of no great size and the space was a little cramped for such an occasion. The meal had been cleared away and the officers were seated round a candlelit mahogany table, with fruit and nuts before them and with decanters still in circulation. The stern windows looked out on darkness save for a distant light or two on an anchored fishing boat. Conversation was lively and Stirling started an argument when he suggested, with a hint of Scots pedantry, that the new century would really begin twelve months hence, but the others agreed to dismiss this idea as heresy.

'What matters', said Mather, 'is the way we date our letters. All our lives we have been writing '17 something' but from tomorrow it will be '1800'. We must feel that we are entering a new period of history.'

'What will be new about it?' asked Stirling. 'We shall still be fighting the same war.'

'And why not?' said Delancey. 'War is our trade and I, for one, have no other. I give you a toast, gentlemen: to the fall of Valletta!'

The toast was drunk with enthusiasm but Northmore added a word of complaint.

'For my part, sir, I can't see why the place has not fallen already. Here are all these Maltese eager for battle or anyway hating the French, and the French troops must be a starving handful.'

'Perhaps you were never there,' said Mather. 'The ramparts must be seen to be believed. You would think them the work of giants, not of men. An assault, believe me, is out of the question.'

'That's true enough,' agreed Langford. 'The fortress is a masterpiece, no question of that. I saw it once in peacetime and have never forgotten it. And this General Vaubois won't give in easily.'

'I suppose', said Mather thoughtfully, 'that he hopes for relief, a convoy from France with naval escort.'

'He is going to be damned hungry until it comes,' said Stirling.

'I think his worst trouble will be lack of fuel,' said Mather. 'It's a curious fact that men cannot eat grain – supposing he *has* grain – without cooking it. And the cook can do nothing without fuel, whether wood, charcoal, oil or coal. Malta has little fuel of its own at the best of times and Valletta, of course, has none.'

'Guernsey, where I grew up,' said Delancey, 'is much the same, with driftwood at a premium. We burn furze there and sometimes seaweed. But you are right, Mr Mather. Even rats have to be cooked. Don't you agree, Mr Northmore?'

'Well, sir, I have heard that rats are eaten sometimes in the gunroom but I have never seen it. I think it's a yarn told to youngsters who have just come aboard.'

'Well, it's more than a yarn so far as the French are concerned in Valletta,' said Stirling. 'By the time they surrender they'll have tried everything.'

There was, however, no shortage at Delancey's table that night and the glasses were all filled afresh as the hour of midnight approached. Then the conversation died away and there was a minute of silence before the ship's bell sounded and everyone cheered. Delancey then proposed the toast 'To the new century!' As he did so there came the distant sound of church bells ashore in Gozo and the crackle and bang of fireworks from the fishing harbour. Delancey then excused himself and went off to visit the other messes, proposing the same toast at each of them.

He afterwards resumed his place and saw to it that glasses were refilled for the loyal toast, the first of the new year. After rapping on the table and calling for silence, Delancey said 'Gentlemen, the King!' All remained seated, as was the naval custom, and all responded 'The King!' or, in Mather's case 'The King, God bless him!' Young Topley, nerved by an unaccustomed allowance of wine, remarked that the loyal toast was never drunk in the mess of the Royal Fusiliers – they had been told by a previous King that they need not show their loyalty – it was not in question.

Conversation became general again and was at its height when a monster rocket exploded over Gozo, lighting the shoreline that could be glimpsed through the stern windows. For an instant the whole anchorage was as light as day. Then it was dark again and there suddenly came an outcry from on deck and the noise alongside of splintered woodwork.

'See what it is,' said Delancey to young Northmore, who was gone in an instant. 'That rocket must have been costly! The Maltese and Gozotans have a great love of fireworks, I hear. They are usually reserved for the saints' days but the new year is evidently observed as piously.'

'I can never understand', said Stirling, 'how they can afford what they spend in this way. These Maltese scratch a poor living out of a stony soil. One wouldn't suppose that they had sixpence between them.'

'If they saved up for the celebration of the new century,' said Mather, 'they would know at least that it wouldn't happen too often.' There was some laughter over this, which ended rather abruptly with Northmore's return. If he had been merry, he was quickly sobered.

'Beg pardon, sir. There's a Frenchman been taken in a boat alongside. His craft was sunk with a round-shot and he has been taken prisoner.'

'This is where our party must end,' said Delancey, 'I'll bid you good-night, gentlemen. It would seem that the year 1800 has brought me work to do.'

It was the gunner who had been standing anchor watch and it was he who brought the prisoner below under escort. He was something over twenty years old, an apparently nervous and shifty character, painfully thin and apparently starving, wrapped in a blanket but still blue with cold. With a thin and sallow face, hollow eyes and untidy hair, the prisoner did not make a favourable impression.

'A Frenchman, sir,' reported the gunner, 'deserter from the *Boudeuse* frigate.'

'Thank you, Mr Helliwell. Have you searched him for arms?'

'Yes, sir. He had a thing like a midshipman's dirk and I took it from him.'

'Good. You can leave the prisoner with me and the escort outside the door.'

The prisoner was told to sit down and the interrogation followed, in French, Delancey making notes as he went on.

'Who are you?'

'Giuseppe Pozzo, Enseigne de Vaisseau.'

'Of what ship?'

'The *Boudeuse*, frigate.'

'What is your function on board that ship?'

'None, sir. She has been broken up for firewood.'

'So you were serving ashore?'

'As Aide-de-Camp to Admiral Decrès.'

'And yet you are a deserter. Why?'

'News came recently to Valletta that this man Napoleon has come to power in France.'

'How did the news come?'

'In a fishing boat from Napoli.'

'I see. But what difference does this make to you?'

'I also come from Corsica and I know the Bonaparte family – a vile, avaricious and thieving tribe of banditti. I could suffer starvation for the people of France and even for the leaders of the revolution, but for one of the Bonaparte – never!'

'So you deserted in a small boat. Where were you going? To Gozo?'

'God, no! They would kill me there. I was hoping to find a ship from Naples or Sicily. This was the ship I tried first.'

'Does she *look* like an Italian merchantman?'

'It is dark, sir. I smelt cooking and could not tear myself away. I have had no proper meal for weeks – no, for months.'

'Not even on the Admiral's staff?'

'For us it was worse. The Admiral was setting an example.'

'I see. What would you have done had you not been seen?'

'I should have tried these other ships, between you and the shore.'

'And when you found they too are British?'

'I should have given myself up to the British, never to the Maltese. You will at least treat me as a prisoner of war.'

'Don't be too sure of that. I could send you back to Decrès to face a firing squad.'

The young man looked terrified, his voice now shrill with alarm and protest:

'You have sent no other deserters back.'

'No other officers have deserted. My Commodore, Sir Thomas Troubridge, is a disciplinarian above all else. He has no sympathy for deserters. He will send you back under a flag of truce.'

'How can I save myself? What do you want from me?'

'Information.'

'I'll tell you all I know. We are starving, as you can see for yourself. We have been reduced to eating horses, dogs, cats – even rats.'

'Which meat do you prefer?'

'Asses' meat is best when you can find it, provided that the beast is not more than three or four years old.'

'How interesting. But that is not the sort of information I want. My mind is dwelling, I find, on a different problem. General Vaubois has been summoned to surrender but he has refused with scorn. Why? Because he expects relief. And I feel, myself, that he is right: that an attempt to relieve the fortress must soon be made. He and Admiral Decrès must have been told that help is on the way. When is this convoy to sail and from what port?'

'How should I know, sir? I am an officer of the lowest rank, what you would call a midshipman, not one who would attend a Council of War.'

'Listen, Citizen Pozzo, Signor Pozzo or whatever you prefer to be called. You fail, I think, to realise your position. You may be dead within a few hours.'

'I don't believe that your Commodore will send me back to Valletta. You are just trying to frighten me. Sir Troubridge would not stoop to murder.'

'You feel sure of that? Perhaps you are right. My better plan, in that case, is to hand you over to the Maltese.'

'You can't do that!'

'Why not? Can't I ask our allies to accept the custody of a prisoner of war?'

'It would be murder!'

'Look, young man. You are an enemy, you say, of Napoleon Bonaparte, for whom this fortress is being held. You must therefore want to see the fortress capitulate – with, of course, the honours of war. Now, think again. You will either talk or take the consequences. I have never supposed that Admiral Decrès is a very sympathetic type – but you, of course, will know him better than I do. As against that, the Maltese have no reason at all to like the French. General Bonaparte behaved so badly – don't you think? – while here! In your place, I should decide to talk.'

'But what should I know?' The young man's knuckles whitened as he twisted and untwisted his hands.

'As A.D.C. to Rear-Admiral Decrès, you must know when the relief attempt is to take place. That is a fact about which we need not argue. Allow me to refresh your memory. . . . Sentry! Pass the word for my steward.' Teesdale appeared as if by magic.

'Steward, is there something left over from our supper?'

'Yes, sir. There is soup, a chicken and half a leg of lamb. I could hot it up in a minute, sir.'

'Do that and put a decanter on the tray – with a little

cheese, perhaps, and a few dates.'

Teesdale withdrew and Delancey, gazing out of the stern windows, began to think aloud:

'If I were Bonaparte, I should make my relief attempt in January while the nights are long, or perhaps early in February. I should collect a squadron of some strength and a few good transports laden with ammunition and essential supplies. But I should realise that a simple plan must fail, the relief being expected. So all must depend on choosing the right commander; perhaps a junior Rear-Admiral, perhaps a Commodore. He must combine daring with caution. Or would two men be better, one to direct and the other to dash in? I have somehow to remove the blockading squadron before my supply ships can enter Grand Harbour. How? By defeating it? Or could I gain the same result by allowing it a victory?

'I have another squadron – I remind myself – under the guns of Valletta, including one very powerful ship. How is that squadron to be used and how can I bring it into action at the right time? That is, I tell myself, a difficult problem. I might begin – no, I will put it more strongly, I must certainly begin – with a clever deception plan. A young officer, to begin with, might fall into the enemy's hands. How? He could be a deserter with a personal grudge against me. For this role I might well choose a Corsican, one who could tell some story about a family feud. There are such feuds in Corsica, as all the world must know. Many people have read that book by James Boswell . . .'

Delancey rambled on intentionally, remembering as he did so that other scene, years ago, when he had been the prisoner and a Spanish colonel had played with him the game of cat and mouse. He might not himself be the world's best interrogator but he had at least been taught by a master. One began gently, mildly, applying the pressure later on. In this instance the pressure would be applied by Teesdale. It was, in fact, already being applied. A smell of roast mutton and chicken was in the air and the prisoner had begun to react. He might be bogus, he might be a liar – and Delancey thought that he probably was – but his being famished was a fact.

'If such a young officer were to tell a story that he knew to be false, he would suffer for it. I don't pretend to know – I should prefer not to know – what the Maltese would do to him. But what if he changed his mind and told the truth? He might, in the first instance, be asked to supper. Oh, it could be nothing elaborate, of course, just a matter of pot luck; a little soup, a fowl perhaps, a glass of wine. . . .' The words reinforced the smell and the young man almost whimpered.

'Now, about this squadron under orders to sail from – Toulon, shall I say? (the prisoner nodded) – it might sail at the end of January or perhaps, again, at the beginning of February . . . early February? (the prisoner nodded) . . . Just so. I seem, however, to have forgotten the name of the commander. Perhaps you could prompt my memory?'

There was at this moment a knock on the cabin door and Teesdale, told to enter, came in with a tray of covered dishes. The young man started to his feet despite himself but Delancey waved him back to his chair. The tray was left on the table and the steward withdrew.

'Wait, my friend. The food will keep hot. I may even have to send it away. . . . Now, where was I? Ah, I remember now. We were discussing, were we not, the name of the officer who has been chosen to relieve the fortress of Valletta. It would be a Rear-Admiral, we agreed . . . called . . . *called*?'

'Perrée.' The young man spat the name out with a grimace.

'But of course! Stupid of me to have forgotten. A very able officer and a very good choice. He was captured by us and since exchanged. Now, I can't imagine that the Contre-Amiral will simply sail for Valletta. The plan needs to be more subtle than that, as I'm sure you will agree. So the relieving force will sail in two divisions, or even perhaps in three?'

'No, just the one.'

'With troops as well as supplies?'

'There are troops, yes.'

'And what is the plan?'

'I know nothing more.'

'Not even the name of the ships?'

'It was not yet decided.'

'So that is all you know?'

'All – I swear it.'

Pozzo had revealed something, whether true or false, and had earned his reward.

'Thank you, Citizen, for reminding me of a few facts which had escaped my memory. I think you need a change of clothes and then some supper. "Steward!" ' Teesdale appeared in an instant. 'Supply this young officer with something to wear from the slop chest. Put his uniform somewhere to dry. Then bring him back here as soon as possible.'

Nothing more was learnt from Pozzo that night and the *Merlin* was under sail at daybreak, presently joining the Commodore off Grand Harbour. After an exchange of signals the *Merlin*'s longboat pulled over to the *Culloden* with Delancey in the sternsheets and Pozzo beside him. The squadron was in precise formation under a leaden sky with the wind rising and the spray flying over the boat. Pozzo had a brief interview with Sir Thomas and was then taken away by a French-speaking lieutenant called Revell. Delancey found himself with the Commodore, the *Culloden*'s captain and members of the Commodore's staff.

'Now tell me again,' said Sir Thomas in his usual gruff tone, 'how exactly did this man fall into our hands?'

Delancey explained, realising as he did so that Pozzo's story was not very credible. The Commodore exposed its weakness in an instant.

'This boat of his, sunk alongside, must have been quite small?'

'A sort of skiff, sir.'

'Could he have rowed in it from Valletta?'

'No, sir. Perhaps from the nearest port of Malta, and that only on a still night.'

'But he claims to have come from Valletta?'

'Yes, sir.'

'So we know that Pozzo is a liar?'

'Undoubtedly, Sir Thomas.'

'But you still think the intelligence he brings us may be important?'

'Even liars sometimes tell the truth.'

'As, for example, about the French plans?'

'His story about the expected relief is at least plausible.'

'Deception plans are usually at least plausible. Leave friend Pozzo with me and return to your ship. Reconnoitre the entrance to Grand Harbour and then come to dine with me this afternoon. I'll tell you then what we have decided.'

Back on his own quarterdeck, Delancey reflected on the mistake he had made. He had been so eager to learn about the next relief attempt that he had neglected the more immediate question of how Pozzo had reached Gozo. Troubridge, with his greater experience, had fastened at once on the weak part of the story and Delancey could see that he was right. He felt, nevertheless, that some attempt to relieve Valletta would have to be made.

It was for Troubridge to decide whether Pozzo was an actual deserter or a patriot who had volunteered for a dangerous mission. Was his information planted, and if so why? Granted that Pozzo's skiff could not have come far, it followed that he had come from Valletta in a larger boat with the skiff on board. That larger craft might have been a Maltese fishing vessel or could as easily have been the launch from a French man-of-war. Which was it? Not for the first time in his service career, Delancey was glad to think that it was not for him to decide.

An hour later the *Merlin* was close in to the harbour entrance and Delancey was studying Valletta at fairly close range. To starboard, he could see, was Fort St Elmo, the seaward end of the peninsula on which the city was built; a towering fortification under the French flag. To port, as he knew, were the other cities; Kalkara, Cospicua, Senglea, defended by Fort St Angelo. Everywhere the cliffs were crowned by honey-coloured battlements. The harbour was completely landlocked and heavily defended by hundreds of cannon. He had heard that the place was impregnable and he could well believe it. But how could a relief convoy enter the port? There was only the one entrance to Grand Harbour and a British squadron to watch it.

The problem would have been simpler if the French had control of a second port or more of the island. But this was the gauntlet they had to run. Their only chance was to send enough men-of-war to engage Troubridge in battle, followed by merchantmen who could slip into harbour while the battle continued. Or could Decrès make a sortie to cover the convoy's approach? The difficulty about that would be one of timing. Delancey went in as far as he dared, being finally checked by a single shot from Fort St Elmo. It was wide but provided proof that the sloop was within range. Delancey at oncc gavc the order to tack, needing no second hint, and no other shot was fired. The French clearly had no ammunition to waste.

Aboard the *Culloden* again, Delancey was hospitably entertained at the Commodore's table. There was no sign of Pozzo, nor was his name mentioned until after dinner when Sir Thomas took Delancey aside and motioned Lieutenant Revell to join them.

'Tell Captain Delancey what we know now about your prisoner.'

'Well, sir, I told him at first that we should send him back to Valletta. He then tried to kill himself but was prevented. I took this as proof that he is really a deserter. I then established by questioning that his story about his feud with the family of Bonaparte is rubbish. He left Corsica as a young child and knows very little about the island except from hearsay. He was no longer Aide-de-Camp to Admiral Decrès at the time of his desertion. He had been caught drawing rations for a coxswain who had actually died. This led to dismissal from the Admiral's staff and to a month as duty officer in the forward position. He was worried, I think, lest some other indiscretion should come to light, earning him further penalties. So he bribed a fisherman to take him and that skiff (which he stole) to the island of Comino. He was not seriously trying to reach Italy. His intention all along was to give himself up as a prisoner of war. I do not see him as a heroic character.'

'And what about the expected relief attempt?'

'I think that story may be true. It fits in with other intelligence reports.'

Delancey was relieved to hear this, glad to think he had not been entirely wrong and that Pozzo was the deserter he claimed to be. He would, nevertheless, be more cautious another time.

'I should be interested to know', he said, 'why a man who had lied about everything else should tell the truth about the expected relief.'

'Well, sir, it is a matter of opinion. You should know, however, that he now denies the statement he made to you. He says that you starved him into saying something about the French plans. He realised that the interrogation would go on until he provided you with some information. He says now that the information he gave you was false.'

'I think it was true and that he is lying now. He was under pressure, as he says, and those few facts were forced out of him. Yes, I agree with you: his subsequent denial adds weight to the information he gave at first.'

'If we accept that reasoning,' said the Commodore, 'we have the point of departure, the commander's name and the approximate date. I don't accept Pozzo's statement that the convoy will sail together. I should assume that the convoy will be in two divisions, possibly in three.'

'Have you decided, Sir Thomas,' asked Delancey, 'how to deal with the situation?' He knew as he said it that he had spoken out of turn.

'It is not for me to decide,' replied Troubridge, shortly. 'The decision rests with Lord Keith, who is quite as experienced as you or I. You did well, however, to bring us that prisoner and better still to question him before he had recovered from the shock of capture. Back to Gozo now and remain there until your supply ships are ready to sail.'

Once more in his own cabin, with the *Merlin* at her old anchorage, Delancey thought that the new century had so far been kind to him. An action was to be expected and he might play some part in it. He had already perhaps done something to influence the British deployment. As against that, he had made two mistakes, the first in his interrogation of Pozzo, the second in this last conversation with Troubridge. The moment he had asked the question he realised that he should not have done so. Would it count against him? On the whole he thought not. But he must never again speak out of turn. This was something to have learnt.

He opened the general chart of the Mediterranean and plotted the obvious course from Toulon to Malta. Perrée's alternatives were two. He could follow the coast of Italy, pass the Straits of Messina and approach Malta from the north, or else he could go south of Sardinia and through the Sicilian Channel, making his approach from the west. He pondered these alternatives and decided, finally, that the simpler plan was the best. Whatever route Perrée might choose he would finally have to enter Grand Harbour and there, just out of gunshot, Lord Keith would be waiting for him. To waylay the French convoy outside Toulon was a theoretical possibility but there was no time for that. No, the entrance of Grand Harbour, the position where the *Merlin* had drawn the enemy's fire, was a focal point towards which all routes must lead.

In a few days' time the Malta convoy would have sailed. At much the same hour Lord Keith would be approaching from the opposite direction. Lord Nelson might also be on the way and heaven knows what other ships had been ordered to the same rendezvous. For the convoy to reach Valletta the first necessity had been to keep the plan secret. With secrecy lost, Delancey could not see that the relief attempt could have the slightest chance of success. But the French must have foreseen the dangers. Their plans must surely involve the convergence of several squadrons; one to give battle, one to lead the pursuit away from Malta and a third to make a dash for Grand Harbour.

Some such plan might succeed against an opponent endowed with plenty of enthusiasm. It might just possibly succeed against Lord Nelson. But he was not the Commander-in-Chief. The man to be outwitted was that stolid Scotsman, Lord Keith, whose place – Delancey guessed – would be in the harbour mouth; a position from which he would not be lured by any alarm or excursion. Studying the chart and surveying the battlefield, Delancey came to what he thought might be a valuable conclusion. In warfare, he pondered, one of the worst mistakes is to be too clever. The next few weeks, he guessed, might prove the truth of this.

CHAPTER FOUR

The Malta Convoy

The orders from the Directory were clear and emphatic. Valletta was to be relieved by a squadron and convoy which would land there three thousand troops with ammunition and supplies to last the garrison for another ninety days. The gallant General Vaubois must not be left to his fate. Something must be done for the honour of France. The naval commander of the escort was not to seek an engagement but the First Consul realised that some sacrifices might have to be made.

The Malta convoy sailed as planned on February 7th, its plans perfectly well known in the streets of Toulon. The vessels were all appallingly overcrowded and the morale of the soldiers was low. They knew that they were being sent to reinforce a garrison already on the point of starvation. Supplies were being shipped at the same time, as they knew, but their own arrival would double the ration strength and shorten the period over which the supplies would last. If the voyage were unduly prolonged, moreover, the greater part of the provisions would be consumed at sea. It was again a question of whether the convoy would reach Malta at all. The likelihood was that Perrée would encounter opposition before he even sighted the island, for the British naval superiority was known to be overwhelming. The Rear-Admiral had good reason to choose the shortest route but was unable, of course, to go any faster than his slowest ship, the heavily laden *Ville-de-Marseilles*.

Knowing roughly what he was to expect, Vice-Admiral Lord Keith was off Grand Harbour with his flagship, the three-decked *Queen Charlotte* mounting a hundred guns. That kept

Decrès's flagship the *Guillaume Tell* in check and placed the goalkeeper in position. Rear-Admiral Lord Nelson, with his flag in the *Foudroyant* of 80 guns, cruised to windward of the port with *Audacious* and *Northumberland* under command. The *Alexander* cruised still further to windward and the *Lion* with the *Sirena*, Neapolitan frigate, and *Gannet*, sloop, watched the passage between Malta and Gozo. Of the remaining two sloops, *El Corso* was used as the connecting link between Nelson and the *Alexander*, the other, the *Merlin*, cruised to the north of Gozo. As the final touch the *Success*, frigate, was stationed off Sicily to give warning of the convoy's approach. Although barely on speaking terms, Lord Keith and Lord Nelson were unlikely to make any tactical error. They waited patiently for their victim to fall into the trap.

Rear-Admiral Perrée was off the coast of Sicily on February 13th. He was sighted by the *Success*, which raced back with information for Lord Keith. Captain Shuldam Beard reported one ship of the line, one frigate, two corvettes and a large transport. He did not sight the second division of the convoy, which was about five hours behind the first. As the *Success* crowded sail and finally vanished Perrée must have known that his convoy was doomed. If he had ever had a chance of success it had depended upon approaching Grand Harbour in darkness. There was no point in that after his position was known to the enemy. Turning to his flag-captain he gave orders to shorten sail. He then made a signal to the *Vestale* to the effect that an enemy frigate had been seen, ordering her to repeat that message to the *Corbière*. Morel, he reflected, would know what to do.

'I have had to make a change of plan,' Perrée then explained to his staff. 'We shall approach Malta at daybreak on the 18th. We can see then what force we have to encounter.'

'It may be no more than a frigate squadron,' said his flag-captain hopefully.

'To blockade Decrès? No, citizens. We have to face Lord Keith and that frigate has gone to tell him of our approach.'

'In that event, Citizen Rear-Admiral, you might be justified in turning back before it is too late.'

'How can I do that? I have been ordered to relieve Valletta. Were we to sail back to Toulon I should have to say "The task was impossible. There was an enemy squadron in the way." Then I should be asked "Of what strength?" To this my reply would be "I have no idea because I didn't actually see it. All I saw was a frigate." I know perfectly well that Lord Keith is outside Grand Harbour. Where else could he be? I know that he is waiting for this convoy. What else could he do? But I can't explain that to a court martial. I can turn back *after* sighting a superior force but not *before*.'

'By the time we see it we shall have lost our chance of escape.'

'Undoubtedly. That is a drawback inherent in my mission.'

All Perrée's fears were shown to be justified at daybreak on the 18th. There was a whole squadron waiting for him off Malta's south-eastern coast. The slow *Ville-de-Marseilles* was taken at once by the *Alexander*. Two corvettes managed to escape southwards but the *Généreux* fled towards Sicily, pursued by Lord Nelson in the *Foudroyant*, with the *Northumberland* and *Success*. She was actually engaged by the *Success* before the pursuit began, the frigate firing several broadsides to good effect, and it was during this exchange that Rear-Admiral Perrée was mortally wounded. The crew would seem to have been discouraged by this disaster and the *Généreux*, when overtaken, hauled down her colours after firing a single broadside. After the prizes had been secured, Lord Keith sent ships in pursuit of the two corvettes and others again to escort the prizes to Palermo or Syracuse. The effect of Lord Nelson's success was very much what Perrée had expected. The British squadron was greatly dispersed and the blockade correspondingly weakened. Unchanged, however, was the position of the *Queen Charlotte*, still flying Lord Keith's flag and still in the harbour mouth. Some other ships were also where they had been posted and among them was the sloop *Merlin*.

The sound of the gunfire which dispersed and destroyed *Perrée*'s division was faintly heard on board the *Merlin*, at anchor off Comino Island in the strait between Malta and

Gozo. The south-easterly wind brought a distant rumbling which gradually died away. The day was overcast with an occasional gleam of sunshine between the rain squalls. In the distance could be glimpsed the citadel of Victoria in Gozo, with the cathedral dome rising above the ramparts.

Not for the first time Delancey wondered how the islanders could find money enough to build a cathedral. They had, as he realised, a wonderful material in which to work. Their limestone, fresh from the quarry, could be sawn, planed, drilled or carved with ease. Placed in position it would then harden and keep its shape for centuries. How different from Guernsey granite!

Comino, in the foreground, was bleak and windswept, crowned by an old derelict castle. There was talk, he had heard, of using it for the safe custody of prisoners of war. In the other direction the waves were crashing on the rocky shores of Malta, beyond which rose the brown deserted hills. Through his telescope he could see two horsemen at a landing place, one of them presently boarding a small boat which headed now for the *Lion* (64), which lay at anchor further to the south. Captain Ball, commanding ashore, had watchers posted on the cliffs and would have the latest news about Perrée signalled to Lord Keith but sent by mounted messenger to the *Lion*. There were two other men-of-war in the strait, anchored further to the eastward, the *Gannet* and the *Sirena* perhaps five miles away.

Half an hour later came the expected signal for the captain of the *Merlin* to report to the *Lion*. The gig soon swept alongside the larger ship and Delancey was received with ceremony. The boatswain's pipe was heard, some boys manned the side and the first lieutenant met him with a salute at the entry port.

As he had approached and now, as he looked about him, Delancey could see that the *Lion* was splendidly maintained and manned; a crack ship with every rope in its place and not so much as a blister on the paintwork. Manley Dixon was among the finest officers afloat, so Delancey had been told, and he could well believe it. There had been no previous meeting, however, and each had some interest in the other. Once in the forecabin, Delancey was greeted by a vigorous well-built man with piercing eyes, very much the seaman and as obviously a man of breeding and intelligence.

'Good-morning, captain. Pray be seated and join me in a glass of Marsala. And allow me to congratulate you on the appearance of your sloop. She looks like a smart frigate in miniature, ready for anything but handled like a yacht.'

'Thank you, sir. I am fortunate in my officers but would not venture to compete in smartness with the *Lion*.'

'Thank you in turn. It is, however, the enemy with whom we now have to compete. I expect you heard the gunfire this morning? I have since had a letter from Captain Ball. He tells me that a big French transport, the *Ville-de-Marseilles*, has been captured, with two thousand troops aboard. The other ships have dispersed and their flagship is being pursued towards Sicily and will undoubtedly be taken. She is assumed to be the *Généreux*, flying the flag of Rear-Admiral Perrée . . . I hope you find the Marsala drinkable?'

'It is some of the best I have tasted, sir.'

'Ninety-seven is reckoned a good year. Well, the attempt to relieve Valletta has failed. On the basis, however, of intelligence obtained by you from a prisoner of war, we suspect that the convoy may have sailed in two divisions. Should it have done so, when are we to expect the second division?'

'Tonight, sir. I can't swear, of course, that my guess is correct; nor would it be surprising, for that matter, if the enemy plans had been changed. For all we know, the ships needed may have been lacking. But if a second division is to profit from the situation created by the first, it must arrive before the pursuit is over; and that means, tonight.'

'I agree. And what plan would you expect the enemy to adopt?'

'With the wind backing nor' easterly, my guess is that he would approach Grand Harbour from the north, keeping close under the land.'

'And so into the arms of Lord Keith?'

'Of whose presence he may not be aware. He would also

reckon to be covered by the shore batteries for the last mile or two.'

'That's true. But one question remains. Which side of Gozo? Through this strait or round the north?'

'Had I to do it, sir, I should pretend to go one way and actually go the other.'

'Yes, but which?'

'Damned if I know!'

'Look at it again then from our point of view. If we had only the one ship, where should we station her?'

'Just to windward of this strait, ready to intercept the enemy in either direction.'

'Very well, then. The enemy, knowing that, must conclude that we shall be watching the strait. So his convoy will pass north of Gozo.'

'After making a feint in this direction?'

'Something like that. Here, then, is my plan: the *Lion* will stay in or near this strait. The *Merlin* will cruise to the north of Gozo, the *Gannet* further to the east, the *Sirena* to the south.' Manley Dixon had the chart in front of him and marked it in pencil. 'What I have now to arrange is a code of signals. You and I will have the island of Gozo between us but we shall be able to see each other's rockets. White flares will mean nothing. If we locate the enemy – one red rocket. Then, to describe the enemy's strength one blue for each man-of-war and one green for each transport. Two red if I want you to join me. Is that clear?'

'Yes, sir.'

'We neither of us know if your guess is correct. Should we sight the enemy tonight, however, their convoy must represent the last French effort to save Valletta. When it fails – if it has not already failed – Vaubois will ask for terms. Before they capitulate, though, the French will try to save the *Guillaume Tell* but without, I think, the least prospect of success. You can tell your men that the fate of Valletta may well be decided tonight. Have they fought a night action before?'

'No, sir.'

'Then exercise them beforehand and make certain they

know what they are doing. All sorts of things can go wrong and it is all too easy to fire at your own side. You will look foolish in the morning if it turns out that you have sunk the *Gannet*.'

'Aye, aye, sir.'

On his way back to his ship, Delancey gave thought to all that Manley Dixon had said. His men had never fought at night and he realised now that they had been trained almost entirely in daylight. It was partly a matter of routine and partly a matter of checking mistakes more easily. Exercising the great guns and small arms normally took place immediately after Divisions (Four Bells in the Forenoon Watch or 10.0 a.m.) or else after dinner at 1.30 p.m. To fix an unusual hour and one after dark would have interfered with other duties and would have been impossible, of course, after hammocks had been piped down. And yet a night action was quite likely, bringing with it problems of its own. Too little thought was given to this and he had himself been as much to blame as anyone else.

On board his own ship again, he explained the situation to Mather and Stirling and added that he would clear for action at nightfall, inspect the guns and talk to the gun captains. It was far from certain that the enemy would appear, but the result of the action, if there was to be one, would be terribly important. A single vessel breaking the blockade and entering Grand Harbour would have a big effect on the morale of the garrison of Valletta, suggesting to them that what could be done once might be done again. That could be enough to prolong the siege for another thirty days. No single enemy craft, therefore, not even the smallest, must be allowed through.

The order to clear for action was given after the crew's supper and there followed a careful inspection of the men and the equipment. Each gun had a crew of nine, numbered off so that each man knew exactly what he had to do. Number One was responsible for the priming wires, tube boxes and vent bit, Number Two for the vent plugs and spar breeching and so down to Number Nine, who had the powder box. The gun would be virtually out of action if the spike and mallet were lost or if Number Six was without his sponge, rammer or worm. Nor was it merely a question of keeping the gun in action. Half a dozen possible mistakes could result in blowing up the whole equipment and leaving the crew dismembered, blinded or dead.

Delancey made his rounds with Topley at heel as his A.D.C., explaining to the youngster how vital it was to have everything in its proper place, from the lantern to the shot grimmet. When he was finished with the guns, Delancey went on to inspect the magazine, of which the gunner had the key, and made sure that the carpenter had the sounding iron and shot plugs, that the riggers had their stoppers and tackles. There was a great deal to do, from extinguishing the galley fire to sanding the decks, and it all had to be done in a matter of minutes. When Delancey was satisfied with the ship's state of readiness, he collected the gun captains round him and gave them some words of warning:

'You all know that the French are besieged in Valletta. The fortress is too strong for us to storm, so we are starving them out. They made this morning what may have been their last attempt to break the blockade. Their convoy was intercepted by Lord Keith and Lord Nelson, their ships were chased off and probably made to haul down their colours. It seems possible, however, that a second convoy may be following the first, hoping to find the coast clear. We don't know that this is their plan but we think it possible. But they won't find the coast clear. They will be confronted, in fact, by the *Lion*, by the *Gannet* and, above all, by the *Merlin*. If they attempt to enter Grand Harbour it must be tonight. In that event we shall intercept them and that means a night action.

'As you can see for yourselves, it is a dark night, moonless and overcast. It is not going to be simple to see the target. Under such conditions it is easy to waste ammunition, firing at nothing. Our only remedy is to fire at the flashes of the enemy's guns. You will all be on your own so far as that goes, and I rely upon each of you to aim carefully, taking your time. It is useless to fire into the darkness, hoping that the enemy will be there. That is what we might expect the French to do, but we must be wiser. We shall use flares at first, enough of them to distinguish friend from foe. After that we must rely upon good eyesight, careful aim and steadiness under fire. If you have questions to ask, now is the time for them.'

'Begging your pardon, sir,' said an oldish gun captain called Dyer. 'Shouldn't we do better to close with the enemy and deal with him at half-pistol-shot range? That way, we couldn't miss, not even in the dark!' Some of the others murmured agreement with this, one of them adding: 'Aye, sir, close range is what the Frenchies don't like!' 'Least of all', said a third called Philips, 'if we load with nails and bolts and bits of hoop iron!' There was some laughter at this and scattered applause. 'That's the way to give them a belly-ache!'

'Listen, men,' replied Delancey, 'and take heed of what I say. First, I won't fight at close range and I'll tell you why. Any ships sent to relieve Valletta will have troops on board, scores or even hundreds of them. Come to close range and we shall have muskets against us in numbers we can't match. So I shall keep out of musket shot. There are risks enough in battle without adding that one. Second, I'll have no firing of scrap metal. Why not? Because these fragments may wedge the cannon-ball. What happens then? You burst the gun. Oh, I know what the old seamen say! But it's a fool's trick, really, and I'll not allow it.'

'Can you tell us, sir, whether we shall have men-of-war to beat or merely transports?' The question came from one of the younger men called Gilling.

'I've no means of knowing but I should guess that there might be both. If I have a choice, I'll take the transports, since they are of more value, probably, to General Vaubois.'

There were no more questions and Delancey dismissed the gun captains, telling them to pass on the information to their gun crews. Looking along the deck, he could see each group collected under a lantern, the warm light revealing the sun-burnt faces. He could have addressed them all together but the way he had done it had given more authority to the gun captains. He had tried to make them feel that it was their battle and he knew that this was the fact.

The *Merlin* was cruising north of Gozo, alone in the

darkness, her position verifiable only from a few scattered lights ashore. The only sails seen at sunset had been those of Maltese fishermen. The sloop was cleared for action but the men had been told to lie down between the guns and take what rest they could. As time passed men on the look-out strained ever harder to pierce the darkness and Delancey, pacing the quarterdeck, came near to exhausting his patience. Mather joined him and they discussed for a while the likelihood of action before daybreak.

An hour or so passed and then, suddenly, the sky was lit beyond Gozo and there was the distant boom of a gun. There was another flare soon afterwards revealing the hills of Gozo in sharp silhouette. It might, of course, be some trading polacre that the *Lion* had sighted. Ten minutes later, however, a third flare was the prelude to some more persistent firing, four or five shots in succession. Then there followed what Delancey had been waiting for, a single red rocket.

'Mr Langford – a white flare, please.' The shores of Gozo were lit for an instant and Delancey glimpsed a sail off the island's north-westerly point.

'Mr Mather. Beat to quarters!' The drum beat urgently to bring the men to their guns.

'Pass the word for Mr Stirling.'

When both lieutenants were there Delancey told them what little he knew.

'One enemy sail has been sighted from the *Lion*. My guess is that there are others and that some of them will prove to be transports, more important to the enemy than their men-of-war. They must be prevented, at all costs, from entering Grand Harbour.'

'With respect, sir,' urged Sitrling, 'couldn't we leave the merchantmen to the *Sirena* and the *Gannet*?'

'I wish we could. But the *Gannet* is rather distant and a Neapolitan frigate is a doubtful quantity. She is or appears to be in tolerable order but her crew, I would guess, have never been under fire. What is her accuracy of shooting at night? We don't even know that her men can hit anything in daylight, or have ever, for that matter, fired her guns at all.'

The conversation died away but there was a further flare from the *Lion*'s direction, to which the *Merlin* replied in kind. With night-glasses already focused in the right direction, Delancey and the other could now distinguish three sail where one had been seen before.

'A schooner in the lead,' said Mather, 'followed by two ships, one a corvette, the other a merchantman.'

'Agreed,' said Delancey. 'A red rocket, please, Mr Langford. Pause for one minute and then let us have a blue and two green.' The rockets soared and burst overhead, conveying their message to Delancey's senior officer. From the *Lion*'s direction there came, in reply, a single green rocket.

'Now, gentlemen,' said Delancey, 'we have the complete picture. The convoy comprises a corvette and three merchantmen or transports. Of the three, one should fall to the *Lion* and the other two to us.'

Despite the problems which were going to face him – and he had already begun to foresee them – Delancey had a certain feeling of satisfaction. He had formed a theory about the French plan for the relief of Valletta and he had been proved right. Their convoy *had* sailed in two divisions and here was the second division, already more or less trapped. Whoever commanded it must know by now that he had been seen. What would he decide to do?

CHAPTER FIVE

The Fall of Valletta

Delancey's plan was to wear when abreast of the convoy and then close on the leading vessel, the schooner. But the next flare revealed the enemy's response to his expected move. The three vessels had begun to scatter, the schooner heading nearer the coast, the leading merchantman coming closer to the wind and the corvette holding her course as if to challenge the *Merlin*. The purpose of the manoeuvre was clear enough. If Delancey fought the corvette the other two would race for Grand Harbour under every scrap of canvas they could spread. If the *Gannet* intercepted one of them it would be the schooner and the other and larger vessel might still get through.

'Damnation!' said Mather, softly. 'We are made to take our pick.'

'Could we cripple one and take t'other?' asked Stirling.

'What – at *night*?' was Delancey's reply. He needed to say no more because the task of shooting down an opponent's mast, difficult enough in daylight, was plainly impossible in the dark when the gunners had little or nothing to aim at.

'Not even if we closed the range?' asked Stirling.

'Against a ship carrying infantry? It would be madness. Haul close to the wind, Mr Mather, and aim to intercept the merchantman on our starboard bow.'

Delancey left the quarterdeck, with young Topley at heel, and made a tour of the main deck, having a final word with each gun captain. 'Aim at the flash,' he said to each of them, 'but if you can't see anything, don't waste your shot.' He asked himself, meanwhile, whether he had made the right decision. The enemy had wanted him to fight the corvette, which was enough in itself to make him decide against it.

But could the French be more subtle than that, guessing that he would turn aside from the challenge? The merchant ship was certainly bigger but what if the corvette were laden with the more vital supplies, the more important men; medical stores, mortars, explosives, artillerymen, engineers and staff? In that event he himself could be made to look too clever and perhaps too cowardly. Anyway, he had made his decision and he knew that, in war, any decision is better than an inability to decide.

Back on the quarterdeck and peering once more into the darkness, he had now to wrestle with a problem in mental arithmetic. At the time of lighting his last flare the enemy transport had been, he guessed, about six miles away. What was his own speed? There was a stiff breeze blowing but he was close to the wind . . . call it, seven knots. Allow the enemy the same speed – no, five knots, more likely – and interception should take place in half an hour, say, after the last flare. That had been fifteen minutes ago. He must give it another five minutes. To light his next flare too soon would be a mistake, revealing his plan before it was too late for the French to change theirs. To leave it too late, on the other hand, would be worse still for he might cross his opponent's wake without firing, or even collide with her and see his crew massacred by small-arms fire.

Straining his eyes afresh he could see nothing in the darkness except the foam on the nearer waves. He forced himself to wait another three minutes. It was, however, the Frenchman whose nerve failed first. A flare was lit on board the corvette, now on the *Merlin*'s port quarter, and the momentary light revealed the French transport, less than half a mile away on the port bow, nearer than Delancey had expected and crowding all the canvas she had.

'We are forereaching on her,' said Mather, and Delancey could see that this was true. He would cross her bows in about four minutes' time and at a distance of two cables. That was not, however, what he wanted for he would have to tack immediately afterwards and might even be caught in irons.

'Helm hard up!' he shouted and then, 'Steady as she goes,' and 'Another flare, Mr Langford.' The Frenchman was now close on the *Merlin*'s starboard bow. 'Tack!' he yelled and there was frenzied activity as course was altered and the yards braced round. 'Helm's a-lee,' called the quartermaster and 'Another flare!' shouted Delancey. The *Merlin* had lost ground and was about to cross the French ship's wake. Being now, however, on the same tack, Delancey could afterwards engage her from to windward, choosing his own range. Ten minutes later he judged that the moment had come.

'Flare, Mr Langford,' he shouted, and then, 'Fire!' This last order was addressed to the gun captain of the after carronade on the quarterdeck. Firing this weapon was the signal to the rest, who would fire as they sighted the target. There was no attempt to fire the guns simultaneously but even a ragged broadside heeled the ship over for a minute, making the last shots go too high.

Then the helm was put up and the next flare revealed the French ship ahead of the *Merlin* at three cables' distance and on a parallel course to leeward. The enemy guns fired at that moment but were poorly aimed. There was a simultaneous crackle of musketry, some of the bullets thudding into the *Merlin*'s timber. Delancey's small-arms men prepared to reply but Delancey told them to hold their fire, since the enemy was out of effective range.

Until the action began the two sides had seen nothing of each other except by the light of flares but each ship was now faintly visible to her opponent. There was a battle lantern beside each gun and the glimmer from the ports could just be seen. Because of the smoke added to the darkness the gun captains could see less than anyone but the French ship's musketry marked her position, the sparkle defining the length of her deck. It was now Delancey's duty, as he knew, to assess the weight of the enemy's broadside. So far as he could make out, the French ship had nine ports a-side on her main deck, four a-side on her quarterdeck. It seemed, however, as if her midship ports were empty, leaving her with only five main-deck guns to the *Merlin*'s eight but with four on the quarterdeck to the *Merlin*'s three; eight all told against eleven.

In calibre the guns on either side were probably much the same but the French ship must be cluttered with stores for Valletta. So, given a higher British rate of fire (which could be assumed) the enemy should be beaten in about thirty minutes. Calling for another flare, Delancey could see by its light that the French corvette was still heading southwards and that the schooner, still more distant, was doing the same. His immediate opponent was to be left to her fate while the other two (or three?) made their dash for Grand Harbour.

Firing as blindly as they were, the guns on either side were slow to find their target. From being to leeward, the French guns tended to have too much elevation, some of their shot going through the *Merlin*'s sails but more of them going into the void. The first serious damage that Delancey saw was the destruction near him of a quarterdeck carronade. A shot hit the muzzle while the men were reloading, driving the piece off its slide and across the deck. The two men unhurt carried the other two below, one bleeding profusely and the other badly mangled.

Other shots had penetrated the main deck where another gun had been put out of action and more damage had been done to the forecastle. Delancey assumed that his guns were at least as effective but a long time passed before he could see any actual damage. Then the Frenchman's mizen-topmast went over the side, causing an immediate loss of speed. The *Merlin* went ahead of her opponent and Delancey was able to cross the Frenchman's bows, firing a raking broadside and then crossing again to give her the other broadside. The French captain did not wait for any further treatment on these lines, preferring to turn into the wind and engage on more equal terms. The move was reasonable in itself but marked the abandonment of the enemy's original purpose, which was to reach Grand Harbour. Delancey followed suit, coming into the wind at about two cables' distance.

Five minutes later the French guns fell silent. 'A flare, Mr Langford,' shouted Delancey, and the whole scene was momentarily lit, revealing the fact that the tricolour had been lowered.

'Cease fire!' Delancey called to the gun crews near him and then repeated the order from the break of the quarterdeck, sending young Topley to carry the message forward. The guns' thunder died away and the men cheered briefly, concluding that the battle was over. A distant sound of gunfire with flashes glimpsed to the southward proved that this was not entirely true. For Delancey, however, the immediate problem was to secure his prize.

Sending for the boatswain and carpenter, Delancey called for a report on the ship's boats. All, it seemed, had been more or less damaged but the carpenter could make the longboat watertight in perhaps an hour. Telling him to get to work on it, Delancey made a quick inspection of ship and crew, collecting returns of casualties and damage. Then Mather and Stirling joined him on the quarterdeck and Delancey issued his orders.

'We have sustained more damage than I thought and there is a lot of work to do. Your task, Mr Mather, will be to have the ship ready to renew the action. Your task, Mr Stirling, will be to take possession of the prize, disarm the enemy, send all their small-arms back in the longboat together with the ship's captain and officers, and have the prize fit to make sail by daybreak. As we have no boat ready, however, I propose to close with the enemy and cover her at short range before you take possession. The prize crew will include Mr Northmore, a boatswain's mate and twenty seamen, half from each watch, and all fully armed.'

Orders were now given to wear ship, the foretopsail being braced round until the ship was under way. Then the *Merlin* sailed a neat circle, coming once more into the wind but now within pistol shot of the prize. All the guns were manned on that side and there was light enough to see that the French ship had been considerably damaged. From amidships on board the *Merlin* came the sound of hammering as the longboat was being repaired. She would be ready to lower in another fifteen minutes.

At that instant the French ship fired her broadside. Her bulwarks sparkled with a volley of small-arms and the musket balls swept the *Merlin*'s deck. With a sense of shock, Delancey realised that he had fallen for the oldest ruse in the book. 'Load with grape-shot!' he shouted to the quarter-deck gunners and then hurried down to the main deck, repeating the same order: 'Grape-shot – fire at the enemy's deck!' By the time he reached the forecastle, the carronade there was already being served with grape-shot.

Dashing back, he called out 'Small-arms men!' They were collected in the waist and he sent them up the foremast. 'Clear the enemy's deck!' he yelled after them. Then he sent Mr Northmore to the foretop with orders to direct their fire on the enemy's quarterdeck. 'Take three men to the maintop, Mr Topley. Issue them with grenades and try to reach the enemy's deck.' The situation was extremely dangerous, as everyone could see. If Delancey tried to make sail, half his topmen would be killed or wounded. If he closed with the enemy his crew would be overwhelmed by superior numbers. His only course was to fight until the enemy surrendered.

Raging along the line of the guns he called on his men to make the effort of their lives. 'Come on, men,' he yelled, 'it's us or them! Fire and reload!' The deck was bedlam, the noise shattering, the smoke collecting in between decks and the musket-balls thudding into the timber. Back on the quarterdeck, he found only two carronades in action. 'Bring another over!' He pointed to the carronades on the disengaged side and a group of seamen began to drag one of them across. Grabbing a musket and bandoleer and telling young Topley to grab another, he sprang into the mizen shrouds. Once in the fighting top, he fired a couple of shots and then told the youngster to carry on.

A minute or two later he was on the forecastle again, helping to drag another carronade across the deck. 'Grape-shot and canister!' he shouted as he scrambled down the ladder. 'Teach the frogs a lesson!' For the next twenty minutes he tried to be everywhere at once, ending once more on the quarterdeck, sweating, dirty and hoarse with shouting. There were three carronades now in action and two small-arms men firing and reloading as fast as they could – one of them the cook and the other the purser's steward. There was no one, he thought, left out of the battle. His men were giving of their best.

The action ended as suddenly as it began. Looking across, Delancey could see that the enemy had again ceased fire. Someone amidships was waving a white cloth. The tricolour, which must have been rehoisted, was being hauled down. So much could be seen by the light of a fire which men on the forecastle were trying to extinguish.

'Cease fire!' called Delancey, and sent a man forward to repeat the order. A few more shots were fired from the fighting tops and another grenade exploded on the Frenchman's deck. Then the firing died away and all was silent, even the distant gunfire having died away. 'A flare, Mr Langford! And pass the word there for Mr Stirling – yes, and for Mr Corbin!'

Preparations began once more for taking possession of the prize. The longboat, oddly enough, had sustained no further damage and was almost seaworthy. After being patched in a couple of places, the boat was lowered and manned. Delancey had a final word with Stirling. 'We have found that these men are not to be trusted. We shall be ready to open fire again as soon as you fire a musket.' Delancey watched as the boat rowed across and was glad to see that the fire was being brought under control. In a quarter of an hour the boat returned with the French officers and a first consignment of muskets.

The captain, it appeared, was a Capitaine de Corvette called Bisson, who first saluted and then gave up his sword. Delancey replied rather curtly, asking him why he resumed the action after his surrender. 'No, no!' Bisson protested, 'I had not struck my flag! It was shot away. When I realised what had happened, I hoisted another.' It was a lame story but not easy to disprove. Having sent his prisoners below, Delancey and Mather began putting their ship to rights. There were hours of work to do, beginning with a new collection of reports and going on to the replacement and repair of sails and cordage.

Delancey had then to visit and condole with the eighteen men wounded. Of the seven men killed two had been petty officers, whose vacancies had to be filled. The gunners came to report on the expenditure of ammunition, which had been considerable, and the quantities still remaining. The carpenter reported that the ship was leaking and that there must be a shot-hole he had not yet located. A number of hammocks had been shot through in the nettings and more would have to be issued. There were reports to come in from the sailmaker, the armourer, the cooper and the cook. Bloodstains had to be removed from the deck – they were bad for morale.

Then came Stirling's report from the prize, named at last as *L'Antelope*, transport, armed with twenty guns and carrying a hundred and forty soldiers in addition to her crew. By comparison with the *Merlin* the French ship had sustained heavy casualties and a great deal of damage. With so many on board, however, she had enough men to man the pumps and was in no immediate danger of foundering. Repairs were urgent, nevertheless, and Stirling would have the French carpenters at work for the rest of the night. It was indeed a hard night's work for everyone.

Delancey made sail at daybreak, with his prize in company, and finally joined the *Lion* at anchor in the lee of Comino Island. The *Gannet* and *Sirena* came into the anchorage soon afterwards and Manley Dixon made the signal for all captains. Short of sleep as he was, Delancey had managed to shave, wash and change into a clean uniform. He now saw to it that his boat should be first alongside.

'Good-morning, captain,' said Manley Dixon, looking as smart as his visitor. 'Allow me to congratulate you on the part you have played in the siege of Valletta. I was less fortunate and have nothing to show for my night's work. It remains to see how the others have fared. Have some coffee in the meanwhile. Steward!'

Next to arrive was the sharp-faced and wasp-like Captain Farrant of the *Gannet*, tired, unshaven and cross.

'I saw all your fireworks up north', he explained, 'and realised that you were in action. So I kept close in with the land, thinking that any French craft bound for Grand Harbour would do the same. Sure enough, there was a schooner, obviously French and heading south. I fired a red rocket and went in chase. She edged closer to the rocks, so close that she only just cleared the north point of Salina Bay. Then I opened fire with my bow-chasers and she ran straight into a reef –'

'I know,' said Manley Dixon, 'the Ghallis Rocks.'

'That's right, sir. Her mast went over the side and I could see that she was a total loss. By the light of a flare I saw that some of her crew were reaching the shore in a boat.'

'You didn't try to save the rest?' asked Manley Dixon.

'No, sir, I did not. I wanted no closer acquaintance with the reef, being close enough as it was.'

'I see. That accounts for the schooner. The craft that I sighted was something even smaller, a cutter. After drawing attention to herself she made off northwards. I did not follow and must suppose that she will reach Egypt.'

At that moment the captain of the *Sirena* was shown into the cabin, a far from presentable man from Naples; dirty, nervous, shabby and evasive. He was called Victor Ricasoli and was accompanied by a young man from Palermo who acted as his English interpreter and made the following report:

'The captain says that he sighted a French frigate last night, one of the largest class, mounting forty-four guns. He made sail to intercept her after lighting flares and sending up a blue rocket. He fired several shot with his bow-chasers but the French avoided action, crowding sail to the south-east and away from Malta. The French frigate fired only her stern-chasers, which were eighteen-pounders, and the captain could see, through his night-glasses, that she was filled with troops. He presumes that she will make her way to Egypt.'

'Thank you, captain,' said Manley Dixon. 'That accounts for the second division of the French convoy: one ship taken, one schooner wrecked, one man-of-war and one cutter escaped. No single vessel has broken the blockade and Valletta should fall in a matter of months, following the last act of the drama.'

'What act, sir?' asked Farrant.

'The attempted escape of the *Guillaume Tell*.'

Captain Ricasoli was the first to go, after paying the proper compliments through his interpreter. Farrant looked after him with a glance of contempt.

'So the *Sirena* chased off a French frigate of the largest

class! Fiddlesticks! I saw her only in the distance by the light of a flare but she was nothing more than a corvette of eighteen guns at most. The truth is that our Neapolitan friend let her go, a ship half the size of the *Sirena.* My guess would be that the Signori Capitano is not exactly spoiling for a fight.'

'Be fair, captain,' Delancey protested. 'Neither he nor his men have ever been in action. I doubt if they have even so much as fired their guns in a practice shoot. Would you yourself risk a night action with an untried crew?'

'If need be,' replied Farrant. 'I shouldn't suppose that the French corvette would be any better trained.'

'And yet she should be better than *L'Antelope*,' said Delancey, 'a ship which left me with seven killed and eighteen wounded – two of them since died!'

'I'm a little surprised, captain, that you didn't go after the corvette yourself. You might have been made post if you'd taken her.'

'Don't you think Delancey knew that?' Manley Dixon asked. 'He chose the transport because she was laden with vital stores for General Vaubois and *L'Antelope* is pierced in fact for twenty-four guns, being a bigger ship than the *Merlin.*'

'Oh, well, I'm sure that Delancey had his reasons. I could do with some prize-money myself.'

Farrant took his leave and Delancey thanked Manley Dixon for his support.

'Do you think, sir,' he went on, 'that some officers will hold this against me? Or shall I be given credit for making the right decision?'

'Neither one nor t'other,' Manley Dixon laughed. 'The affair will be forgotten in a month; sooner, indeed, if anything more dramatic should happen. We have provided a mere prelude to the great moment when Valletta capitulates. And how else could the story end? For Bonaparte to hold Malta without a fleet in the Mediterranean is impossible. We may have hastened the capitulation by a month or so, maybe even by three months. We should be foolish, however, to claim more than that.'

As an immediate sequal to this action Delancey was ordered

to take the *Merlin* to Palermo for repair. He did so after landing his prisoners and wounded on the island of Gozo. During a week spent ashore in Sicily he wondered, for the hundredth time, how he could have made the mistake which cost so many lives. To think the battle won before it is over must be the most elementary blunder.

He could find a little consolation, however, in two circumstances. First of all, his men did not blame him for anything. They cursed the French, to be sure, for a treacherous lot of landlubbers but they thought him perfectly justified in closing the range. In the second place, he knew that he had made the right decision when the French opened fire again. The alternative had been to make sail and withdraw out of musket shot but he reflected now that this would have been fatal. Casualties apart, it would have been bad for morale. As things were, the French had been fairly beaten and his men were all proud of themselves. They owed the victory to their own rapidity of fire, not merely to their captain's cleverness (clever though he might be). Mather reported that the men were in good heart, cheered by the prospect of prize-money. In her class and for her size the *Merlin* was becoming a crack ship.

This did not save her, however, from routine work in trade protection. News came of the *Guillaume Tell*'s capture while attempting to escape, followed by the capture of the *Diane*, frigate, also out of Valletta. It was evident in August that the fortress was about to fall and it was late in that month that Delancey was ordered back to Malta, escorting some victuallers which would feed the prisoners after their capitulation.

At the last moment Delancey was ordered to give a passage to a Captain Laurence Savage, ranking commander but about to be posted. He had recently come from Malta and was able to give Delancey the news. It also transpired that he was a Guernseyman from St Sampson's, Le Sauvage being the original version of his surname. He dined at Delancey's table soon after the *Merlin* sailed from Palermo. He was short, burly, grey-haired, with a scarred face and a slight limp. Congratulating him on his coming promotion, Delancey asked him what ship he was to command.

'A 64-gun ship called *Athénien,* which belonged to the Knights of Malta and is now at Valletta. After the fortress falls and provided the French haven't burnt her for firewood – after she has been repaired, moreover – I am to sail her to England.' He heaved a long sight, closed his eyes and opened them again and said with tired satisfaction, 'Then I shall go ashore and stay there.'

'Why not remain in the service, sir, and see your flag hoisted?'

'Me? I'm too old for that, spent too many years as a lieutenant. I should be Rear-Admiral at the age of ninety. No, I'm fifty-six and have been at sea for forty-three years. I've battled the watch for long enough and it's time to quit. The time comes when you can't climb the rigging, can't see the signal and don't hear the breakers on the reef. It's time then to drop anchor in a country cottage and grow cabbages. Still, I am grateful to Sir James Saumarez, who brought me into the service and to whom I owe this final promotion. As a Guernseyman, you will have met him, I expect?'

'No, sir. I know him only by reputation. He is Guernsey's hero, of course.'

'A fine seaman is Sir James. He fought at St Vincent and the Nile and must be near the top of the captain's list. He doesn't make friends too easily, though.'

'A contrast to Lord Nelson?'

'He could hardly be more so. Nelson is all emotion and pathos, now sorry for himself and now angry with Lord Keith for being born a dozen years earlier and commissioned seven years sooner. Nelson can be childish at times, as in wanting to capture the French ships which escaped him at the Nile. The *Généreux* was not important in herself but he wanted her to make his victory more complete – yes, and wanted to make the capture in person. Once she was taken he pleaded sickness and went off home. But don't mistake me about Nelson. He has no equal in battle. His weakness is in wanting to be liked, honoured and recognised, as also in being sulky when asked to take second place.'

'He is popular with the seamen, I believe.'

'Nobody could be more popular but his fleet was one which

St Vincent and Keith had disciplined. Sir James is very different, as you'll find for yourself some day. He always shows interest in anyone from Guernsey.'

Thinking about this conversation afterwards, Delancey reflected that Sir James Saumarez's patronage had done little to hasten Savage's promotion. Was that because Saumarez would admit no favourites and had no followers? Or was it because Savage had been too outspoken? He was now on the point of retirement but Delancey suspected that he had been incautious all along. To speak as he had done of Lord Nelson was taking a risk. If Lord Nelson's preference for another man's wife were as notorious as his neglect of his own, the wise officer was one who knew nothing about it.

So far as patronage went, Delancey was barely known to Lord Keith and to Troubridge. Lord Nelson he had not so much as seen and to other rising men like Sir John Borlase Warren or Sir Edward Pellew he was not even known by name. If Saumarez came to the Mediterranean it might make some difference to his prospects. There was no certainty of patronage from that quarter, he told himself, but it represented his best chance. He could certainly expect no help from anyone else.

Soon afterwards the *Merlin* entered Grand Harbour, Valletta, and Delancey found himself in one of the finest harbours in the world, a pattern of deep-water creeks flanked by jetties and warehouses, sheltered by high ground and protected by towering honey-coloured ramparts and bastions. 'It looks like the towers of Babylon!' he said to Savage. 'Just think of this as a naval base', he went on, 'midway between the western and eastern halves of the Mediterranean, impregnable, secure, and ours for as long as we have a navy.'

'The fortress is breath-taking,' Savage agreed. This impression was strengthened when they went ashore to call on the Governor at St Anton Palace. They were astonished to see the depth of the moat, cut deep into the solid rock. Seen close at hand, the defensive works were tremendous. Captain Ball received them cordially and had a kind word to say about the part played by the *Merlin* in frustrating the last French attempt to relieve Valletta. 'When that failed,' he said,

'General Vaubois knew that the end had come.'

Delancey and Savage dismissed their carriage in Valletta and walked through the city, passing the Opera House, with its fine classical columns and pediment, and finally emerging from the main gate. Looking again into the moat, Savage exclaimed: 'You could lose a church in that ditch and never know where it had gone.' They walked on through Floriana; in concept at least, the finest shopping street in Europe, lined on either side with a superb colonnade. Then they went down to the quay-side where their boat was waiting.

'Now to find the *Athénien*!' said Delancey. They eventually found her in Kalkara creek, a fine ship but in great need of repair. After going round her decks, Savage expressed his relief: 'She is in fairly good shape, after all. She will be able to reach England under her own sails. I shall reach post-rank yet!' Delancey left his friend on board and was rowed back to the *Merlin.* He had found in Savage a man he could like and respect.

For the rest of the year 1800 the *Merlin* was based on Malta, employed in routine duties and commerce protection. At one stage Delancey had parties of men working on board the *Athénien,* which had to be rigged for sea. This work was finished early in 1801 and Savage invited Delancey to dinner on the day before the *Athénien* was to sail.

'Welcome aboard! Have you heard the news?'

'That Spain has declared war?'

'Yes, and Bonaparte is to buy six Spanish sail of the line, now at Cadiz.'

'So with his three French ships at Toulon –'

'And six more ships under the Spanish flag –'

'He will have a fleet again, and one big enough to attempt the rescue of his army marooned in Egypt!'

'So it is a question of whether Portugal can remain our ally, withstanding Spanish pressure. If not, we have lost the use of the harbour at Lisbon.'

'Altogether, then,' Delancey concluded, 'the balance of power in the Mediterranean is tilting again in Bonaparte's favour. Thank God we have Valletta! He won't recover that in a hurry. There could, however, be another siege of Gibraltar, and it mayn't be too safe a passage for the *Athénien*.'

'I shall make it, never fear! And now you must meet my other guests.'

It was a convivial party but with all the talk about the new situation. The British had not lost control of the Mediterranean but the likelihood was that they would have to fight for it again. Among naval officers, and even to some extent on the lower deck, the prospect was more attractive than otherwise. There was every likelihood of action but the centre of interest was moving westwards towards the Strait of Gibraltar.

It became known in May that the French ships at Toulon were fitting for sea and had been placed under the command of Rear-Admiral Durand Linois. Secret agents added the intelligence that Linois was to sail for Cadiz in June. Senior naval officer at Malta was then Rear-Admiral Sir John Borlase Warren, who decided to send this news at once to Gibraltar. Delancey was sent for on board the *Renown* and was given his orders by the Rear-Admiral's flag-lieutenant. The Admiral he did not see but his outer office was a scene of almost frantic activity, with orders being written and messages dispatched and received.

'The Admiral has an urgent dispatch for the senior naval officer at Gibraltar. Is the *Merlin* ready to sail at once?'

'I can sail tomorrow morning.'

'Very well, then. Here is the dispatch, sir. You will realise that the situation is changing rapidly and that you will have to keep a sharp look-out for the Spanish as well as the French, more especially as you approach the Straits. We suppose that Linois is still at Toulon but plans could have changed and he might be already at sea. As against that, the Spanish ships at Cadiz could have been ordered to Toulon, in which case you might sight them.'

'I shall bear that possibility in mind.'

'Sir John supposes that a flag-officer will be on his way to Gibraltar and should be there before you. In a postscript to his dispatch, Sir John authorises that officer, whoever he may be, to retain the *Merlin* with his flag, at least for the time being. He feels that the flag-officer in question may have dispatches for England and no other sloop at his disposal.'

'That is fully understood.'

'I should perhaps tell you, sir, in confidence, that Sir John had meant to entrust this dispatch to Captain Lord Cochrane of the *Speedy*, but that sloop has not returned and is indeed some weeks overdue.'

'Let us hope she has not been taken.'

'The Admiral would not be heartbroken if she were. The trouble we have had with Lord Cochrane is past my powers of description. His exploits may be dramatic but he is never there when wanted. When he is present we soon wish that he weren't. Earlier this year his lordship attended a ball in Valletta, organised by French royalists, and ended by fighting a duel with one of them.'

'He makes a lot of prize-money, I have been told.'

'He does, indeed, sir. He is chasing enemy shipping when under orders to protect our own. That is what he will be doing now and that is why you will have to take his place.'

'Don't grieve too much on my account. I think that Gibraltar may be the scene of action in the near future and I would rather be there than here. I shan't waste time, I promise you, in the pursuit of Spanish coasters. In return for that undertaking, you might tell me which Admiral I am likely to find there.'

'We have no means of knowing, sir. The change in the situation must compel their lordships to send a squadron to Gibraltar. The flag-officer selected will not be one of those on the station but one chosen for this particular service.'

'So you have no idea which officer is likely to be chosen?'

'No, sir. Considering the strength of the squadron which will be needed and listing the senior officers likely to be available, Sir John made a guess but it is no more than that.'

'And whom did he think would be chosen?'

'Sir James Saumarez.'

CHAPTER SIX

Raid on Majorca

'I should esteem it a personal favour', said Colonel Windham, the Acting Governor of Minorca, 'if you would afford protection to the *Venturer* of Whitehaven.' Delancey had noticed the ship in harbour but her importance had not been obvious. His passage from Malta had been uneventful and his dispatch for Minorca had been delivered. It looked now as if his further voyage was to be complicated by the need to escort a merchantman. It was an unwelcome prospect but he made no immediate comment. He merely looked inquiringly at the Colonel, who realised that some further explanation was wanted.

'She will carry the mails and, what is more to the point, a quantity of military stores. Her safe arrival is a matter of some consequence.'

Delancey would have liked to ask 'To whom?' – suspecting as he did that the Colonel had a personal interest in the *Venturer*, but decided against being too inquisitive. It was none of his business and the request, in itself, was perfectly reasonable. He had brought a small convoy from Malta and had hoped to sail for Gibraltar without any such encumbrance. He now resigned himself to the inevitable.

'Very well, Colonel. I'll see to it that the *Venturer* arrives safely.' Relieved on this point, the Acting Governor began to look on Delancey with more favour.

'That's most kind of you, captain. I'm vastly obliged, I am indeed. A merchantman to escort is a confounded nuisance, as I fully realise, limiting your freedom of action. But I have some intelligence which may interest you. It has come to my knowledge that some Spanish coasters have put into Pollensa

Bay at the east end of Majorca. Why don't you cut them out before that fellow Cochrane forestalls you?'

'With the *Venturer* in convoy?'

'Oh, I can arrange that. I have reason to believe that one of these craft has on board some deserters from the garrison. I shall request you, in writing, to take them into custody.'

'And bring them back to Minorca?'

'Yes, but the chances are against your finding them.'

'But what news do you actually have?'

'None at all. They deserted, five of them, and are no longer in this island. I must presume that they left in some coasting vessel; of just such a type as those reported in Pollensa Bay. They may well be aboard one of them. Nothing, in fact, could be more probable. I shall act on that assumption.'

'And they might, of course, be killed while resisting capture?'

'Nothing could be more likely. Dine with me tomorrow and we can settle the details over a glass of port. I shall also invite the master of the *Venturer*, quite a decent fellow but rather lacking in experience. And, er, there is one other thing . . .' He hesitated a little with just a hint of embarrassment. 'I have staying with me an elderly Oxford don, the Reverend Doctor Daniel Rathbone. Could you oblige him with a passage to Gibraltar? He could sail in the *Venturer*, of course, but he was tutor, it seems, to the present Lord Chancellor and came here with a whole sheaf of introductions, one even from royalty. You will find him a very interesting man, I give you my word, and one with influence.'

Delancey's distrust of the lean and hawk-faced Colonel was instinctive and immediate. He accepted the dinner invitation, however, and was glad to meet Mr Gosling, captain of the *Venturer*, before the other guests arrived. It appeared that Gosling had been a surgeon in the slave trade, having qualified at Liverpool Infirmary. He ended as master of a slaver after the other officers had died, and had since obtained his present command. He could be no older than about twenty-four but made up in confidence for what he lacked in knowledge. He complained about having no mate on whom he could rely, his first being no more than a promoted boatswain and his second a mere boy. When dinner was announced, Delancey found himself next to Dr Rathbone, a gnome-like figure with a mane of white hair, wizened features and a head too large for his very slight body and legs. However odd in appearance he turned out to be a good conversationalist and one whose chief interest lay in North Africa or at least in its classical history.

'I owe my antiquarian interests', he explained, 'to the late Dr Thomas Shaw, Regius Professor of Greek and Principal of Edmund Hall. You will, no doubt, have read his *Travels*, published in 1783.'

'And what, sir, aroused Dr Shaw's enthusiasm?'

'He was at one time Chaplain to the English Factory at Algiers. There can never have been a more inspiring teacher. Fired by his example, I have been on pilgrimage to Syrtis Minor and Hadrimetum, to Ithaca and to Carthage itself.'

'In what we now call Tunisia?'

'Yes, sir. My disappointment has been in failing to reach Numidia and more especially Hippo Regius. There, almost due south of this island, are the wonders of antiquity.'

'But surely there are more extensive ruins in Italy, in Rome itself?'

'Extensive, yes, but too often disturbed or hidden by later structures. There are cities in Africa, half buried in sand, which have been deserted by man since the time of St Augustine.'

Delancey, though no classical scholar, was able to show more than polite attention. The old man's interest in the ancient world was infectious and it gained him, on this occasion, a passage to Gibraltar. Delancey could say, in all sincerity, that he would be glad to have him aboard.

'And were we to sight the African shore,' sighed Dr Rathbone, 'I could at least claim to have seen Mauritania from the sea.'

On board the *Merlin* again, Delancey felt that he had conceded a great deal and received little in return. He had, it is true, an excuse to raid Pollensa Bay, but he had only the Colonel's word for it that the operation would be worth while. As for the *Venturer*, he could foresee the greatest difficulty in making her keep station. He had a suspicion that Mr Gosling should have remained a surgeon and that the Colonel had more than had his fill of classical archaeology. He could imagine the practised ease with which Lord Cochrane would have parried the Colonel's request. He should himself have learnt the art – he supposed that titled folk were born with it. . .

That evening, Delancey broke the news to Mather and Stirling, telling the latter that he would have to give up his cabin for the next few weeks. 'We shall have trouble, I fear, with the *Venturer*. In the meanwhile, I shall make a raid on Pollensa Bay. It should take place at dawn the day after tomorrow. The attack, I suspect, could well prove a waste of time, for the coasters there may be in ballast. As against that, the operation should afford useful experience for our young officers, more especially if we bring the prizes out. You, Mr Mather, will direct: Mr Langford will lead, with Mr Northmore and Mr Topley each commanding a boat. We shall anchor the *Venturer* at a distance, adding to our appearance of strength. If there is serious resistance, I shall make the signal of recall. I don't want to lose men for nothing.'

Mather's face lighted up when he heard of the plan and Delancey knew that the others would react in the same way. It would be the sort of affair in which young officers would be given their chance.

Delancey made his approach to Pollensa Bay in darkness, the coast of Majorca just visible under a crescent moon. The *Venturer* dropped anchor on his signal and then the boat's crews were mustered and inspected. Under reduced canvas, the sloop drifted silently inshore with three of her boats towing astern. Mr Mather took his junior officers to the forecastle and studied the Bay as it opened. At length he lowered his night-glass and said quietly, 'Well, they are there all right.' He handed the night-glass to Mr Langford, who passed it in turn to Northmore and Topley. 'Well, gentlemen?'

'There are five coasters in all, anchored pretty close to the shore. Three of them are quite small vessels, lateen rigged. Of the other two, one is a bark and the other a brig.' Langford was confident so far. With a little hesitation he added, 'I should guess that the brig has a cargo aboard. The others are riding light.'

'Have they seen us yet?'

'Probably not, sir. They should see us against the sunrise in another quarter of an hour.'

'So they should. But how are they armed, Mr Northmore?'

'The bark shows a broadside of seven gunports, sir, but some of them will be dummies. The brig shows six gunports but she is low in the water and her guns will be cluttered with deck cargo as likely as not. The smaller craft seems to be unarmed.'

'Anything else?' Langford and Northmore shook their heads but Topley looked through the night-glass again.

'I can see no shore batteries, sir,' he said at length, 'but there are some light-coloured patches on the headland to the north. I wondered, sir, whether they might be tents?'

'Let's suppose that they are. What then?'

'We should keep close to the south headland, sir.'

'Just so, Mr Topley. Any other comment?'

'Well, sir,' said Northmore, 'the Spanish could pitch their tents on one side and put their soldiers on the other.'

'They might, but they wouldn't. We know about our attack, but they don't. Let's not try to be too clever.'

Mather told them to continue studying the ground while he reported to the captain. Delancey listened carefully and gave an order to the helmsman.

'Very well, we'll keep to the south side of the bay. But that confounded brig lies to the north!'

'We shall leave her to the last. I notice, sir, that young Topley shows signs of promise. It was he who thought of studying the coastline while the others merely looked at the coasters.' There was a gradual lightening of the sky astern and Mather observed that the sloop must be all too visible.

'I know that,' said Delancey, 'but the enemy will have the sun in his eyes when we pull out again and that is the dangerous time, after the surprise effect has been lost.'

Mather now ordered the boats to be manned while Mr Stirling backed the topsails. Langford went in Topley's boat,

Mather took the gig and Northmore the boat which would bring up the rear. A few minutes after they pushed off there came the distant sound of a bugle call. 'That will be the alarm,' said Delancey to Stirling. The alarm it was but the Spaniards were slow to react.

'Odd that the bark has not opened fire,' said Stirling.

'How could she?' replied Delancey. 'The bark is a merchantman and had no reason to expect an attack. Half her crew are still in their hammocks. Her guns are unloaded. Where is the gunner? Who has the key to the magazine? Has anyone seen the linstock? She won't fire a shot for another ten minutes.'

Dr Rathbone came on deck at this moment with his overcoat thrown over his nightshirt. White-haired, venerable but eager, the old scholar looked remarkably out of place.

'Good-morning, sir,' said Delancey. 'We may be under fire presently. Perhaps you should stay below?'

'And never know what it is like to be in battle? No, Captain. I have the childish notion of playing the hero when I return to Oxford.'

'But if you were to receive a mortal wound?'

'I should make history, sir. It rarely happens that a Doctor of Divinity is killed in action.'

Watched by those still on board the *Merlin*, the boats were pulling shorewards in line ahead. At a hail from Mather's speaking-trumpet they now fanned out, each boat offering only a single target. They had nearly reached the bark before the first gun was fired. Four other guns went off in a ragged sequence and without effect, followed by a volley of small-arms. Northmore's boat was steered, undamaged, for the enemy bows, and Topley's boat rounded her stern in the smoke, followed by the gig, evidently to board her from the shoreward side. Two minutes later her flag was hauled down. Small-arms fire continued, however, probably from the smaller vessels. Then the firing died away and the *Merlin* came slowly inshore, steering so as to place the bark between her and the brig. Delancey focused his telescope on the shoreline to the north.

'Is the battle over?' asked Dr Rathbone in a tone of disappointment.

'No,' replied Delancey, handing over the telescope. 'Look at the vessel on the right.' The classical scholar focused with difficulty and then exclaimed: 'Soldiers!'

'Just so – soldiers. Some along the shore and some being rowed out to the brig. Perhaps a company all told. Mr Stirling! Fire a gun and make the signal for recall! Lower and man the other gig. I'm going in.'

Fifteen minutes later, Delancey stood on the quarterdeck of the captured bark, which was, he found, the *Santa Catarina*. Mather, beside him, explained that he was about to obey the signal, having manned the three smaller vessels. He was reluctant, however, to leave the brig untaken, having so far not lost a man.

'We could capture her easily and at small cost,' he pleaded. 'We can fire this ship's guns and board her in the smoke. We can take her in five minutes.'

Delancey had been studying the brig through his telescope, which he now closed with a snap.

'No, you couldn't, Mr Mather. You would lose ten men and I can't spare them. Her capture is out of the question. Tell me, though – with what cargoes are the smaller vessels laden?'

'Two are in ballast and one, the *San-Felipe*, partly laden with a few barrels of olive oil.'

'Is she, by God? Oil! And to whom did you give the command?'

'Mr Northmore, sir.'

'Tell him to come within hail. What have you done with the prisoners?'

'I have kept a few to help with the sails and have sent the rest ashore.'

'Very well, then. We shall quit this bay together in fifteen minutes' time. Get ready to hoist sail aboard this vessel and convey the same order to the two in ballast.'

At this moment the brig opened fire on the *Santa Catarina*, following up her cannon-shot with a volley of small-arms. Delancey took Mather's speaking-trumpet and hailed the

San-Felipe during a moment's lull in the firing.

'Mr Northmore!'

'Sir?' came the distant reply.

'Put the *San-Felipe* on course for the brig, set her alight and return in the launch. Is that clear? Use *San-Felipe* as fireship to destroy the Spanish brig. SET HER ALIGHT!'

'Aye, aye, sir!' The young man would seem to have heard and understood the order, for the lateen sails were being set and the *San-Felipe*'s cable was being cut. Using the light southerly wind, the coaster had begun her last voyage. Northmore could be seen forward with an axe, staving in a barrel. The launch was being hauled alongside. A few minutes later seamen could be seen tumbling into the boat with some alacrity and Northmore, still forward, was fumbling with flint and steel. Delancey wanted to tell him to use his pistol but there was now a continuous noise as the brig engaged this new assailant with musketry. It was probably a musket-ball which touched off the blaze for Northmore was evidently taken by surprise. Seeing the fire in the vessel's waist, he jumped overboard and swam back towards the launch.

'Make sail, Mr Mather!' shouted Delancey and there was frantic activity on board the *Santa Catarina*. She was no longer under fire and the Spanish gunners on board the brig, while aiming at the *San-Felipe*, were being enveloped in a drifting cloud of smoke. The Spanish cannonade was now at random and the withdrawal took place in good order, almost without hindrance from the enemy. Followed by the two other and smaller prizes, the *Santa Catarina* slowly left Pollensa Bay and headed for the open sea.

Look astern through his telescope, Delancey could see that the brig was fairly alight and that her crew and soldiers had taken to the boats. They had made little effort, seemingly, to put the fire out.

'Mr Mather!'

'Sir?'

'Ask your prisoners about the brig's cargo.'

There was some difficulty, but Mather managed to put the question in Spanish and returned with the answer.

'Like the *San-Felipe*, sir – oil.'

'Thank you, Mr Mather.'

Inwardly, Delancey cursed himself. He should have guessed what her cargo would be. Of course, it *would* be oil! She would blaze for hours, sending up a column of smoke which would be visible for thirty miles in every direction – no, further still to leeward. This would attract the attention of cruisers on either side, the last thing he wanted. Had he been on his own, he could have made all sail to leave the scene of his minor exploit but he was hampered and delayed by the *Venturer*. The barks he might have scuttled but he could not avoid responsibility for the ship he was escorting. He had the uneasy feeling that he had made a mistake.

Back on board his own ship, he set a course to the south-east and signalled the *Venturer* to take station in his wake. It took Gosling half an hour to get under way and Delancey used the time to send their gear to the prize-masters, Langford, Northmore and Topley, together with a rendezvous in case of separation. By the time he could pause for breath he found Dr Rathbone at his elbow.

'Congratulations, captain! You took what you could and burnt what you couldn't.'

'Thank you, sir. You will observe that we had no killed or wounded on this occasion.'

'I fear that I may forget that when I come to tell the story in the fellows' parlour at Edmund Hall. I may even be tempted to give myself a conspicuous role, as perhaps in tossing overboard a mortar bomb with fuse alight.'

'And indeed, I recall the incident,' said Delancey, smiling. 'What better witness can you have?'

At that instant, the look-out hailed from the mast-head, reporting a sail which was seen at the same instant from the deck. The ship was rounding the northern headland and was already within signalling distance. She was a British man-of-war and an exchange of numbers revealed that she was the 14-gun sloop *Speedy*, commanded, as Delancey knew, by Lord Cochrane.

Her arrival was unwanted and he regretted still more the

column of smoke which had probably attracted Cochrane's attention and might well attract the enemy as well. His only consolation lay in the fact that Cochrane was a few months junior to him in the Commander's list. The young man had a great reputation as the officer whose 14-gun brig sloop had actually taken a Spanish frigate of thirty-two guns. No one could doubt that he would have a brilliant career but the fact remained that he came at this moment under Delancey's orders.

Through the telescope the *Speedy* looked a queer craft, originally, he guessed, no more than a merchant brig. She had done good service under the command of Captain Brenton, that much he knew, but there was something odd about her rig. She seemed to be overmasted with too big a spread of canvas for her tonnage. This perhaps accounted for her endless list of prizes but it would require superb seamanship to handle her. That Cochrane was exceptionally able was undoubtedly true but Delancey knew that he was unpopular in some quarters. With his little squadron hove to, Delancey waited for the *Speedy* and finally signalled her captain to come aboard.

Lord Cochrane turned out to be a tall, handsome, red-haired man in his middle twenties. He had a Scots accent, an aristocratic manner and no particular love for officers who might be senior to him.

'Thomas Cochrane, sir,' he introduced himself, 'at your service. I saw the smoke and sailed to investigate. It is evident that I am too late to be of any assistance. Perhaps I could interest you, sir, in another enterprise?'

'I am glad to make your lordship's acquaintance. If you will step into my cabin I might be permitted to offer your lordship a glass of wine.' Delancey had no aristocratic friends and found it difficult to strike a balance between the claims of seniority and social position. He apologised for the austere furnishing of his day-cabin, assuming that his guest was accustomed to something better.

'I assure you, captain,' said Cochrane, with disarming frankness, 'that you are better accommodated than I am. I don't even have headroom in the *Speedy* and am confoundedly short of money. All my inheritance consists of is a ruined castle and a heap of debts. There is nobody so poor as a man with a title and without a fortune. Much is expected of him and he has nothing to give.'

'You have my sympathy, Lord Cochrane,' said Delancey rather coldly, 'but I should rather suppose that you have good prospects of promotion.' He thought inwardly that he would not be Cochrane's senior for long.

'I could wish that you were right!' Cochrane continued in a very open manner. 'I have some influential friends and relatives, to be sure, but this can tell against me. If too many people approach the First Lord on my behalf, he may well resent it and say "No".'

Not entirely convinced, Delancey asked him about the project he had mentioned.

'Well, sir, I have long had my eye on a French privateer called *L'Espoir* and presently based on Cagliari in Sardinia. She is not valuable in herself but would be fit for purchase into the service as a sloop. She is too fast for me and needs to be trapped between two pursuers. I observe, sir, that you have an English merchantman in company?'

'Yes, the *Venturer* of Whitehaven.'

'I would suggest using her as bait with this ship, disguised, in company. Then I would place the *Speedy* between the privateer and her base.'

'I am sorry to disappoint your lordship, but the *Venturer* is bound for Gibraltar, carrying the mails.'

'But of course! This would be only a minor detour, hardly out of her way. Her master could have no reasonable objection.'

'I regret that the first objection comes from me. I am bound in the opposite direction.' Delancey spoke rather stiffly, perhaps in a chillier tone than he had intended. He was having to resist Cochrane's social position and undeniable charm.

'No doubt of it, sir. But an officer must be allowed to use his initiative. I have intelligence, moreover, that the French are at sea. I learn – and this from a reliable source – that

Admiral Linois has sailed, or is about to sail, from Toulon, bound for Cadiz with a squadron destined to co-operate with the Spanish fleet. He may be already between us and the coast of Spain. A detour southward, therefore, and a passage along the African shore would be justified on grounds of caution.'

'So it would, my lord, but the same could not be said of a preliminary detour eastwards. I thank you for your suggestion and I sincerely hope that you capture *L'Espoir*, but my answer to you is "No".'

'I must confess, sir, that I am disappointed. You have a reputation for activity and I had counted on your co-operation.'

'It is with infinite regret that I decide against sailing with you.' Delancey knew where his duty lay and felt that his decision was inevitable. But Cochrane's powers of persuasion were considerable and Delancey had no love for the part he was playing. Was he unimaginative and dull, pleading prior orders and behaving like a prig? He had made his choice, however, and Cochrane had risen, plainly showing his resentment and contempt.

'You will allow me, sir, to take my leave?' he said coldly. 'I must make some other plan for the capture of *L'Espoir*.'

'I am confident that your lordship's abilities are more than equal to making the capture without such help as I could offer.'

The two captains parted coldly and Delancey wondered afterwards whether he had been unwise to antagonise Lord Cochrane. He would have been wrong to go against the orders he had received but could he not have found a better way of saying "No"? He would have handled the situation better if the other man had not been a lord. He called himself a fool and returned to his work. He and his group of vessels kept close to the wind and the *Speedy* was soon hull down to the north.

At dinner that afternoon Dr Rathbone was Delancey's guest, with Mather and Northmore to complete the party. It was a better meal than average, with a piglet from Minorca, with plenty of fruit and some Maltese wine.

'Thank you, sir, thank you,' said Dr Rathbone as his glass

was filled, 'I was agog, I own, to see the celebrated Lord Cochrane, the hero of so many exploits. He makes a striking figure, to be sure. I should suppose that we shall hear of him again, perhaps some day as an admiral.'

'What did you make of him, sir?' asked Mather, looking to his commanding officer.

'I was impressed, Mr Mather, I must admit. He is undoubtedly an outstanding seaman and officer. It seems to me, however, that he is too much the partisan, too eager to distinguish himself and too keen to make money. The one thing he fails to capture is the good opinion of the flag-officers under whom he is placed.'

'I am interested, captain, in your verdict,' said Dr Rathbone, 'but I should have thought that his success would be enough, in itself, to gain their approval. They have their share of the credit and also, I believe, of the money. Is that not enough for them? What more can they ask of him?'

'What they ask', replied Delancey, 'is that he should do as he is told. We all have to decide, at one time or another, whether we are fighting our own war or whether we are serving the King. It so happens that I have done both in my time. I have been tempted – and shall no doubt be tempted again – to ignore my orders and go after prize-money. My conclusion is, however, that it is wrong and that it does not even pay in the end. Our duty is laid down for us in orders and we neglect them at our peril. As for Lord Cochrane, my belief is that he will play his tricks once too often.'

'He is not much in favour, sir, with the Admiral's staff at Malta.' Northmore's comment was echoed by Mather who added that Cochrane seemed to do as he pleased.

'It sometimes looks like that,' Delancey admitted, 'but these things are remembered. Should there be a court martial its members may start with an impression of an officer's character based on past events.'

'Had Lord Cochrane any news of the French, sir?' asked Mather.

'He repeated what we had already heard – that the French are planning to send a squadron to Cadiz. His intelligence went a little further, however, suggesting that Linois may have sailed already. I should suppose that this could be true and I am setting our course accordingly.'

'So we are heading south and will be sailing close to the African coast?' asked Dr Rathbone hopefully.

'With your interest in mind, my good sir,' said Delancey. 'We hope to increase our knowledge of classical antiquity.'

'What astonishes me', said Mather, 'is the evidence on the African coast of a former and prosperous civilisation. To judge from its present state, as we read about it, there is hardly more arable land than will support a few villages. Can the climate have changed?'

'I have been told', said Northmore, 'that it is the Arabs who have done the damage, their camels and goats having destroyed the trees.'

'I too have heard that,' Delancey replied, 'and they will have destroyed the vineyards on principle.'

'What, sir, has history to teach us?' the tactful Mather addressed Dr Rathbone directly.

'We know all too little about it, gentlemen. I believe myself that the camels and goats must take part of the blame. The fact is, however, that the fertility of the land declined under the Roman Empire during its later years. I incline to suppose that the land had been overcropped.'

'You would maintain, sir, would you not', asked Delancey, 'that the population of North Africa must once have been considerable?'

'There is no doubt about that, captain,' Rathbone replied. 'I have examined the ruins in the vicinity of Tunis. Quite apart, however, from these traces of antiquity, who has not heard of Carthage, a power sufficiently strong to have sent its army to attack Rome by crossing the Alps? Who has not heard of Hannibal? No campaign of that sort could have been based on a few square miles of desert.'

'Hannibal is certainly a name that has never been forgotten,' Mather admitted. 'We have a ship of the line called *Hannibal* – a 74-gun ship built just after the last war, a sister ship to the *Thunderer*.'

'We might drink a toast presently to Hannibal's memory,' said Delancey, 'but I shall first propose a toast to our guest, Dr Rathbone, hero of the Battle of Pollensa. I need hardly remind you, gentlemen, that he saved my life while we fought the enemy hand-to-hand.'

'Boarding the *Santa Catarina* of a hundred guns,' cried Northmore, 'it was he who cut down the Spanish Admiral with his cutlass.'

'It was to him that Don Whiskerandos, their Vice-Admiral, finally surrendered his sword!'

'A health, gentlemen, to our own Don!'

Dr Rathbone took the joke in good part, finally asking Delancey whether the skirmish had served its purpose. He did not see that the captured vessels could be of much value and the only laden coaster had been destroyed.

'A good question, sir. The purpose of the raid was to teach my young officers. Each of them had to steer a boat under fire, boarding an enemy merchantman. Mr Northmore here had the task of burning that brig. Each is now in sole command of his own prize, responsible for keeping station. Tomorrow I shall have the chance to exercise the squadron, giving these young men more to think about. They all did well, they are all gaining confidence and they can all learn from my mistake.'

'What mistake, sir?' Mather was pained and surprised.

'The mistake of burning a ship before you know what her cargo is. That coaster was laden with oil, sending up a column of smoke which could be seen for miles and marked our presence for hours. I shan't make that mistake again, nor will my officers.'

Next day's exercises began with the *Merlin* closing each of the other vessels in turn and providing each with a description of the signals which would be used. The *Venturer* was directed to take station ahead, and Langford, Northmore and Topley were told to assume that she was a valuable prize taken from a superior enemy squadron and that the manoeuvres which followed were to prevent her recapture.

Gosling was ordered to follow a given course, ignoring the

others. If the exercise was not concluded by sunset, he was to display a stern light, allowing the squadron to re-form in his wake. If contact were lost, all ships were to rendezvous next day off Cape Cavallo, going no further westward except under escort. The beginning of the exercise was indicated by the firing of a gun. Since all the other young gentlemen were out of the ship, young Stock was made the acting signals officer and found himself a key figure in the exercise.

David Stock had been overwhelmed and mostly silent during his first months at sea but he was now beginning to emerge as a personality, as a boy with some initiative and a sense of humour. This was his first taste of responsibility and the result was a delay over each signal. But Mather was a good teacher and coaxed Stock into seeing the logic of the code in use. 'What does the man want to know – the one to whom you are signalling?' he asked patiently. 'First of all, I mean?'

'Whether the signal is for him, sir.'

'Exactly. It can be for all ships and we have a way of indicating that. Or it can be just for one ship. How do we explain which?'

'By her number, sir.'

'But what if the ship is not a man-of-war? What then?'

'I don't know, sir.'

'Well – think.'

'Spell out her name, sir?'

'Won't that take rather a long time?'

'Well . . .'

The lesson continued, the signals were made and corrected, cancelled and repeated and eventually acknowledged. The signals were even obeyed, though seldom quickly and not always correctly. With inexperienced officers and minimal crews, there could be no very smart response to signals. With difficulty, however, and with frequent errors, the three prizes struggled into position, wore together and tacked in succession. They improved, moreover, and Delancey felt encouraged to attempt the last movement he had planned; the formation of line abreast. Young Stock did not panic even when he realised that Mr Mather had disappeared.

'Now,' said Delancey, 'the squadron will form line abreast. Make a signal, Mr Stock.' This time the flags were hoisted without more than a brief hesitation. Delancey ignored what delay there was and explained the exercise to Dr Rathbone.

'This is not a battle formation. It can be used, however, to intercept enemy stragglers or, as in this exercise, to protect what we are treating as a valuable prize.'

'Why is it never used in battle?' asked Rathbone. 'The ancients regarded it as the normal formation. It was used, I fancy, at the Battle of Actium.'

'Because of the danger of firing into our friends,' said Delancey. 'Rowing galleys used to fight in line abreast even in modern times, but this was because their guns were all mounted in the bows. We fight today in line ahead, manoeuvring so as to have the enemy on our beam. In line ahead, we may fail to destroy the other side but we are safe at least from destroying each other.'

While the exercise continued, the *Venturer*, having no manoeuvres to perform, drew slowly ahead of the rest. By evening she was only just visible in the failing light. Delancey cursed inwardly and brought the exercise to an end by firing three guns. By the time his prizes were once more in station the *Venturer* could not be seen at all. 'No stern lantern,' said Delancey to Mather. 'That man is an utter fool.'

'Completely witless, sir. We shall sight him again at first light.'

'What if we don't? Can we trust him to make the rendezvous and stay there?'

'God knows, sir. I can't see what he has to gain by sailing alone.'

'To gain? Near Algiers? The man must be out of his mind.'

'The Dey of Algiers will not attack a British ship, sir.'

'That's true. But the Dey's subjects are not to be trusted when out of his sight. The Arabs on that coast would have no mercy on a ship in distress, under any flag. Should the *Venturer* be lost I shall be held to blame.'

Delancey turned in that night with a sense of failure. The raid on Pollensa Bay had been a mistake. He had turned aside from his clear duty, which was to reach Gibraltar as soon as possible, ensuring the safe arrival there of the *Venturer*. He had resisted the worse temptation of joining Lord Cochrane in his wild operations. So far his common sense had triumphed. But he had lost a whole day with little to show for it and now he had lost touch with the merchantman he had to escort. It was quite true what he had said to Rathbone, that the raid had afforded valuable experience for his young men. So it had and so had the subsequent exercise.

But the fact remained that he had risked the capture or destruction of what was supposed to be a valuable cargo. He would not be court-martialled for it even if the *Venturer* were taken, so much he knew. She was laden with military, not naval, stores, and any senior officer would accept his explanation that Gosling was to blame, as indeed he was. But a successful leader is not a man who offers good excuses for failure. He is one, rather, who habitually reports his success.

He made a vow then and there to reject every temptation which could distract him from the line of duty. Rumour had it that Lord Nelson had been led astray by a woman. His guess was that Lord Cochrane had been led astray by his need for money. He was in no position to blame either of them. But he resolved never to repeat his own mistake. Tossing and turning, he wished repeatedly that he could undo the damage. In future, he resolved, he would sleep soundly in the knowledge that he had done his best, that he had obeyed his orders. He did not fall asleep until the small hours and was called a minute later, as it seemed, by young Northmore, knocking at his cabin door.

'Beg pardon, sir, it is first light. Mr Stirling presents his compliments and begs to report that the *Venturer* is not to be seen from the mast-head.'

'Thank you, Mr Northmore. Return my compliments to Mr Stirling and tell him that I shall be on deck in five minutes.'

As Delancey reached the quarterdeck there was a hail from the mast-head. 'Land ho on the starboard bow!' Telescopes were focused in an instant. Lowering his again, Delancey said 'Good-morning, Mr Stirling. That is Cape Cavallo and the *Venturer* is not in sight.'

CHAPTER SEVEN

Salvage

Delancey's conclusion was that the *Venturer* had parted company through sheer incompetence. He had to assume that she had gone too far westwards, cutting the corner, as it were, and that Gosling had mistaken some other feature for Cape Cavallo. If their error was in the other direction, Delancey could do nothing more. He was certainly not going to head back for Tunis.

'She couldn't be astern of us, sir?' asked Mather.

'No,' replied Delancey. 'We were in line abreast when he parted company. We shall now keep close in with the land. Were we distant we might fail to make her out against the coastline. And if she were attacked by Algerine pirates, it would be the result of her going too close inshore. So we'll make a coastal passage to Gibraltar, keeping just clear of the shoals. With luck we'll find the *Venturer* to seaward of us somewhere off Dellys, where I shall tell young Gosling exactly what I think of him.'

By the evening of that day, which had been very hot, the *Merlin* was off Algiers or Djegairi-gharb, the well-guarded and warlike city. Sailing close inshore with a wind off the land, Delancey studied the harbour through his telescope. The masts of shipping showed above the seaward fortifications. Behind the waterfront the whitewashed houses covered the hillside so as to form a triangle topped by the citadel. Beyond the surrounding fields and woods the more distant hills rose brown and yellow, barren and dry.

'It looks', said Delancey to Dr Rathbone, 'like a ship's topsail spread out on a green field. There is no sign of the *Venturer* in harbour.'

'A formidable looking place.'

'It's as strong as they can make it. Or did the Romans begin the work before the days of Islam?'

'Apparently not, captain. The harbour is artificial, I believe, built since Khair-ed-din captured the place in 1529. The Roman harbour on this coast was farther westwards and was ruined, they say, by an earthquake.'

The Algerines ignored the *Merlin*, recognising her flag as that of a power they had learnt to respect, and the sloop sailed on under reduced canvas. Delancey did not want to pass the *Venturer* in the dark. Nor did he do so. She was sighted at daybreak, close in with the land. Stirling laid down his telescope and busied himself with the chart.

'We must be twenty leagues west of Algiers,' he reckoned. 'The village we can see must be Cherchell, and my guess is that the *Venturer* is hard aground.'

As the distance lessened, the fate of the merchantman became increasingly clear. She was motionless, not far from a small island, her sails furled and her foremast over the side. Two or three Arab craft were circling round like vultures and there were signs of activity ashore. No efforts were being made to refloat the ship and Delancey guessed that her crew were exhausted by their labours during the night. She must have been miles off course. With a light wind it was another hour before the sloop and her consorts dropped anchor well to seaward of the wreck. Dr Rathbone had breakfast with Delancey and they came on deck together soon after the ship had anchored.

'Now, doctor, this is Cherchell. Is this the Roman seaport you mentioned?'

'It certainly is, captain. I have been studying my books and it is quite evident from them that this is the site of Julia Caesarea, later called Jol. The ancient city was destroyed by an earthquake, the site being occupied by an Arab town, but that too was destroyed by an earthquake as recently as 1738. What village there is would seem to have a pleasant surrounding country, with plantations stretching up to the mountains. There should be an aqueduct somewhere . . . might I borrow your telescope?'

After a careful study of the landscape, Rathbone had to express his disappointment.

'I can see no aqueduct. Over to the left somewhere is the river Hashem and its water used to be brought to the city by an aqueduct. The city was well fortified but rather shut in by the mountains. Procopius tells us that the Romans came to Caesarea by sea, the passes in the interior being held by hostile tribes, perhaps not unlike the Beni Menasser of today.'

'But where would the city have been?'

'I should suppose that much of it lies under the sea, since the ground-level fell dramatically during the earlier earthquake.'

'Very well, then. I shall presently have a boat lowered so that I can visit the *Venturer*. If you care to come with me, you may be able to see something of the old city by peering into the water. We luckily have an almost dead calm.'

In detailing a boat crew, Delancey added the ship's carpenter and his mate together with an able seaman called Wishart, known for his skill as a diver. It was a half-mile pull under a hot sun and Dr Rathbone could at first see nothing, the water being too disturbed by the boat itself. As they approached the stricken *Venturer*, the dejected figure of Gosling could be seen on the quarterdeck, and the ensign drooped spiritlessly from the stricken gaff. There was no sign of any effort being made to save the ship. Delancey went on board, followed by the old carpenter, Nathaniel Corbin, and Isaac Denny, his mate. Dr Rathbone remained in the boat, looking fixedly over the side. Gosling met Delancey at the main entry port and attempted some form of salute.

'Tell me, Mr Gosling, what brings you here?' he was asked. 'Why did you fail to light a stern lantern? Why did you lose touch? Why did you not shorten sail? How did you fail to reach the rendezvous? What game do you think you are playing? And how, sir, do you propose to refloat your ship?'

There followed some stuttered excuses, received in silence. Then Delancey spoke again, after a pause:

'What water have you forward and aft? Is your hull damaged beneath the waterline? Have you done anything to lighten the ship? What have you done, sir, and what do you mean to do?'

Gosling muttered something about lowering a boat. Delancey ignored him and told Corbin to survey the position and make a report. Then he called down to his boat and told Wishart to dive under the ship and report back. He finally told the coxswain to sound with the hand lead both ahead and astern of the ship. A minute later, Wishart had thrown off his shirt and dived overboard.

Realising that some action was expected of him, Gosling collected a party of his men and began swaying up and emptying the water casks. His first mate led another group forward to cut away what remained of the tangled foremast rigging. The *Venturer*'s carpenter began to sound the well and the boatswain started examining one of the boats with a view to lowering it. Half an hour later Delancey had some idea of the wretched ship's predicament. There was deep water astern but none ahead of her. There must have been a higher water level when she grounded, probably the result of an onshore wind. She was not badly damaged below the waterline but was firmly wedged where she was. Then Wishart came aboard with a really startling report.

'It's not a reef, sir. It's more like a building with solid walls still upright under the water.'

'Like a house, you mean?' asked Delancey.

'Well, sir, it put me in mind of St Martin-in-the-Fields at Charing Cross.'

'There are columns, you mean?'

'Pillars, as you might say: all broken, to be sure, but with carving like they have on the stern of an old flagship – foliage and suchlike.'

'Is there just the one building, or are there others?'

'I think there are others, sir, like as if it had been a city. The ship is wedged, seemingly, between two of 'em.'

'Well done, Wishart.' Delancey walked to the entry and hailed his boat. 'My compliments and I should be grateful if Dr Rathbone would come aboard.' When the old scholar had joined him, he asked whether he had heard Wishart's story.

'I have indeed and it's the most amazing thing. It seems to me that this merchantman is wedged in between two Roman buildings, one of them a temple. Heaven knows what other remains of antiquity are around us! We have blundered into Julia Caesarea! I was never so excited in my life. . . . If only I could see below the water!'

'A strange discovery indeed! It happens, unluckily, that my task here is to refloat the *Venturer*, which is going to be problem enough. But I'll do what I can in the pursuit of learning. We'll talk of this again when we are aboard the *Merlin*. I have had an idea!'

There followed a conference on board the sloop at which Delancey explained what had to be done. The crestfallen Gosling was present and Delancey forced himself to be civil. He would need the man's help if the wreck were to be saved.

First, he explained, the *Venturer* would have to be lifted by the 'camel' method. The two smaller prizes would be brought alongside her and her cargo mostly transferred to them. When these two craft were deeply laden they would be lashed firmly to the *Venturer*. When thus secured, the two prizes would be unloaded into the third. Empty, they should have buoyancy enough to lift the *Venturer* clear. It would mean hard work for everyone and the task would begin immediately. Part of the ship's cargo would have to be jettisoned – he would be more precise about that after he had seen into her hold.

'A final warning,' he concluded. 'The Arabs ashore may have been regarding the *Venturer* as a gift from Allah. The boats withdrew when we came on the scene but they won't regard our salvage work with any favour. If they think that we are succeeding in our efforts they may stage an attack, most probably after dark. So keep an eye on them and have small-arms within reach. We shall row guard from sunset. In the interests of safety, I shall bring the *Merlin* closer to the wreck.

'Mr Mather, you will have charge of the *Merlin* while the rest of us are out of the ship. Mr Gosling, you will command the *Venturer*'s crew and you will have Mr Langford's help. Mr Corbin, you will repair the damage to the *Venturer* so far as it is possible. Tell the sailmaker that we shall fother the leak – and tell him what size of sail we shall need; using the *Venturer*'s own canvas of course. And tell Isaac Denny to report to me – I have a small task for him, as also for James Wishart. Gentlemen, detail your men, have all boats manned – my gig excepted – and start the work as soon as possible.'

An hour later, the boats having towed the *Merlin* to within two cables' length of the wreck, the sloop was almost deserted and the *Venturer* had become the scene of furious activity. Delancey now turned to Dr Rathbone and said: 'And now we'll pay a visit to Julia Caesarea!' His meaning became clear when Denny came up to him with a glass-bottomed wooden box which he had just finished making. 'Thank you, Denny. With this device we can see below the surface, cutting out reflections and distortions. Man the gig now and we'll take you to join Mr Corbin aboard the wreck.' The gig was rowed over by Wishart and Delancey's steward.

After Denny had been returned to duty, Delancey said, 'Now we'll see what we can see!' He was almost in a holiday mood, directing the oarsmen while he took the tiller himself. 'Now, doctor, push the box a little below the surface and tell us what you can see through the glass!' After a brief experiment, Dr Rathbone looked up with a startled expression. 'A Roman temple!' he gasped. 'A pile of shaped stones but with the pediment clearly visible and the capital of a Corinthian column!'

Having surveyed the position of the *Venturer*, they worked ahead of the ship, where other buildings could be glimpsed in shallower water. One of them looked rather like a gateway with flanking towers. Further to the left was a smaller structure grouped round a courtyard; perhaps a priest's dwelling.

At this point Dr Rathbone came up with a theory which was to prove extremely valuable. 'The ship is not wedged, I think, between two buildings. There is a temple with a portico formed by columns and a pediment. The roof has gone but the walls are still there.' Delancey looked puzzled and the old scholar turned to paper and pencil. 'Here is the temple, just like a barn but with a detached line of six columns across one end, the columns supporting a pediment, like this. . . . There is no roof now but the pediment remains and the ship is jammed between the pediment and the end of the building.'

'How wide is the gap, then?'

'I don't know. About the length of a tree-trunk.'

'Which is the breadth of a ship. But why is this important, Dr Rathbone?'

'Because while the building may be solid the pediment, unsupported, should yield a little. Given good luck, it would even fall down.'

'I see what you mean. . . . So the ship might wriggle out of the gap.'

Further study through glass showed that Dr Rathbone was right. Then the boat went a little ahead of the *Venturer* and Delancey looked again at the house and courtyard. Glimpsing something of interest, Delancey told Wishart to investigate and the seaman dived again, remaining under water for about a minute.

After his third dive he reported a discovery. He had found a statue in two halves – the statue, he thought, of a child. 'How big?' asked Delancey, and Wishart made gestures to indicate a figure about three feet high. 'Could you tie a rope to it?' Rathbone asked eagerly. Wishart thought this possible and dived next time with a rope in hand.

He was below for a longer time and surfaced with a gasp and a splutter. 'I've bent the rope to his ankle,' he explained at length. Gently and slowly the rope was hauled in, bringing with it the lower half of a nude and male figure, delicately made in what people often call a 'late' or 'decadent' style. After something of a struggle the other half of the marble boy came to the surface, a flute-player, almost undamaged. 'This is incredible,' whispered Dr Rathbone. 'But it must be enough for the time being,' replied Delancey. 'There is some activity ashore and I don't like the look of it.'

Exactly what was happening ashore was far from obvious. A small crowd of men had gathered round the local fishing boats and some of them were seen to point seawards.

Gradually, however, the crowd dispersed again without taking action, perhaps through failure to agree or perhaps – who could tell? – because action had been postponed. Delancey boarded the *Venturer*, sending the gig and its cargo back to the *Merlin*.

On board the merchantman, barrels and crates were being swayed up by means of a tackle at each yard-arm. The craft alongside were already lower in the water but the *Venturer* showed no effect of lightening. Delancey asked Mather how the work was going.

'We began well,' Mather answered, 'but the sun is hot and the men have begun to tire.'

'We'll stop work for dinner in half an hour. She's still hard aground, I see.'

'Yes, sir. No sign of movement underfoot.'

'There won't be until tomorrow. And I suspect that the Arabs may attack us in the meanwhile.'

'We'll beat them off, sir.'

'No doubt. The trouble is that we can't beat them off and shift cargo at the same time. If they make trouble enough we shall be here forever.'

'We could bombard the village, sir.'

'And have the whole Algerine navy here? No. We may have to buy them off. We could give them some of the ship's provisions: although not the salt-pork.'

'They're welcome to the *Venturer*'s provisions or to all I've seen of them. I take it, sir, that we shall not be working after sunset?'

'No, but the watch on duty will be mounting guard.'

Work resumed after dinner and Delancey addressed a few words to the *Venturer*'s crew. 'I hear that you are not working as hard as my boatswain would like to see. Some of you have pointed out to him that you are not subject to naval discipline. That is perfectly true.' He paused and two or three of the men sniggered. 'But when we reach Gibraltar you will be liable to impressment. Once entered on board the *Merlin* you will meet Mr Bailey again. You will find then that you *are* subject to naval discipline, And if you have been listed now as insolent and idle you will have reason to wish that you had never been born. So work now as you have never worked before. If you don't, you'll wish, by God, that you had!'

The men sweated after that but there was much to do. By sunset the *Venturer*'s hold was little more than half-empty. Mather called a halt and detailed the boats' crews who would row guard after dark. The rest went thankfully to their hammocks.

The attack when it came was a half-hearted affair. The Arab craft were sighted before they came anywhere near the *Venturer.* When fired upon, they fled, but renewed their efforts within the hour. Watching and listening, Delancey came to the conclusion that the object of the raid – if it could be called that – was merely to keep his men awake. By the small hours he had endured all he was prepared to endure. The firing had died away but he guessed that there would be more trouble at first light. He decided to make his own move first. Sending for Stirling, he told him the situation.

'I have decided to take a hostage. Watching movements ashore I have come to the conclusion that the chief here, the magistrate, whatever he is called, lives in a house to the west side of the landing place and perhaps five hundred yards inland. I could not see the house very well because of the trees on this side of it, but there has been a great deal of coming and going of people in that direction. Our neighbours have disturbed us for half the night and have now gone to bed. So it is our turn to do something. I want you and Topley to take twenty men on shore with Tanner as coxswain, find the town hall or whatever it is, capture the magistrate or mayor and bring him on board the *Merlin* with as little noise as possible. A second captive would be useful, I think. He could be released later and might explain the situation to the rest. So kidnap the town clerk or tipstaff, whoever might serve our purpose. We shall then have something to bargain with. Aim to be back here before daybreak.'

Delancey quietly paced the deck, listening to the dwindling sound of muffled rowlocks. Then all was silent except for the lapping of the water and the faint sound of wind in the rigging.

There was a scent from the land – was it peach or apricot? How recently had he been the one to go ashore on this sort of raid. Now he gave the orders but remained on board the ship, waiting for the report of success or the rattle of musketry which would tell of failure. He would never have believed, as a youngster, that the waiting role was the more difficult. This he had come to know. He also knew, however, that Stirling was reliable and intelligent.

The worst thing that could happen – well, almost the worst – was an assault on the wrong house; the kidnapping of some nonentity or some unpopular character to whose fate the inhabitants were utterly indifferent. But how would the house be recognised? Over two hours had passed that there were the first signs of dawn. Beyond the river Hashem were the hills and beyond them again was the Ras el Amoush. Yes, there was a lightening of the sky in that direction and he could imagine the first stirring of the birds. No shots had been fired, so his boat *must* be returning.

At last he heard the sound of the oars. Then the boat was alongside, with three passengers in the stern-sheets, two of them with the Arab headgear. He made his voice sound casual as he asked Stirling whether all had gone well. There had been no real difficulty, he was told, they had found the house and the only two guards had been asleep. Their chief prisoner was the Alcayde, the other Arab was probably his clerk, the third man a Jewish merchant from Tetuan, who was being held prisoner and who might be useful as an interpreter. No alarm had been raised and nobody had been hurt on either side.

'Well done, Mr Stirling,' said Delancey. 'Secure the two Arabs under an armed guard and send the Jew to my day-cabin.'

Ten minutes later he was faced by a small, bearded man with dark skin, bright eyes, aged about fifty and shabbily dressed in black. Tanner and the escort remained outside the cabin door. Delancey's clerk prepared to take notes.

'Who are you?' asked Delancey.

'Isaac Sulman of Tetuan, merchant.'

'Your trade extends to Gibraltar, perhaps?'

'That is how I come to speak English.' Though somewhat ruffled by his unexpected situation, Sulman had a brisk, businesslike manner that inspired confidence.

'Why were you a prisoner?'

'I was here on business and some of the Arabs said that I owed them money,' he made a gesture of resignation. 'Anything said against a Jew is always believed.'

'What would have happened to you had we not interfered?'

'I should have promised them some gunpowder. They would have let me go when it came.'

'They are short of powder then?'

'They are always short. They waste it firing in the air.'

'Firing in the air? What do you mean?'

'They have a game on horseback, to gallop fast, stop suddenly and fire. It is very wasteful and it ruins their horses.'

'But Arab horses are famous, surely.'

'When properly trained. The Arabs work them too hard before they are fully grown, know no pace between the gallop and the walk and wear them out in a few years.'

'So there is a perpetual shortage of gunpowder.'

'Yes, sir. They make none themselves and have to import it.'

'Now, Mr Sulman, you will perhaps understand why I have brought the Alcayde on board this ship.'

'As a hostage.'

'Will this be enough to keep the Arabs quiet until I have the merchantman afloat?'

'Perhaps not. Achmet bin Abu Said is not much liked. He is greedy and mean and inevitably has made enemies.'

'What if I left two small merchantmen behind?'

'With cargo on board?'

'No, in ballast.'

'With gunpowder on board?'

'One barrel in each.'

'That could be just enough, I think. What reward do you give me for acting as your agent?'

'What do you ask?'

'A free passage to Tetuan.'

'Agreed. So go now and talk to the Alcayde. I shall hang

him if we have any more trouble. I shall leave two coasters behind if his people will let us alone. His clerk I shall release and he can carry the Alcayde's orders to his deputy.'

'And what if the Arabs refuse your offer?'

'I shall burn the merchantman and sail with the first fair wind for Gibraltar. And our Consul at Algiers will complain to the Dey about the conduct of his subjects at Cherchell.'

'Very well, sir. I'll tell the Alcayde what terms you offer. May I have paper, pen and ink? He will want to send a written message ashore.'

'Go with Mr Sulman', said Delancey to his clerk, 'and see that the Alcayde has what he wants. Bring Mr Sulman back to me when the business has been concluded.'

When Sulman returned it was to report that all was agreed and that the clerk was ready to go ashore with the Alcayde's message.

'I used my discretion, sir,' said the Jew, 'in one respect. I said that the two coasters would have gunpowder aboard. I did not say how much. The Arabs are free to suppose that the vessels are laden with gunpowder.' There was a slight pause and he added, 'I did not say that; not in so many words.'

'Thank you, Mr Sulman. I congratulate you upon the success of your negotiations. You are a free man and our guest until you go ashore at Tetuan.'

Delancey turned in as the boat left for the shore hoping to snatch an hour or two of sleep before he was needed again. There was a distant sound of musketry but it died away and all was quiet as the sun rose. It was a hot day and almost windless.

A little before noon the *Venturer* was as empty as she was going to be, her valuable cargo shifted to the vessels alongside, her provisions mostly dumped overboard, nearly all her water casks emptied but kept for further use and her guns tipped over the side. The two 'camels' were low in the water and now Mather gave the order to secure the 'camels' to the *Venturer* by ropes which passed, some of them, under the keel. That done, he ordered the men to begin shifting cargo to the third and larger prize, which had to be moved periodically from one side to the other. Delancey and the carpenter rowed round in the gig, marking the ship's side and hoping to find her higher in the water as the work went on.

'We need to lift her three feet six inches', said Corbin, 'according to Wishart, but she hasn't moved an inch so far. She is wedged, sir, I reckon, held as if in a vice.'

'How big is the vice?'

'She is gripped from a point amidships to a point some fifteen feet forward with deeper water under the bows and stern.'

'Is she leaking much?'

'Not more, sir, than the one pump can deal with.'

After dinner and a double rum ration the work was resumed with urgency. The buoyancy of the 'camels' as they emptied was applying a great upward pressure but the lift could not overcome the jamming effect of the Roman walls. The *Venturer*'s waterline was exactly where it had been when the ship struck. The men were tiring and even the officers were discouraged. Delancey had foreseen that this moment would come. He played what was almost his last card, ordering all men aft on the quarterdeck.

'Listen, men. We have now to work the ship loose from the stones that are gripping her amidships. When I give the word, every man aboard will run forward as if to the heads in a moment of urgent need. When I give the word again, every man will run aft as if he were about to splice the mainbrace. In this way we shall rock the ship and work her clear. One – two – three – GO!'

The men rushed forward and aft, once, twice and a third time. The ship did not move but Delancey felt (or did he imagine?) a slight tremor underfoot.

'Now, men – our last chance. Each man will fetch two 12-pounder shot from the *Merlin* and we shall repeat this exercise carrying that extra weight.'

With a lot of mock despair, the men piled into the boats and rowed back to the sloop. Whatever they might say, this last game was better fun than shifting cargo. Their morale had risen since the rocking attempt had begun. The boat returned and a sling from the yard-arm rigged to sway the round shot aboard. Then the crew reassembled on the quarterdeck, each man loaded with twenty-four pounds dead weight. The load was too much for two of the boys, whose load was halved, Delancey taking a full load himself.

'Once more!' he shouted. 'One – two – three – GO!' This time he ran with the rest, arriving very short of breath on the forecastle. 'GO!' he shouted again and found himself on the quarterdeck with his lungs about to burst. Setting an example was all very well but he felt that he had gone too far. . . . His next 'GO!' was in more of a conversational tone, and the one after that was no more than a whisper. By the fourth rush, this time aft, he had given up all hope of success.

Then, quite suddenly, it happened. The deck heaved beneath his feet, the whole ship wobbled and shuddered and everyone knew that she was afloat. There were spontaneous cheers, which ended only when Delancey had breath enough to order the manning of the boats.

The *Venturer* was pulled stern-first off the stonework by which she had been trapped. Once she was in deep water her anchor was dropped and a fothered sail pulled over the place where the leak had been found. The men were too exhausted to do more, so Delancey thanked them and announced the splicing of the mainbrace. The pumps had to be kept going and the boats had to row guard, but the crisis was over and most people could sleep.

There was silence ashore and no native craft so much as put to sea. Delancey invited his officers and Dr Rathbone to join him in a glass of wine. They drank his health with words of congratulation. His salvage operation, said Mather, had been a miracle of seamanship. 'More credit goes to Mr Stirling,' he replied, 'whose raid had been the turning-point.' He thought inwardly that he himself deserved no praise from anyone. It was his fault, indirectly, that the *Venturer* had been wrecked in the first place. Looking up, he found that Dr Rathbone was looking at him curiously as if he had guessed his train of thought. 'May I suggest, captain, that we do not judge a man's quality from the way he wins a victory but from the way he recovers after a defeat.'

'I am entirely of your opinion, doctor. I only wish we

could go fishing again for classical sculptures!'

'I wouldn't dream of suggesting it, sir, God knows your men have done enough.'

'We shall be tolerably busy tomorrow and will do well if we can put to sea by nightfall. Let's agree to come here again in time of peace.'

It was a long day of effort before the *Venturer*'s cargo had been shipped again but the task was completed somehow and the ship fitted with a foremast. A few casks were placed in the two smaller prizes and filled with sand taken after dark from the beach. They were each then topped up with about an inch of gunpowder. After being shown this treasure trove, the old Alcayde was taken ashore and released with a great show of politeness. With a look of bitter hostility, he disappeared among the trees, leaving young Gosling to complain about the loss of his casks. He was told that his supply of water could be replenished at Tetuan, which would be the next port of call.

Soon afterwards the *Merlin* made sail, heading northward with the *Venturer* astern and the *Santa Catarina* bringing up in the rear. The Algerine coast was soon lost to sight and Delancey expressed the hope, inwardly, that he would never be in such a position again.

After three days' sail along the African coast there was more shipping to be seen. The shores of Spain and Africa were now closer together, converging on the Straits of Gibraltar, squeezing the traffic into what would become a single shipping lane. Anxious for news, Delancey spoke with a Danish brig, from which he learnt that Admiral Linois had been seen off Cartagena, heading south, and could not be very far away. This intelligence was confirmed by a Portuguese coaster and again by a privateer out of Gibraltar. But the privateer had other news, having spoken to a British sloop the day before. 'She was the *Speedy*,' said the privateer captain, 'commanded by a lord with a Scots accent. She is well named, I should say, for she carries a big spread of canvas. Which way? She was heading south but in search of a Spanish merchantman. I could not help him there and might not have wanted to. I have my own living to make.' Later the same day, the *Merlin* fell in with an

American brig. She had actually been intercepted by the *Speedy* and two of her men had been impressed as deserters from a British man-of-war. 'Were they? It would be hard to say. They all tell lies, don't they?'

Delancey pored over the chart, marking his own position and course and lightly pencilling in the possible track of the French squadron. He had many doubts and queries but had already decided that his approach to Tetuan would have to be in darkness. The ease with which he obtained news about Linois would be matched by the ease with which Linois would have gained intelligence about the *Merlin*.

Luckily, the Frenchman was less likely to be interested, presumably being intent on reaching Cadiz. It sounded as if Cochrane was taking risks but then he always did. When another sail was sighted, Delancey swore to himself. Ships were jostling each other like pedestrians at Charing Cross.

Next morning, July 3rd, yet another sail was sighted, a cutter with the mails from Gibraltar to Minorca. The news she brought was second-hand, obtained at daybreak from a Maltese coaster. Some Spanish merchantmen had been driven ashore near Alicante and had been set on fire. One of them was laden with oil and had blazed all the previous night. Delancey asked the cutter's master whether it was a British man-of-war that had burnt them. Seemingly it was, said Delancey's informant. There had certainly been a sloop in the vicinity. It was Cochrane again, Delancey thought, and he had failed to learn from example when it came to burning a prize with cargo unknown.

Going back to the chart he drew a semicircle with thirty miles' radius and with centre at Alicante. Then he drew another semicircle with the same centre and fifty miles' radius. Then he prolonged the estimated course he had pencilled in for Linois, finding that it cut both semicircles. After a few more calculations involving wind direction and speed, he came to the conclusion that Linois must have seen the blaze and that the *Speedy* would still be within the larger semicircle. On paper Cochrane's chances of escape looked very slight. He was, of course, a magnificent seaman and had every chance of knowing that a French squadron was in the area. He would escape if anyone could, but the wind was failing and might die away to nothing.

Then came the sound which Delancey had been expecting; the distant rumble of gunfire. The sound came from the north-west and was spasmodic, single guns firing and the occasional broadside. People not on duty came on deck to listen and Delancey found that Dr Rathbone was among them. The old scholar asked him whether a battle was in progress.

'Not a battle, doctor; perhaps a pursuit.'

'Should we not expect then, that the sound of gunfire would approach or die away?'

'What would you say was happening?'

'Why, sir, I picture a single ship trying to escape from a squadron.'

The distant thunder dwindled, resumed fitfully, came and went. After about four hours, the sound came to a climax with a series of broadsides. Then the firing ceased abruptly and there was silence. 'He was too self-centred', thought Delancey 'and too cocksure.' He hoped at the same time that Cochrane had not been killed. He thought, on the whole, that he was the sort of man who would survive.

Shortly before nightfall, Delancey intercepted a small Spanish coaster, releasing her again as valueless. She was heading eastwards and her master had seen the recent action. He spoke a Catalonian dialect, knowing only a few words of Castilian, but eked out his story with gestures and a rough diagram.

He conveyed the idea of three big ships hunting a small one which twisted and turned in its efforts to escape. In the end, he indicated, the small ship had been taken. Yes, she was English and about the same size as the *Merlin*, maybe a little smaller. Her pursuers were French sail of the line, one flying a Rear-Admiral's flag. Had the sloop been greatly damaged? The Catalan thought not. Her sails and rigging, yes, but not much otherwise. The conflict had been so unequal that he and his men had wanted to see the English escape even if they were not Christians, for the French these days were not Christians either. Avoiding any theological discussion, Delancey thanked his informant and made him a present of a captured barrel of wine.

Delancey now kept closer to the African coast, not wanting to share Cochrane's fate. Next day he was off Mellila with an easterly wind and every hope of reaching Tetuan by daybreak on the following day. He sent for Isaac Sulman, who had been sick for most of the voyage, and told him that he was nearly home.

'Tell me about the watering place.'

'Yes, captain. You should anchor off the river Boosega or St Martin and fire three guns as a signal to the British Vice-Consul, a relative of mine. You will then be eighteen miles from Tetuan and six miles from the custom house and fort. While you are watering, it would be wise to call on the officer who commands at the fort. The Vice-Consul, a very good man, will be there to meet you. If the Governor is in residence the Vice-Consul will arrange for you to visit him. The captain at the fort will expect, as a present, a cartridge of powder.'

'How long will it take to water the ship?'

'Two days or a little longer. You will perhaps allow me, meanwhile, to show you round the city? It is a good place for silverwork, leather and saddlery.' Delancey accepted the invitation with pleasure, he and Dr Rathbone questioning Sulman about the sights and looking forward to going ashore.

Early next morning, the *Merlin* was nearing the coast with a stiff breeze and Delancey surveyed the wild landscape with interest. There were high mountains inland, formed of barren rock but clothed with undergrowth on the lower slopes. In the foreground the foothills were green and dotted with occasional buildings, all white or nearly so. Delancey thought that he would some day like to paint the scene, which had a dreamlike beauty in the early light.

Sulman came on deck to act as pilot, pointing out the river mouth and indicating the usual anchorage. The sails were furled smartly, the anchor dropped, and three guns were fired which echoed back from the hills. Delancey turned to Sulman with a word of thanks as he watched the *Venturer* and *Santa*

Catarina drop anchor in turn. He made a mental note that Langford and Northmore had both done extremely well.

'Well, here we are, Mr Sulman,' said Delancey. 'You have had your setbacks, but you are safely home at last.'

'Home?' repeated Isaac Sulman sadly. 'I and my people have no home.'

CHAPTER EIGHT

Slave Market

Delancey's journey to Tetuan began from the custom house, where he met with Mr Levi Manasseh, Vice-Consul to Mr Matra, Consul at Tangier. Landing with Delancey were Dr Rathbone, Mr Sulman, Mr Midshipman Topley as A.D.C., Luke Tanner and John Teesdale. Delancey would have liked to take a lieutenant with him but Mather was needed to command the ship in her captain's absence and Stirling was needed with the watering party, now ashore under canvas. After a meal at the custom house of roasted fowls and fried sardines, they were mounted on horses and their luggage strapped on mules. Each horse had an enormous high-peaked saddle and bucket-shaped stirrups. Delancey's horse was a grey and distinguished by a scarlet saddle cloth.

Returning with them to Tetuan, Mr Manasseh rode an easy paced mule and was attended by a servant, similarly mounted. The road was abominable but the country was very attractive, with pastures along the winding river backed by plantations of olives, as also (rather surprisingly) by vineyards. Above all were the sunlit mountains, across which cloud shadows chased each other. Ahead lay the walled city, looking like an illustration to the *Arabian Nights*. There were eighty thousand inhabitants, the Vice-Consul explained, and a fourth part of them were Jews, who were made to live in their own quarter. The Governor, under Muley Solyman, Emperor of Morocco, was Sidi-Ash-Ash, whose authority extended to Tangier. He was not at the moment in residence.

'I am sorry to hear that,' said Delancey. 'I have brought a present for him: four barrels of gunpowder.'

'It will not be needed,' said Mr Manasseh. 'It will,

however, have a ready sale.'

'It is sold already,' said Mr Sulman. 'I will pay whatever price the Vice-Consul considers fair.' Some discussion followed and the price was agreed at what seemed to Delancey an unusually high figure. The powder had come from one of the prizes left at Cherchell and its value could be added to the amount of prize-money which would come from selling the *Santa Catarina* when she was condemned at Gibraltar.

Delancey had been told that the city was wealthy but he could at first see no sign of it. The streets were narrow and filthy, the houses were so many blank walls, almost joining overhead, and the only buildings of note seemed to be the mosques and a castle or citadel sited on high ground and commanding the city centre. No particular notice was taken of the Europeans and Delancey presumed that they were often seen there while purchasing supplies for Gibraltar, but one or two pebbles were thrown at Sulman by jeering urchins. He took no notice and presently led them to the Jewish quarter, entered by another gateway which was shut, he explained, each night.

His own home looked like all the rest but his wife, who greeted her guests at the entrance, was able to show them a luxurious interior. Sulman answered Delancey's compliments by saying, 'Ah, we were rich, some of us, before Muley Yazid plundered us ten years ago.' His wife was a beautiful woman and some of the other womenfolk had fine features and clear complexions. Among those who greeted Sulman, congratulating him on his safe return, was an Arab called Ali ben Ismail who seemed to be his partner.

Delancey had been invited, with his party, to dine at the Vice-Consul's but it was now agreed that he should first visit the markets and shops. Setting out again, this time on foot, and guided by Sulman, Delancey was taken to the central bazaar, thronged with people and offering, among other things, silks and carpets. Distinct from this was a produce market with meat, poultry and vegetables for sale and distinct again was the Socco, used for sales by auction.

Delancey passed through these colourful scenes with an

appreciative eye but aware of possible theft. He was carrying an unusually large sum of money, received from Sulman and decided to entrust this to Luke Tanner as a precaution against pickpockets. After admiring cattle, sheep, horses and mules, the party was brought to a momentary halt by Sulman.

'I hope you will forgive me, captain, if I take you a little out of the main street. There is a mosque just ahead of us. As a Jew I am compelled to pass it barefoot. So I usually follow this lane to the left, rejoining the shopping streets a little further down. Would you mind . . . ?'

Delancey had no objection and they passed through an almost deserted alley, which echoed to their footsteps. They turned right, then left and right again and presently came into a square, through which they had to pass to regain the high street. People were collecting there on the shady side, as if to watch a performance staged under the hot sun. Sulman made a gesture of annoyance.

'I did not know that there was to be an auction here today. It is not a place for visitors. How stupid of me!'

'Why don't you bring visitors here?' asked Delancey with amusement.

'Well, captain, this is the Basistan or slave market. Visitors must be shocked at something so uncivilised. It won't be too difficult, however, to push our way through, especially if I make Ali ben Ismail go first.'

'What slaves are sold here?' asked Dr Rathbone.

'Poor creatures from other parts of Africa – a few Berbers and a few black men brought across the desert.'

As if to prove the truth of this, the auctioneer's men led in the first slaves for sale, arranging them on a paved area higher than the pathway and forming a kind of permanent stage. The luckless slaves were made to walk up and down, to show their paces. Others were half starved or ill and squatted listlessly where they were put. Dealers and possible buyers came to the front and the auction began.

'What a terrible sight!' exclaimed Dr Rathbone.

'Heathen goings-on!' growled Luke Tanner.

'Poor creatures!' muttered coxswain Teesdale.

Disapproval was unanimous among the Europeans but nobody made a move, all being fascinated. Rather reluctantly Sulman began to explain how the auction was planned.

'The cheapest are sold first. Then come the stronger slaves, thought to be good workers, the more valuable household slaves, and last of all, the women who might do for the harem. Slaves of the better sort are usually bought by dealers known as *tegorarini*, who fatten them up for sale to particular clients.'

'Are there Christians among them?' asked Dr Rathbone.

'Sometimes,' Sulman admitted. 'After prizes have been captured. I doubt if there will be any today.'

'You say that dealers sell to particular clients,' asked Delancey. 'In what way are they particular?'

'Well,' began Sulman hesitantly, 'there are people who are known to have certain tastes. They like young girls with no experience or else they are cruel, or perhaps they prefer boys.'

'Monsters!' groaned Dr Rathbone, but he too was rooted to the spot.

As the auction proceeded, Delancey identified the dealers who chatted to each other, finding little of interest even among the household slaves. Their attention was caught, however, by the appearance of a strikingly beautiful woman with a fair skin, clad like the others in a rough piece of sacking.

'Is she Christian?' asked Delancey sharply.

'Oh, no,' Sulman replied. 'With that colour and those eyes she surely comes from Mequinas. Women from Fas are fairer still but less lively. I don't know how she comes to be a slave but she will bring a high price.'

Bidding was brisk and the girl was knocked down to a dealer, who instantly paid in cash. Doing mental arithmetic, Delancey thought she had fetched the equivalent to five and a half barrels of gunpowder. To judge from her bright eyes, he guessed that she might be about as explosive.

Mr Midshipman Topley moaned a regret that he had insufficient funds for such an investment. There was a pause in the proceedings and several dealers, including the successful bidder, left without showing any further interest. Delancey was about to do the same when a final lot was announced. She was a girl aged about twelve, a mere child, miserably thin and downcast. She was not exactly pretty but her skin appeared to be fair under the dirt and her hair was possibly more brown than black.

'Italian, surely?' asked Delancey.

'I think – perhaps,' replied Sulman, 'or mixed a little, Italian and Arab.' Delancey was thinking about what Sulman had said about clients with known and peculiar tastes. Without making a conscious decision about it he found himself saying 'Buy her for me.'

'Buy her?' asked Sulman, astonished. 'I couldn't, being a Jew.'

'Ali ben Ismail can bid for me.'

There followed a whispered conversation between the two partners.

'Ali thinks that the girl will go to Abdul Hassan, acting for Ibrahim Mansour.'

'Can't I outbid him? You know, Mr Sulman, how much money I had from you.' There was a further discussion and Ali finally nodded.

'Ali thinks "perhaps" but he will want a commission.'

'He can have it within the limits of what I have.'

Delancey had a dreadful feeling that his behaviour was idiotic. Who was he, a poor man, to indulge in such a mad scheme as this? He was spending what little he had – and maybe more he would have to borrow – on trying to save this unknown child from an unknown fate. He could sense Dr Rathbone's disapproval. He could feel Topley's surprise. Why in heaven's name had he done anything so foolish? Whatever his second thoughts – and his heart was beating unusually – it was now too late; his decision had been taken.

Sulman explained the situation to Ali ben Ismail and they apparently reached agreement, for Ali walked deliberately away from Sulman and Delancey, taking up a position further forward and to the left. The auctioneer was making the girl walk up and down, emphasising her good points, no doubt, and explaining that she would be a good investment. He did his best but was aware that several of the dealers had gone.

Delancey hoped that Abdul Hassan was among them. Then the description ended and the bidding began.

Ali ben Ismail may have been no more than Sulman's junior partner, a Muslim to put forward when a Muslim was needed, but he certainly knew how to bid at an auction. His intervention came late and his manner was deliberately casual. Abdul Hassan was present, as soon became obvious, but Ali never glanced in his direction. He was bidding on impulse, and was backed, it was obvious, by unlimited funds. Chatting with an Arab acquaintance, he almost forgot to bid at one point and then raised his opponent (for he had only the one) by the value of a single small coin. People laughed and the auctioneer looked rather hurt.

His next bid marked a substantial rise. Abdul hesitated for a minute and finally shook his head. The auctioneer shouted, the deal was made, the auction ended and the girl was Delancey's property. Luke Tanner went over to Ali ben Ismail who made payment on the spot and retained his own commission. Sulman looked anxious. 'It would never do,' he explained, 'if I were thought to have outbid an agent acting for Ibrahim Mansour, who is a powerful man in this city. If you are known to have bought a slave, that is another matter. The law is doubtful – I don't know for certain what the position is.'

After a short discussion it was agreed that Delancey should go with his party to the Vice-Consul's house for dinner but that Ali ben Ismail should take the slave girl (named Souraya, it seemed) back to his own room where he lived with his wife Aisha and servant Mustapha in a corner of what had been a large mansion. Aisha would bath the girl and tell her that she was free. It would then lie with Delancey to decide what he was going to do with her.

In the meanwhile he faced the unspoken disapproval of Dr Rathbone and the shocked silence of the others. Was he, they were wondering, the man of iron they had thought him to be? Had he given way to sentimentality – or to some even more deplorable emotion?

Delancey would have been more than human if he had not considered, fleetingly, the advantages of possessing a slave girl.

The drawbacks were more obvious, however, as soon as he sat down to dinner at the Vice-Consul's house. He told Mr Manasseh what had happened and hoped that there would be no legal or political complications. 'I should suppose that the girl is Italian. I could not allow her to be sold as a slave.'

He realised, as he said the words, that his actions might be misunderstood. He also realised that it was a thoroughly quixotic gesture hardly becoming to a man in his position. The Rev. Dr Rathbone looked at him almost accusingly, Mr Midshipman Topley with a touch of envy. 'I propose to leave her with some family in Gibraltar', he went on, 'and have no doubt that she will be treated kindly.' Mr Sulman looked worried and Mr Manasseh expressed his doubts.

'People here cannot object to a Christian slave being redeemed by a European. Slaves are often thus ransomed by the Redemptionist Fathers and the practice is clearly within the law. We have to be certain, however, that she is not a Muslim. If she is, we shall have trouble. And you say, captain, that her name is Souraya?'

Discussion continued during dinner and Delancey realised that his rescue of the girl would not be complete until she was on board the *Merlin*. Abdul Hassan was an awkward customer and Ibrahim Mansour was a sadistic bully. In their hands, the child's fate would have been unmentionable, as Sulman had to admit, but it remained a problem how to smuggle her out of a walled city. A first precaution might be to disguise her as a boy.

As they were finishing dinner, a servant came in saying that a messenger had arrived with news for Mr Sulman. 'I feared as much,' he muttered as he excused himself. He was back in five minutes, looking more worried than ever. 'It is Mustapha, sent by Ali ben Ismail to say that Abdul Hassan has collected his friends, that they are at the outer door of the house and demanding that Souraya should be given up to them. They will go to the judge and demand that she be taken into custody. They claim that she is a Muslim and that she was bought illegally by a Jew.'

'Not by a Christian?' asked Delancey.

'No. It is always easier to raise a mob against the Jews.' Sulman spoke without bitterness, resigned to his position in a harsh world.

'I see,' replied Delancey. 'I shall fetch Souraya and make it clear that she belongs to me and not to you. While I do this I want you to provide horses and mules for our return to my ship.'

'That is easy,' said Sulman. 'They are already collected at my house, ready for your departure in the morning.'

'No good. They must be somewhere *outside* the gates and ready for our departure tonight. I know the gate by which I came from the harbour – the east gate, I suppose. Is there another gate from which I could reach the river mouth by a less obvious route?' Some argument followed but it was finally agreed that the south gate would be best. Given a reliable guide, he could reach the Marteen from there, although it would mean a longer ride. He could reach even sooner, however, the place where his men were camped ashore.

'Very well, then. I owe you a thousand apologies, Mr Sulman, for all the trouble I have caused. I can't explain – it was something I had to do. And now I must ask you, Dr Rathbone, to take command of the horses, and have them in a place of concealment about half a mile from the south gate. I shall be there, I hope at about nightfall, when the gates are closed. I think that Mr Sulman can provide you with a guide. How far is it from the place where Ali ben Ismail lives to the south gate?' There was a short discussion about routes and distances and Delancey formed a fairly clear idea of what had to be done and when.

'I don't like this at all,' Mr Manasseh sighed. 'You may be set upon by the mob and then there will be bad relations with the Governor. The British are well liked, as things are, and this could spoil everything.'

Delancey made his apologies over this and set off down the street with Mustapha for guide and a total force of three. They left the Jewish quarter and passed through the main bazaar which was coming to life after the midday rest. They skirted the fish market and the leather-sellers' street, and were nearing their destination when Mustapha paused to listen. From beyond the next turning came the angry sound of voices. 'Bad, bad,' said Mustapha, 'Allah, preserve us!' Then he went on and Delancey came in sight of the riot which was so far, he was glad to see, on a small scale.

Some twenty people were gathered at the door of what seemed to be a large house, one which presented an almost blank front to the street. One was hammering on the door and several were shouting insults towards a small first-floor window. The rest were expressing their support in a less active way. Delancey guessed that more would join in the fun when the siesta was finished.

Seeing so small a demonstration, he walked on quickly, followed by his A.D.C., coxswain and steward. Touching nobody except merely to brush him aside, he pushed his way through and found himself in front of the door. He realised at this point that things might be difficult if the door remained shut and barred. But those inside were expecting Mustapha's return. The moment he shouted his name the door opened and Mustapha darted in. The two seamen followed, then the midshipman.

Delancey looked sternly at the crowd, entered quite slowly and closed the door. It was quickly bolted by Ali ben Ismail, who remained there on guard. In theory, the followers of Abdul Hassan should have fallen on the Englishmen and prevented the closing of the door. In actual fact, they were taken by surprise. They had been told that a wicked Jew had bought a Muslim slave. They knew nothing about any European being involved. Giving way, at least momentarily, to an officer in uniform, they did not connect him with the outrage they had come to prevent. He could have been there on some other business. By the time they had made him the villain of the story it was too late. The door was strong and it was closed. After a pause of a few minutes, they resumed their aimless knocking and shouting.

Once inside, Delancey found himself in a square chamber serving as porch which was in the corner of what proved to be a large and formerly luxurious mansion. Led by Mustapha, he and his followers passed a door opening and found themselves at the foot of the staircase. Another opening on their right led into a spacious courtyard centred upon a disused fountain and surrounded by a gallery resting on Moorish arches. The place had become a sort of tenement, evidently housing a number of families, and the plaster was flaking off the walls.

Mustapha led the way up the stairs and into the gallery. Passing a series of half-doors and curtains through which dark faces peered at them, Delancey followed his guide to a room diagonally opposite the entrance; that is, in the far right-hand corner of the building. He was met there by Ali's wife Aisha and by another woman, possibly Mustapha's wife, called Muni.

With them was Souraya, clean, reclothed in local style but still barefoot, inarticulate and shy, with eyes downcast. The difficulty which now became apparent was that Delancey and his men knew no Arabic dialect and neither Aisha nor Muni knew any language but their own. Souraya wanted to say 'Thank you' and Delancey wanted to say 'Don't be afraid – we are friends,' but there was no way of conveying any message to anyone.

It was no time, in any case, for idle talk, for the noise from the front door was on the increase. Bowing to the women and leaving Topley to guard them, Delancey ran down the staircase to find Ali, who might speak some European language. He did not, as was soon obvious, and Delancey had to ask his question in dumb show: 'Is there a back door?' Distracted as he was, Ali understood nothing at first but Delancey persisted, finally drawing a sketch with his scabbard point in the dirt of the porch floor. Comprehension dawned and Ali nodded repeatedly, pointing to the far left-hand corner of the building.

Going in the direction indicated, watched by many eyes peering from dark recesses, Delancey found that there was indeed a back door. Opening it, he found that it led into a deserted lane. The main problem solved, he went upstairs again and explained by gestures that he would take Souraya to a place of greater safety. Aisha knew at once what he meant and told the others. Within a few minutes the whole party was at the foot of the stairs. Delancey said good-bye to Ali and then led his followers to the rear of the building. But there he met with an unexpected obstacle. The usually docile Souraya refused to go.

Delancey could have picked the child up and carried her but he decided that this would be a mistake. She was explaining something to the two women, who came round, seemingly, to agree with her.

Aisha pointed to the back door, which Delancey opened, and shook her head. Then she pointed to the upper floor as if to say that there was another and better way. Mustapha was about to close the back door but Delancey made him leave it ajar. Then he followed Aisha up to the gallery, leading the others. She did not go to her own apartment but to a point above the back door where there was a ladder, evidently leading to a flat roof. She climbed this as one who knows the way, leaving Muni and Mustapha behind, but beckoning Delancey's party to follow.

They came into sunlight on the roof but the heat of the day was now giving place to the relative coolness of the late afternoon. Without hesitation Aisha went quickly and quietly to the far corner of the roof and jumped a three-foot gap which separated that house from the next. The gap after that was wider but bridged by a couple of planks. The gap after that amounted to nothing. After thus crossing half a dozen rooftops, Aisha led them down another ladder into another house, centred upon a smaller courtyard than the one her own apartment overlooked.

Nothing could be heard of the riot from which they had fled. The women who now greeted Aisha were evidently friends or relatives. She talked to them volubly, pointing to Delancey and Souraya. They tittered a great deal, scenting a romance, but the youngest of them stared with bright interest at young Topley, who blushed uncomfortably. With a final word of farewell, Aisha had gone. Her friends giggled afresh and proceeded to make coffee.

'I've heard tell of all this before, sir,' said Teesdale unexpectedly.

'You have heard of – what?' asked Delancey.

'The rooftops, sir. The Muslim idea is that women stay home and aren't never seen in the street 'cept maybe with another woman and heavily veiled. They are supposed to have no fun until their man comes home, like. All this seems a bit dull, so they use the rooftops as their own street, visit their friends, hear the news and sometimes meet with a man younger than their old husband. They have signals, too.'

'How d'you mean?'

'Squatting on the rooftop, they sing out much as if they were chanting a ballad; not very tuneful, though, and all on a high note.'

'What sort of messages do they send?'

'Gossip, sir, I'm told. Miriam is expecting another baby, her sister has a boy visitor – that sort of thing. They use a code, though, and their menfolk don't understand a blessed word.'

'I've heard of that too, sir,' said Tanner. 'But I'll admit, sir, that I don't like running away from a parcel of Arabs.'

'Nor do I, Tanner,' replied Delancey, 'but fighting would get us into trouble. Tetuan is the place from which Gibraltar receives half its supplies.'

'That's true enough, sir, come to think of it. So we must keep clear of the law and that – avoid being seen?'

'Yes, and we shall need a disguise. I'll try to explain this to the ladies after we have had coffee.'

The coffee, when it came, was hot, black and strong, served in egg-cup sized china. They all squatted on the floor while they drank it. Then Delancey tried to explain what they wanted, showing them what money he had to offer; luckily, a useful sum. It was Souraya who came to his rescue, having some prior knowledge of the situation. With renewed giggles the women finally produced some old pieces of cloth, tattered, worn but very much what was wanted. One after another, the Englishmen were wrapped in shabby material and made to look like Arabs. Thus transformed, they descended to ground-level and headed for the south gate, guided only by the setting sun. They found it before nightfall, not without difficulty, and boldly passed the guard. Luckily for them, the men posted at the gate were watchful over people entering the city but far less concerned about people who were leaving it. Delancey trudged on in a mercifully failing light, hearing the gate close while he was still within earshot. Some half-hour later Dr Rathbone stepped out from the shadow of an old ruin and said that the horses were ready and waiting on the tether. Four hours later and something after midnight, Delancey answered the sentry's challenge and rode into the camp at the watering place.

The Vice-Consul came down to the river mouth before they sailed next day, bringing their luggage and assuring them that all was well. Ali ben Ismail had complained that his slave girl had been stolen by some Europeans, men unknown to him, and his explanation had been accepted. Mr Sulman had been questioned but knew nothing about the girl, not having seen her since the auction, at which his presence had been accidental. Manasseh himself admitted that some English sailors had been ashore, but they had sailed again.

This soon became the truth. The tents were struck, the seamen returned to their ship and the *Merlin* and her consort put to sea with a favourable wind, sure of reaching Gibraltar that afternoon. On the quarterdeck stood a new crate, marked with Dr Rathbone's name and containing a classical statue packed in wood shavings. In the captain's day-cabin, which Delancey had given up to her, Souraya was still asleep. Delancey was pacing the deck with Rathbone beside him.

'Tell me, captain,' asked the old scholar, 'how much does the Admiral have to know?'

'I shall report that we have taken one prize; that the *Venturer*, from Minorca, parted company and grounded on a reef, being refloated with difficulty, and that we called at Tetuan for water. I could add that the *Speedy* has probably been captured but he probably knows that already.'

'A laconic report doing scant justice to the most exciting days I have spent or will ever spend!'

'It was a pleasure to have you with us, sir.'

'I should like to add that I have formed the highest opinion of your professional skill. Should I have the chance to mention your name to anyone with interest in high places, I shall do so in terms of warm admiration.'

'Thank you, sir. I shall be obliged to you.'

'Forgive me, however, if I hint to you that your worldly wisdom falls a little short of your warlike accomplishments.'

'How so, Dr Rathbone?'

'Your purchase of a slave girl is a romantic story that will lose nothing in the telling.'

'But what was I to do? I could not let a mere child be sold like that to an Arab dealer.' Delancey had acted on impulse, as he knew, and it was a lame excuse.

'I know – I know,' said Rathbone. 'But what will people think when she steps ashore at Gibraltar?'

'People? Do you mean the Port Admiral?'

'No, I don't mean the senior officers of either service. I mean their wives. This could ruin your chances of making the right sort of marriage.'

'I see what you mean, sir. I suppose I could smuggle the girl ashore after dark . . .'

'What would be the use? Tetuan is a short day's sail from Gibraltar, forty miles or less, and there is constant communication, with supply ships passing every week. What happens in Tetuan today is known in Gibraltar tomorrow. Come what may, that story will make the rounds.'

'What then can I do?'

'Leave her on board in my care. Find a kind woman on shore and persuade her to visit the ship, bringing with her some clothes and, above all, some shoes. Then they can land together in broad daylight. That will look perfectly proper even if it doesn't prevent the gossip. Do you know a motherly sort of woman who would look after the girl and train her as a maidservant?'

'No, sir, I don't. I have only a small acquaintance in Gibraltar.'

'That being the case, you had best consult with the garrison chaplain. Call on him as soon as you have reported to the Admiral. It will help, perhaps, if you tell him that the girl is aged nine.'

'And you, sir, a clergyman, would have me tell a lie?'

'What lie, captain? What is her real age? Do you know?'

'Of course not, sir. I can only guess.'

'But with no real knowledge. I can guess too and I put her age as nine.'

'I am sure you are right, sir. She might, in fact, be no more than eight.'

Delancey went to visit Souraya at this time and took Dr Rathbone with him. The girl was up and looking out of the nearest gunport with every sign of bewilderment. It could have been, and probably was, her first sight of the sea. Delancey sat near her and talked soothingly, putting all the kindness he could into the words she could not understand. He finally extracted a single fleeting smile, after which she looked fixedly again at the deck. He then realised (with an absurd touch of jealousy) that Teesdale was already a friend of hers and could make her laugh. So he and Dr Rathbone left her in good hands, wondering how the steward had overcome the language difficulty. Overcome it he had, anyway, and he admitted to having a way with children; something Delancey conspicuously lacked.

After dinner that day, a farewell occasion for Dr Rathbone, the Rock of Gibraltar was in sight. Delancey presently spoke with a cutter on patrol and learnt that Linois had not yet been seen but that the *Speedy* was known to have been captured. Asked whether the same admiral was there, the master reported that there was no admiral at all. The flag-officer to whom Delancey used to report had gone home, invalided, and there had been no replacement. The harbour was empty of men-of-war, save for a single sloop. So there was no likelihood of Delancey being asked questions about what he had been doing.

With Linois daily expected, with a crisis at hand, no one would take much notice of Souraya. Thinking it over, Delancey decided that Dr Rathbone had made too much of the problem. He put the matter out of his mind and turned to something of more immediate importance.

'We shall presently be entering harbour, Mr Mather, and I want to do so with credit. Replace the old ensign by the new one. We'll have the sails a little more taut. Be ready to salute the flag and check the appearance of the men. The *Merlin* is no frigate but she can be as smart as any frigate in the list. Here is the place and now is the time!'

CHAPTER NINE

Algeciras

The *Merlin* was rounding Europa Point and Delancey was secretly thrilled, as he had always been, by the sight of Gibraltar, the rock-face rising almost sheer from the sea on the eastern side, the sea breaking over the rocks to the south. The scene was warmly sunlit and he could see the yellow-brown hillsides beyond the Spanish coast. He could almost smell the undergrowth on Gibraltar's rocky slopes.

He had been there during the great siege eighteen years back, gaining his commission just before peace was signed. He had reconnoitred the floating batteries and had served in the gunboats which finally rescued some of the Spanish survivors. He had been at Gibraltar quite recently, for that matter, but his mind dwelt now on that earlier and historic occasion. General Elliott's defence of Gibraltar would be remembered, he supposed, for as long as Britain herself should survive. But war was fought in those days with a sense of chivalry. There were courteous messages and flags of truce and the whole affair ended with an inspection of the garrison by the Duc de Crillon, a polite visitor to the fortress he had failed to capture. The French Revolution had changed all that. So much had changed and so much for the worse. Lord Nelson had learnt from his opponents to aim at the annihilation of the enemy. There had been no thought of that in the previous war. In Rodney's day it had been enough to win the battle; one was not expected to destroy the enemy.

As the harbour came in sight, Delancey saw that the only other man-of-war on the scene was another sloop, a queer-looking craft, probably smaller than the *Merlin.* If her commander were his junior, which was not very likely, he would himself be the senior naval officer at Gibraltar, entitled to open the dispatch of which he was the bearer. As for the squadron sent to fight Linois, there was no sign of it. The *Merlin*'s passage from Minorca had been delayed by headwinds and Delancey guessed that Linois's passage might be slower still.

In the meanwhile, pending the arrrival of other forces, three French sail of the line would be opposed by two British sloops. Coming smartly into harbour, Delancey saluted the flag, dropped anchor, and signalled his number to the other sloop. From her reply Delancey gathered that she was the 14-gun *Calpé*; commanded, according to the List, by the Honourable George Heneage Laurence Dundas, senior to Delancey in rank but almost certainly his junior in age. After issuing a few routine orders to Mr Mather, Delancey went off in a boat to pay his respects and deliver his dispatch. Dundas turned out to be a red-haired young man, aged little over twenty, with a very slight Scots accent, who received Delancey with more than a hint of patronage.

He looked rather prosperous and overweight, to all appearance more of a gentleman than a sailor. His after-cabin was richly furnished with brocade curtains, Persian rugs and silver hanging lamp. Glancing at Delancey's uniform he all but muttered 'Provincial tailoring – it never looks right.' After some slight hesitation he offered Delancey a glass of wine, thinking almost audibly that his ill-dressed visitor would not appreciate good wine when he tasted it and would probably have preferred ale. He broke the seal of the dispatch and then, belatedly, asked Delancey to sit down.

'Pray be seated, captain, while I read this.'

The pause which followed gave Delancey time to look around and admire the prints, the cushions, the crystal decanters. Dundas was evidently a man of wealth. He looked up sharply after he had finished reading:

'You know the contents of this?'

'Yes.'

'Well, there are only two facts I can add. First, Linois has not yet been sighted. Second, there is a squadron off Cadiz commanded by Rear-Admiral Sir James Saumarez.'

'So Linois will have to fight?'

'To reach Cadiz, undoubtedly. But my guess is that he will call at Algeciras. There he will be told that Cadiz is blockaded. It will then be for him to decide what to do next. He might, for example, sail back to Toulon.'

'He will be outnumbered, I take it, by Saumarez?'

'Oh, yes. Sir James has seven sail of the line besides the *Thames*, frigate, and a sloop. He in turn would be outnumbered, of course, by the French and Spanish together.'

'Should he be warned about Linois?'

'Not until Linois is actually sighted. In the meanwhile, you will want to call on the Governor, General O'Hara. With Spain now at war with us, he sees himself as the hero of the coming siege.'

Delancey and his officers dined that day with the Governor, giving him news of Malta. The Governor, for his part, assured his guests that the fortress would be held to the last. Perhaps prejudiced by memories of General Elliott, now Lord Heathfield, Delancey decided silently that he himself would never have entrusted a key fortress to anyone called O'Hara. An Irishman, he thought, would be better leading an assault.

He enjoyed the occasion, nevertheless, and was glad that Dr Rathbone was among those present. The old scholar came across to Delancey when the guests rose from table and said at once 'I want you to meet the garrison chaplain, the Reverend Mr Samuel Slater. His wife, whom I have had the pleasure of meeting, is going to be very helpful indeed. She has a friend, Mrs Hardwick, who would be delighted to provide a home for Souraya. Come and meet Mr Slater before he goes about his duties.'

It soon appeared that Mrs Hardwick was kindness itself and promised to come aboard the *Merlin* next day, together with Mrs Slater, and would bring with her some suitable clothes and shoes for Souraya. Delancey accepted this offer with real gratitude but was not quite as pleased when the actual moment came for Souraya to leave his ship. He realised then that the girl had meant something to him, that he would miss her. He realised as promptly that her sadness, which was evident, was the result of her parting from Teesdale. There were tears on either side and then the parting came. His last glimpse of Souraya was of a small figure on the quayside waving good-bye to Teesdale.

On July 4th Dundas and Delancey watched the French squadron pass Europa Point, cross the bay and drop anchor four miles away at Algeciras. From their point of vantage on the King's Bastion they gazed through their telescopes until the French sails were furled.

'The flagship I take to be the *Formidable*, a seventy-four,' said Dundas, 'with the *Indomptable* and *Desaix*.'

'I believe the *Formidable* is an 80-gun ship, sir,' was Delancey's reply, 'and so is the *Indomptable*. There is a frigate – the *Muiron*, I think, and I suppose the other vessels are prizes.'

Dundas looked a little put out but came back with a comment of his own:

'One of them must be the *Speedy* and the brig is a small merchantman.'

'It looks to me, sir, as if the French men-of-war are in pretty good order.'

'Yes, the *Formidable* is a ship to reckon with and I suppose that the other is a sister ship. I must admit that I never heard of Linois.'

It almost seemed that Linois had been dismissed as a man of no social consequence but Delancey did what he could to reinstate him.

'He was an officer of the old regime, I believe, sir, and served under Suffren in the East Indies. He was promoted quite recently. He is a Breton, I have heard, with a reputation for caution rather than for enterprise.'

They closed their telescopes and walked back towards the harbour, both looking thoughtful.

They provided a certain contrast. Dundas was prosperous and well connected but rather lacking in experience. Delancey was a good practical seaman but had no influential relatives. They were on reasonably friendly terms but with a hint of jealousy on either side, liking each other better when they came to know each other more.

That night was windless and the *Calpé*'s launch was sent off in a flat calm to warn Sir James Saumarez. Delancey was on board the *Calpé* when the dispatch was sent and he remained to discuss the situation.

'This sloop would have been seen at once,' Dundas explained. 'The launch will pass unnoticed.'

'A pull of about eighty miles. . . . And what will Saumarez decide to do?'

'I have been thinking about that. His first instinct will be to prevent Linois joining up with the French and Spanish at Cadiz. His idea will be to destroy the weaker of the two squadrons before it can join forces with the other. That means attacking Linois tomorrow.'

'But Algeciras offers Linois a good defensive position in shallow water, with covering fire from the shore batteries. Saumarez would think twice, surely, before attacking him there.'

'Yes, but what else can he do? Suppose Linois sends a message overland to the Admiral at Cadiz, whose squadron then puts to sea. Then, when Linois himself quits his anchorage, Saumarez would be caught between two enemy squadrons. What chance would he have?'

'What is the Spanish strength, sir?'

'The French and Spanish are said to have about eleven ships between them at Cadiz, but they include three ships of a hundred guns or more. Two of them, we hear, the *Real-Carlos* and the *San-Hermenegilde*, mount a hundred and twelve guns apiece. They must be among the biggest ships in the world and we hear that they are splendidly built.'

'Their crews will have seen little service.'

'And that's the truth. But if you plan for the *Calpé* and the *Merlin* to fight the pair of them, you can leave me ashore. They have another three-decker, incidentally, in the *San-Fernando*.'

'The more pity that we should have lost the *Speedy*. With her we should have had three a-side!'

'Oh, Cochrane would have fought them single-handed, sending half his crew away on shore leave. To be serious, however, Delancey, I don't like the sound of those three-deckers. We have nothing to compare with them and they should be able to blow any seventy-four out of the water. A *hundred and twelve* guns! If it comes to a battle with them, Saumarez would do well to engage at extreme range.'

Early next morning, Dundas and Delancey met again at the King's Bastion, each with a midshipman to carry sextant, telescope and chart. They could see now that the French ships were in a carefully chosen defensive position. After taking bearings, Delancey pencilled them in on his chart. Then he pencilled in the shore batteries. 'There is one on Islà Verda, another on Santiago – perhaps five shore batteries in all. There is a whole flotilla of gunboats – God knows how many but I've seen them exercising – and those three sail of the line are moored in from four to five fathoms. In Saumarez's place I should let them alone.'

'That means facing the Spanish three-deckers. I'll wager that he attacks Linois', replied Dundas, 'and I'll tell you why. Saumarez was at the Battle of the Nile, wasn't he? Well, his idea will be to fight the same battle again. He'll try to anchor between the enemy ships and the land.'

'What, in three fathoms? Opposite the batteries?'

'That's what he'll do, I'll wager five guineas.'

Soon afterwards, the British squadron was sighted in the distance. As they rounded Cabrita Point it became possible to count the ships.

'Six sail of the line,' said Delancey. 'There is one missing, together with the frigate and sloop.'

'The Rear-Admiral may have left them to watch Cadiz, keeping up the appearance of a blockade.'

'That will be his plan. I should expect him now to cross the bay and pick up some local pilots, men with a knowledge of Algeciras. He might then order our two sloops to go ahead of his line, sounding as we go and signalling the depths back to him.

'Let's hope to God he doesn't think of it! We should both be destroyed in the first hour.'

'I doubt if he has even seen us but his leading ship has just sighted the enemy.' Delancey wiped the lens of his telescope and adjusted it again. 'The Rear-Admiral's flag is in the fourth ship and the signal for battle has just been hoisted. It's seven o'clock of a sunny morning and the day is before them . . . I wish to God, however, that the wind would hold. It blows for a while and then dies away.'

'Yes, look at the flag there. It's drooping again. And look at Saumarez's line. His rear ships are miles astern, his leading ship just opening fire.'

The rumble of gunfire could be heard that moment across the bay and smoke began to obscure the view from the Rock of what was happening at Algeciras. Dundas led the way to the harbour, remembering that both sloops should be ready to sail at a moment's notice. The ramparts were lined with people, both soldiers and civilians, and the streets they passed through were buzzing with excitement.

'We can play no part in the battle,' said Dundas, 'but we might have to rescue survivors. I fear that there must be heavy losses on both sides. With the wind as fitful as this, half the ships may fail to engage and those that do may have no chance to withdraw.'

'I submit, sir, that we should do what we can.'

'You are right. We cannot be mere spectators. Bring your officers over to the *Calpé* and I'll explain the situation and the part we may hope to play.'

A conference followed on board the *Calpé* at which Dundas showed the four lieutenants the position so far as he knew it. 'The three French sail of the line were last seen in the position as marked on the chart. It may have been Sir James's intention to anchor between them on the shore. I suspect, however, that his ships are still on the seaward side of them and some of them may be in danger. I shall presently make sail and steer for a position nearly opposite the Isla Verda and astern of where the *Indomptable* was last seen. The *Merlin* will take a more northerly course and should reach a position about a mile to the north of Algeciras town but not too close to the Santiago Battery. Our object on board either sloop will be to offer what help we can to the ships of Sir James's squadron. Having given aid or found it impossible to help in any way, the two sloops will return independently to this anchorage, arriving here in any case before nightfall. Have I made myself sufficiently clear?' All nodded or replied briefly and he went on, 'Very well, then, I shall make sail in fifteen minutes' time and the *Merlin* will make sail five minutes after that. Good luck!'

The sloops were soon under sail, and were cheered by spectators as they left the anchorage. Delancey gave the order to clear for action and hoped devoutly that their intervention would prove useful. Sloops ordinarily formed no part of a battle fleet and, while frigates were often present, they seldom took any part in an action. In the present instance the two sloops might be ignored by the enemy. As against that, either or both might be sunk before they were even identified. The wind was faint and the two craft moved slowly across the bay. What had been a distant rumble of gunfire became more deafening as they approached. Before them, as they diverged, the smoke lay across their bows like a belt of fog, occasionally lit from within by flashes of light. On her more northerly course the *Merlin* was approaching an area where two or three topgallant masts showed faintly above the smoke. From forward came the chanting of the leadsman. The ship was otherwise quiet save for Delancey's orders to the quartermaster at the wheel.

'Steady as she goes,' he said, and then, to Stirling, 'I don't like the look of this. The shore batteries are playing merry hell and the wind has almost died away.'

'Let us hope, sir, that the Spanish artillerymen are new to their work.'

'Likely enough, but Linois will have sent a third of his men ashore to help them. He need only man the one broadside . . .'

To make himself heard, Delancey had now to shout. One or two spent shots passed overhead and one hit the water alongside, ricocheted and sank somewhere astern. The *Merlin* was all too vulnerable on this battlefield. But Dundas had been right. The two sloops had to do something if it was only to rescue a few men from the water. Delancey had often studied paintings of naval battles where a common feature was usually some wreckage in the foreground to which seamen were clinging. But for this device the foreground would be rather blank. Was it, however, as common in fact as in art? There had been such scenes, to be sure, during the siege of Gibraltar in the previous war, but that had not been an ordinary battle.

What about the present affair? He was soon to discover for himself what its foreground would look like. One thing already apparent was the smoke, more of it than any artist could represent without simply spoiling the canvas. Sailors all believed that gunfire tended to produce a flat calm. Whether generally true or not, the faint wind was certainly dying away on this occasion. Moving ever more slowly, the *Merlin* was now entering the acrid smoke of battle. Her bowsprit became indistinct and then her foretopsail, already torn by a stray shot.

Overwhelmingly now came the smell of expended gunpowder. It was sometimes said of a man 'he has never smelt powder.' This could never be said now of anyone on board the *Merlin*, for the smoke was everywhere, making the eyes smart. There came a shout from the forecastle and Delancey snapped 'Hard a-starboard,' hoping that his reaction was the right one. A ghostly ship's boat slid past to larboard but seemed to be empty. Delancey corrected the sloop's course, knowing little by now of his whereabouts save that he was or would soon be in the middle of a battle.

To judge from the tremendous noise there were two ships in action somewhere shoreward of the *Merlin*, each broadside shaking the sloop by mere concussion conveyed through the water. Delancey glimpsed one of them for a minute and saw the muzzle flash from her more distant opponent. He guessed that the British ship might be the *Pompée*.

Five minutes later some wreckage was sighted, a ship's mizen-top with seven men clinging to it. The *Merlin* hove to as Delancey ordered and the men, Frenchmen from the *Formidable*, were rescued. They had gone overboard when the mast fell but could give no information save that the *Formidable* had cut her cable, probably with the idea of running ashore. Firing in that direction was now more distant but the sounds of battle to the northward were intensified.

A boat appeared from nowhere which Delancey recognised as a launch from the dockyard, pulling towards where he had last seen the *Pompée*. She had no sooner vanished than another but smaller boat appeared, evidently damaged and leaking. Her crew were taken on board the *Merlin*, explaining that they had come to help the squadron but had been hit by a stray shot. Delancey held north-westward, the sound of gunfire intensifying, and then the smoke was cleared by a freshening breeze and he could see the *Hannibal* on his larboard bow. The breeze did not hold for long but he could see what had happened.

The *Hannibal* had been heading south, attempting to pass between the French ships and the shore. She had gone too close to the land, however, and had run aground a quarter of a mile from the beach and immediately opposite the Santiago Battery. An attempt was being made to kedge her off but the launch with the anchor was under fire from some gunboats. To judge from the chart, the *Hannibal* must be in three fathoms or less; her attempted manoeuvre having been singularly ill advised.

Holding his course for another ten minutes while the breeze died away again, Delancey dropped anchor at a cable's distance to seaward of the *Hannibal*, keeping her between him and the battery. Then he ordered Stirling to lower a boat.

Coming on board the *Hannibal* with Topley at his heels, Delancey found himself the witness of a scene in hell. Seamen were firing and reloading with top speed but several of the upper deck starboard guns, including Numbers One to Three had been dismounted. Those still in action were undermanned and the blood-stained deck was littered with the killed and wounded. As he hesitated at the entry port, more cannon-balls tore between decks and crashed through the stern. She was being raked by a French ship somewhere on her bows. The ship's hull shuddered under the impact but she was otherwise motionless, a sitting target. Taking a deep breath, he ran aft and gained the quarterdeck, where some of her guns were still in action. A wounded man was sobbing like a child, another was groaning. The only officer to be seen was a lieutenant whose right arm was bandaged.

'Delancey of the sloop *Merlin,* come to see if I can be of service. Are you the captain?'

'No, sir. The captain is below, having a wound dressed.' The man was in obvious pain and was trying hard to keep his voice under control.

'Can I help you lighten the ship? My men could push your guns overboard. She might float then and we could tow you off, stern foremost.'

At that instant the deserted wheel was smashed by a shot which went on to knock splinters out of the mizen, wounding another five men, one of them doubled in agony. The lieutenant winced and tried to focus on Delancey.

'I'll tell the captain of your offer, sir, but I don't think your plan will answer. If we cease fire we shall suffer worse and lack the men to help drag her off. We have lost over fifty killed already. Apart from that, the ship has been holed between wind and water.'

'But the shot holes have been plugged?'

'Oh, yes, sir. But with the water aboard she will be deeper than when we took the ground.'

'And the pumps?'

'Damaged, sir, and only one of 'em working.'

A cannon-ball from the Fort shattered the gangway amidships and another, red hot, lodged in the break of the quarter-deck, where it was dowsed by a marine.

The lieutenant's voice cracked but he remained steady. 'Heated shot, sir; a trick they learnt from us in the last war. They are using explosive shells, too, but so far without effect.'

'If we can't float her, you will have to haul down her colours. Can I help remove your crew?'

'Not without the captain's order, sir.'

'My compliments to him, then, and tell him that I am standing by. I can relieve you a little by giving those gunboats something else to think about.'

'Thank you, sir. The captain will be obliged to you.'

The *Hannibal* was evidently in a bad way, too many of her officers fallen and her men shocked and dazed with bloodshed, noise and fatigue. As he went back to the entry port, calling Topley to follow him, another shot smashed through the ship's side. He glanced in that direction to see what had happened. 'There goes Number Seven Gun,' he said to himself as he scrambled into the boat. 'She can't last much longer.'

Back on board the *Merlin*, Delancey used his telescope to survey the battlefield as a whole. Firing was less intense and a breeze had cleared the smoke away, revealing the full extent of the disaster. A mile to the south was the flagship, *Caesar*, flying the signal to discontinue the action. The *Venerable* and *Audacious* were obeying this signal, the *Pompée*, badly damaged, was being towed out by boats, and the *Spencer*, which had never come to close action, was under sail.

Looking shorewards, he could see that all three French ships were aground in the shallows, all damaged and none in action. The *Hannibal* apart, only the shore batteries were firing. Far to the south was the *Calpé* but heading towards the flagship with several boats in tow. The Spanish gunboats were in two groups, some to the south and others to the north of the Santiago Battery, all firing at the *Hannibal*.

The gunboats were undecked rowing craft, somewhat larger than a ship's boat, each mounting a single cannon in the bows. A group of them, working together, could equal the fire of a warship but they were highly vulnerable and were used only close to the shore. Studying them through his telescope, Delancey made a quick decision and ordered Stirling to make sail. While the sloop gained way he had a hurried talk with Mather.

'We can't save the *Hannibal* but we can drive off the gunboats. If I get the chance I shall try to capture one of them. So I want the launch ready to lower, with crew armed and Mr Northmore to command.'

The *Merlin* swept round the *Hannibal*'s bows and bore down on the near gunboat. For a fatal moment or two these continued to engage the *Hannibal*. Before they could shift to the new target, the *Merlin* had hove to with her port broadside bearing on them. 'Fire!' shouted Delancey and his gunners, inspired by Stirling, produced a rapid and accurate fire, enough to sink one of the gunboats and send the rest pulling out of range with more haste than dignity.

Seeing that group in disarray, Delancey made sail again, circled to seaward of the *Hannibal* and bore down on the other group. 'Heave to!' he shouted, and 'Lower the launch!' The order, being expected, was quickly obeyed and the launch raced after the gunboat which had advanced most daringly. The boat, full of men, might have escaped but a shot from the *Merlin* smashed three of her oars.

Through his telescope, Delancey watched the longboat surge up to her opponent. Northmore was first aboard the enemy, cutlass in hand, and the Spanish were overwhelmed in a matter of minutes. Then the launch was on her way back with the captured gunboat in company.

All this time the guns of the Santiago Battery ignored the *Merlin* and continued to fire steadily at the *Hannibal*. The artillerymen had found the range and bearing of that target and were not to be tempted into engaging any other. Neither the French nor the Spanish had captured a British ship of the line for years. They saw in the *Hannibal* a ship that would have to surrender and they would not cease fire until she did. Their tired gunners were firing slowly but every shot found the target.

A few guns replied from the grounded ship and Delancey could see that Captain Solomon Ferris was on deck again and directing the fire. Delancey did not linger on the scene but made sail as soon as he had recovered his launch. Captain Ferris acknowledged his help with a wave of the hand. The *Merlin* was now headed seawards, lengthening her distance from the *Hannibal*.

'She is striking her colours, sir,' said Mather, and Delancey could see that this was true. Her ensign was rehoisted with union downwards and boats from the French flagship *Formidable* could be seen closing in on her. Half an hour later, while the *Merlin* was on her way back to Gibraltar, with the gunboat in tow, Delancey saw the *Calpé* nearing the *Hannibal* as if to offer help. There was nothing he could do and some gunfire followed as if the *Calpé* were in action. Then all was silent again and the battle was over.

Back in the anchorage at Gibraltar, Delancey went over to the *Calpé* to ask what had happened.

He found Dundas in a smoke-blackened uniform, hatless and bloodstained, struggling to make good the damage aboard his sloop. He was a more convincing leader than Delancey had expected and his exhausted men were doing their best.

'Well,' said Dundas, 'we had done what we could for the other ships, especially the *Pompée*. It was our boats and two from the dockyard which towed her out. We picked up a few Frenchmen from the water. Then, as the smoke cleared, I saw that the *Hannibal* was ashore. I guessed that she would have to strike her colours but thought it might be possible to remove some of her crew first. Her ensign was still flying but, with the wind as it was, I could not see it plainly. I only discovered afterwards that it had been hoisted union downwards.

'By then it was too late. I had sent two of my boats to her assistance. The result was that twenty-two of my men were taken prisoner. I was so furious about it that I fired a broadside or two at their gunboats, which had been beached. The Santiago Battery replied and we sustained damage enough to keep us busy for a week, with seven men wounded into the bargain. How did the *Merlin* fare?'

'We were a little more fortunate, sir. I was on board the *Hannibal* at an earlier hour, before she struck but after she was aground. I drove off the gunboats and captured one of them. We suffered no damage and only two men are slightly wounded.' Delancey felt that his report sounded rather smug. He tried to add the human touch: 'We might have suffered more if the batteries had not been firing at you. We were lucky to escape as lightly as we did.'

'You did well, Delancey. The man I am sorry for is the Admiral, though. We must assume that the French will be claiming a victory and it will be Sir James's task to explain away a defeat.'

'But *was* it a defeat, sir?'

'Well, Sir James had six ships against their three and came off badly damaged, leaving one of his ships in their hands. Men have been court-martialled for less.'

'But look, sir, you were the last in action. What did you see? All three French ships were aground and out of action, masts sprung, topmasts gone. Boats from the shore were taking away the wounded. What you could see, what I had seen a little earlier, was a beaten enemy, unfit to renew the engagement.'

'Very true, but it won't read like that in the dispatch which Linois is writing. France has no excessive number of victorious admirals. Linois, you may depend upon it, is making the most of his opportunity. He has a British ship of the line with the tricolour hoisted above the blue ensign and he wants, above all, to place her out of our reach. She is the proof of his victory. Had I been in Ferris's place I should have set her on fire.'

'With all his wounded on board?'

'No, you're right. He couldn't do that.'

'So Linois has his prize and means to keep her. What will he do next?'

'He will send a message overland to Cadiz, asking the Admiral there to come to his rescue. I should guess that the messenger is already on his way.'

'Then he must have his three ships – no, four, ready for sea by the time the squadron arrives. He will have to work fast.'

'And Sir James will have to work faster!'

'That's true, by God. When Linois sails, Sir James has his last chance to recover the *Hannibal.* I thought of volunteering to burn her tonight but his better plan will be to recapture her.'

'From among all those Spanish three-deckers?'

'It will be his only chance, for all that. The work of repair should have begun by now.'

'It has begun so far as the dockyard is concerned, but the seamen are exhausted, unfit for work until tomorrow. Then they will have to work as never before. It is going to be a race against time.'

CHAPTER TEN

Race against Time

Delancey went aboard the *Merlin* again in thoughtful mood, considering all the problems that were likely to arise. The damaged ships of the line were already being warped into the harbour and he decided, on an impulse, to visit the dockyard and discover, if he could, what the shortages would be.

With him he took young Stock with the idea of teaching the boy something of the shipwright's work. The youngster had so far, he thought, been rather subdued. He had been useful on occasion and he had certainly kept out of trouble – more so, perhaps, than a high-spirited lad should have done – but Delancey rather wondered whether he had given the boy enough encouragement.

'My object in paying this visit is to discover what help I can offer,' he explained. 'A sloop can play only a small part in a general engagement. But we may be able to help in some other way.'

They entered the dockyard gate and picked their way among stacks of timber and coils of rope. 'Where is Mr Evesham?' asked Delancey and was directed to a small wooden hut round which some labourers were collected. Presently the men dispersed and the grey-haired senior shipwright turned to greet his visitors. 'Good to see you again, Captain Delancey. What can I do for you?'

'I want to know about the damage sustained by the *Pompée* and *Caesar*. What state are they in?'

'Well, sir,' replied the shipwright, 'a complete repair of those ships would take six weeks and maybe two months. We are told, however, that Sir James must put to sea in a matter of days; as soon, in effect, as the Spanish squadron arrives from

Cadiz. This is a different undertaking altogether, an all but impossible task. We must patch them up somehow so that they won't actually sink. I don't pretend to like this sort of work, all hurry and bustle, with no time to plan or do things in order, but we are at war – as I have to tell my workmen – and we can't ask the enemy to wait for us.'

'What material are you going to lack? Timber, plank, canvas or what?'

'Compass timber, knee timber, masts and spars.'

'And labour?'

'Not immediately. We'll need every blessed man in the place when it comes to rerigging the ships.'

Delancey reported this conversation to Dundas and asked whether he thought the *Santa Catarina* would be of any value if broken up. 'Too small,' said Dundas promptly. The only source of timber he could think of was a Spanish ship, a merchant vessel taken by the *Speedy*. If she were dismantled, her timber would be very useful indeed.

The trouble was that she was on sale for the benefit of the captors, who were not of course present. Nothing could be done without Lord Cochrane's permission and he, it was now known, was a prisoner at Algeciras. All that could be done immediately was to send the *Calpé*'s carpenter to make a survey of the ship. He returned with a favourable report but no more could be done for the time being. Were Lord Cochrane to be exchanged, as seemed likely, he could agree to a price for the ship and then demolition could follow.

Strictly speaking, Dundas should have reported to the Admiral at this point, explaining that the two sloops were under his orders. He did, in fact, deliver a letter to the Admiral's office ashore, enclosing the order which Delancey had brought from Malta, but he rightly judged that Sir James would be too busy to receive him in person.

Having no particular orders, he set to work on the *Calpé*'s repairs and laid plans for cannibalising the Spanish prize if and when he had the authority to do it. In point of fact, Lord Cochrane was released on parole and arrived next day in Gibraltar. Agreeing at once to sacrifice his prize, and sure that the crew of the *Speedy* would have no objection, he authorised the process by which the old merchantman was pulled to pieces.

Using half his men for this purpose, Dundas began to supply the dockyard with needed material. Tremendous efforts were being made and the greatest ingenuity shown as the men-of-war were prepared for sea.

Since Dundas was thus completely occupied, Delancey presented himself on board the flagship, the *Caesar*, and asked for Lieutenant Donkin, with whom he had some slight acquaintance. That officer was frantically busy and the ship in turmoil, with carpenters everywhere, the decks loud with the sound of the hammer and the screech of the saw. Parties of seamen were removing the mainmast and the ship herself had been given a list to allow of some repairs below the waterline.

'What were your losses in the flagship?' Delancey asked.

'Nine killed, sir, twenty-five wounded and eight missing, probably drowned but just possibly taken prisoner. That makes us forty-two under strength but we were not up to establishment when the action began. Even then we were wanting another dozen, eight seamen and four marines.'

'Have you lost any of your officers?'

'Yes, Mr Graves, the master, was killed. Mr Forster, the boatswain, is ashore in hospital, and Mr Best, master's mate, is among those missing.'

'And what about damage to the ship?'

'The shot holes are already plugged, sir. Where we suffered most was in the masts and rigging. The mainmast is gone, as you'll have noticed, and several of the spars are beyond repair. Sails and cordage are cut to ribbons. What is most inconvenient of all, the boats are all more or less damaged apart from the pinnace and that was sunk. We have borrowed a couple of boats from the dockyard and that is all we have.'

'Damned awkward. I mustn't detain you longer, however. You have work to do.'

Donkin escaped gratefully and Delancey, finding a relatively quiet corner, took down some notes. He then reported to the first lieutenant and asked whether he could call on the Admiral next day.

'You will realise, sir, that Sir James has a great deal to do, both here and ashore.'

'I do realise that but I am under orders to report to him.'

'I'll inform his flag-lieutenant, then. I suggest, sir, that you call early, before he goes ashore to the dockyard.'

'Thank you. I shall not take more than five minutes of his time.'

The first lieutenant hurried off, was stopped at once by the purser with a question for him, and then again by the carpenter. If the flagship were not soon repaired, it would not be for want of effort. Was there not, however, an element of confusion? Delancey sensed a need for better organisation and then remembered the shortage of officers. What a moment, after all, to be without a master or a boatswain! On his way back to the *Merlin* he had a sudden inspiration. He knew now what he had to do. Would he, however, be allowed to do it?

Alone in the wardroom Delancey made some calculations on paper, thought over some problems and ended by making a summary.

When finally admitted to the Admiral's presence he saw before him a handsome middle-aged officer, his face showing signs of strain but his manner deliberate and resolute.

'Yes, Captain Delancey?' the voice was cold. (Couldn't the man realise that a defeated Admiral might be busy?)

'Knowing, Sir James, that you have had some losses, I beg to suggest that you bring your flagship up to establishment. I can supply you with a sailing master, a boatswain, a master's mate, twenty-one seamen and ten marines. For the time you are in port I can furnish you, in addition, with two working parties, each of thirty men under a lieutenant and midshipman, to stand watch and watch. I also beg to offer you two ship's boats, one of which might serve as your barge.'

'Leaving the *Merlin* unmanned?'

'Yes, sir. You have the *Calpé* for any special service, until the *Pasley* rejoins your flag.'

'And who is the sailing master you offer me?'

'I am, sir.'

'You?'

'I am master as well as commander, sir.'

The Admiral stared at Delancey as if unable to grasp his intentions. For a captain to accept a temporary drop in rank was something outside his experience and something for which the regulations did not provide. It was the immediate answer to a problem but dared he accept it? As against that, had he the right to refuse? After looking fixedly at Delancey for a minute or so, he suddenly said:

'Why not? Well, Mr Delancey, I accept your very generous offer and will tell Captain Brenton. . . . Now may I add that I know of no other officer who would come to my aid with as little thought of his rank and dignity. You have my heartfelt thanks!'

Back on board the *Merlin*, Delancey issued his orders and told Mather to pick the best men for the flagship. Then he went to his cabin and sent for Teesdale.

'I have been appointed acting sailing master of the flagship. I want you to remove the gold braid from my old uniform coat and hat. Then pack all I shall need and be ready to come with me. Pass the word for Mr Stirling.' When Stirling reported Delancey went on:

'Take the first party over to the *Caesar* and report to the first lieutenant. Then take the boat ashore and try to find another boat for him, as shabby as it may come but able to carry thirty men. We shall want it for a week. Send Mr Topley to see me.' When Topley reported Delancey continued:

'Mr Langford is going to the flagship, so is Mr Bailey and so am I. Mr Mather and Mr Stirling will be out of the ship alternately, watch and watch, accompanied by Mr Northmore and Mr Stock. That leaves you in virtual command. Your chief task is to ensure the safety of the ship. Your second task is to see that the working parties are fed. Your third task is to make good such damage as we sustained in the recent action, for which purpose you have one week. Pass the word for Mr Corbin . . .' It would be good experience for Topley. More than that, it might be the making of him as a future officer. If he survived this test he would be a man.

In going about the flagship, Delancey's fear was that he would encounter some measure of hostility, especially perhaps from the first lieutenant. There was a possibility after all, that his name might be mentioned in the gazette after that of the captain. He had been careful for that reason, to report in a plain coat as worn by a warrant-officer.

But the actual scene was quite different from anything he had pictured. The flagship represented a nightmare of overwork. So far from being asked who he was, he had become essential in ten minutes, the only unspoken question being why he had been absent on the previous day. As for jealous and sidelong glances in the wardroom, he was scarcely ever there at the same time as anyone else. Officers ate something quickly when they had the time and were gone again in a matter of minutes.

Captain Brenton said a word of welcome when he came aboard but plunged back at once into his task of organisation – eight men to the main hold, six to patch the jib and two more to assist the carpenter's mate....

The panic fear was that the French would quit Algeciras before the British squadron was ready to sail. It was a race against time as everyone knew from the flag-lieutenant to the ship's cat. The wonder was that anyone could sleep during his watch below, such was the noise on deck, but men fell exhausted into their hammocks and proved that they could sleep through anything. What had to be done would ordinarily have taken six weeks at Portsmouth or Chatham. At Gibraltar it was being asked whether they could sail in six days. For the damaged *Pompée* this was clearly impossible. It was a question, for that matter, whether the squadron might not have to sail without the flagship.

The central problem, in Delancey's department, was removing and replacing the mainmast, which had been shot through in five places. Hoisting out the stump was simplified by deciding against attempting to save anything. It was sawn up and removed in sections. Brenton was lucky to have found a new mast ashore but to lower it in by means of an improvised crane was not easy, least of all in a hurry. Then the topmast had to be sent up and the whole mast rerigged, the spars replaced, and the sails bent.

The foremast and mizen-mast had to be fished, the jib-boom replaced, the ropes spliced and the rigging set up. What was astonishing was the way the seamen worked. Saumarez was evidently more popular than he appeared to be at first sight. Apart from that, however, the men had been involved in a defeat – at least by French and Spanish accounts – and were not content to leave it at that. They had actually been beaten off, leaving a British seventy-four in enemy hands, and this result had somehow to be turned into victory.

Major reverses formed no part of recent British naval history and men on the lower deck saw themselves as potential targets for derision or pity, as figures of fun in some future ballad. They worked to prevent this and worked with fury. The task of the officers was to allocate the work and prevent the different parties from impeding each other. There was no need to urge the men on – they were plainly doing all that was possible. Ticking off his list of tasks to be completed, Delancey found himself regularly ahead of the timetable. Even so, the possibility remained that the Admiral's flag would have to be hoisted in another and less damaged ship.

The action at Algeciras took place on Monday, July 6th, and its immediate sequel was a letter, sent overland, from Linois to Admirals Massaredo and Dumanoir at Cadiz, asking them to come and rescue him. Agreeing to this, Massaredo ordered Vice-Admiral Don Juan Joaquim de Moreno to sail for Algeciras on Thursday the 9th with six sail of the line, three frigates and a lugger. By the afternoon of the 9th the Franco-Spanish squadron had reached Cabrita Point, joining forces with Linois. At the same time, the *Superb* (74), *Thames* (frigate) and *Pasley* (lugger) arrived to reinforce Saumarez.

On the Saturday the Admiral paid a visit to the *Caesar*, which was so far from being ready for sea that he reiterated his doubts. His inspection finished, he turned to Delancey and said: 'His Excellency the Governor has been kind enough to invite me to dine with him today, adding that I might bring one of my officers with me. I should like you to be my fellow guest on this occasion. There will be a carriage waiting for us on the quayside in half an hour's time. Perhaps you would like to wear your other uniform?' Delancey accepted with pleasure, standing to attention with the rest while the Admiral entered his barge and was rowed to the *Audacious*. Captain Brenton seized his opportunity and told the men on deck to gather round.

'Listen, lads! The enemy may sail tomorrow or the next day and our Admiral means to go after them. What I fear is that he will leave this ship behind, distributing the crew to the ships that were less damaged in the recent action. He speaks of having to hoist his flag in another ship.' Brenton pointed to the Admiral's barge, 'And you can see which one it will be. Well, lads, what's our answer to that?'

It was Delancey's boatswain, Sam Bailey, who shouted for all to hear 'All hands to work day and night till she's ready!' There was a roar of agreement and a burst of cheering. 'We'll do it, sir!' said Sam. 'All day then,' said the captain, 'and watch and watch at night. Let me see what you can do!' Having heard so much, Delancey made for his cabin for a quick change and a clean shirt, just reaching the quayside by the appointed time. There was the carriage waiting with a small cavalry escort and the Admiral's barge came alongside a minute later.

'Well, Captain Delancey,' said the Admiral as the coach drove off. 'I heard some cheering from the *Caesar* just now. What was it all about?'

'The men have sworn to refit the ship by daylight tomorrow. Captain Brenton told them, Sir James, that the *Caesar* might otherwise be left in port, your flag shifted to another ship.'

'To the *Audacious*, to be exact. I don't know why there is a bitter rivalry between these two ships but there always has been. Brenton's men will have performed wonders by sunset.'

'Perhaps, Sir James, you had no intention of leaving the *Caesar* behind?'

'How could I? The enemy have nine ships to my five. The odds are sufficiently against me as it is. If I sailed with four ships I should be pitting three hundred guns against seven hundred, with far worse odds in terms of men. No, the *Caesar* has to be ready in time and I have not forgotten your help in making that possible. Yours was a timely offer, captain, and one that not every officer would have made.'

'It was made, Sir James, as from one Guernseyman to another.'

'What, are you a Guernseyman? From which parish?'

'Born in St Peter Port, sir. I have a small property on the border of St Sampson and the Vale.'

'And you have spent your life in the Navy?'

'Most of it, sir. I was here during the great siege and was commissioned in 1783.'

'What is extraordinary is that I never heard of you. Perhaps, however, you will have met my old messmate, Laurence Savage?'

'Yes, Sir James. I met him recently in Malta when he was on the point of retirement from the service.'

'He is not to be blamed for quitting the service, his promotions have come so slowly. Let us hope that you are more fortunate and that I may some day have the opportunity of saying a word on your behalf.'

'Thank you, Sir James.'

The carriage rolled up to the front door of the Convent, as Government House at Gibraltar is called, and Delancey, following the Admiral, was once more presented to the Governor. The other guests were Brigadier-General Osborne, Colonel Devereux and the Commissioner of the Dockyard, Mr Hartley. The uniforms were smart and the gold braid glittered but it was not a convivial occasion. There was an atmosphere of tension, perhaps of embarrassment.

'We have only a small company to dinner, Sir James,' explained the Governor. 'I knew that you must be tired. At the same time I wanted you to know that our thoughts will be with you.'

'Thank you, General. I have work enough, as you may suppose and am vexed to think that the French and Spanish are claiming a victory over me. I have no idea how the business may be viewed at home but must rest content in the knowledge that we did our utmost.'

'That you did, Sir James, and your defeat – if it can be called that – was due to bad luck with the wind. The result, we must allow, was unfortunate, but this was due to causes you could not have foreseen.'

The dinner was excellent, the company friendly and the conversation interesting but Delancey grew restive at the sympathy being shown to the Admiral. Sir James, he had come to realise, was rather shy, which made many people think him distant, and somewhat lacking in self-confidence. He was desperately disappointed and tired, all too willing to accept the assurance that he had been unlucky, that all allowed him to have done his best. Over the dessert Colonel Devereux referred, in passing, to 'the recent setback' and Delancey could contain himself no longer.

'Forgive me, Colonel, if I take issue with you over this word "setback" or "defeat". It so chanced that my ship was among the last to quit the battlefield and I take a different view of the matter. We do not claim a victory but our attack did succeed. At the close of the action the enemy were defeated with heavy losses and in no mood to continue the fight.'

'Very well, captain,' said Devereux with a smile. 'I withdraw the word "setback". Will you allow me to call it an indecisive action, one after which both sides claim the victory?'

'No, sir, it *was* decisive, and you will presently see proof of it. Our enemies claim a victory, since three of their ships beat off six of ours, leaving a ship of the line in their hands. They have since been reinforced by six sail of the line, including three of exceptional size. So now they have nine powerful ships opposed by five or six of ours. What should we expect their victorious Admiral to do? He should appear off Gibraltar and challenge our squadron to battle. But will he do that? Or will he use his six new ships to cover the retreat of the other three, bringing his whole force into Cadiz? If he adopts the latter plan – as I think he will – his tactics will be correct for an Admiral defeated on July 6th. What he does will be more significant than what he says. If he has really won a victory he should want to complete it. If he has really been defeated, he will want to avoid another battle.'

'Well said!' exclaimed General O'Hara. 'I think you must confess, Colonel, that there was nothing indecisive about your skirmish with Captain Delancey! Allow me to propose a toast in words which Delancey may be able to accept: I drink to Sir James's completion of the victory he partially achieved on July 6th!' The toast was drunk with applause and Colonel Devereux came up to Delancey afterwards and said, 'I liked the way you stood up for the Admiral.'

The guests had left the table and were chatting to each other while their carriages or horses were being brought round to the door. Reflecting on the recent action, Delancey had come in fact to believe that Saumarez had made two mistakes. He had plunged into battle when he should have paused, reorganised, collected pilots, studied the battlefield and made a plan. He had also convinced himself that he could repeat the tactics which Lord Nelson had used at the Battle of the Nile – tactics which hinged on passing between the enemy and the shore.

The circumstances, however, had not been the same. It was easy, of course, to be wise after the event. We knew now that the squadron at Cadiz was unready to sail. But an Admiral can be criticised for anything he does or neglects. If Saumarez had attacked headlong, without pausing to study the problem, he had erred on the right side and in good company. He was a fine leader, that was certain, and his men were devoted to him.

All the while these thoughts passed through his mind Delancey was paying only partial attention to the Brigadier-General whose theme was the present strength of Gibraltar. 'The Spanish may plan an assault or a siege but we have done a great deal since the last war. It can be held until doomsday.' Delancey agreed rather absently and then became aware that the Admiral was no longer there.

With a word of apology to the Governor he went into the garden and saw that Sir James was looking across the harbour. Even at this distance the ships could be seen to be buzzing with activity, and the noise of work in progress could just be heard. The bushes were loud with insects, the bay was blue under the sun and distant Algeciras was marked by its group of masts. There too it was a time of feverish preparation. What were Shakespeare's words in *Henry V*?

> Fire answers fire, and through their paly flames
> Each battle sees the other's umbered face;
> Steed threatens steed, in high and boastful neighs
> Piercing the night's dull air; and from the tents
> The armourers, accomplishing the knights,
> With busy hammers closing rivets up,
> Give dreadful note of preparation . . . .

Quite without intention Delancey had uttered the last three lines aloud. The Admiral turned with a smile and added:

> The country cocks do crow, the clocks do toll,
> And the third hour of drowsy morning name.

He led the way indoors without further words but presently excused himself, saying that he had work to do. Farewells were said, good wishes expressed and Delancey found himself in the carriage again, going through the streets which led to the harbour. As they parted on the quayside, Sir James said:

' "The day, my friends and all things stay for me . . . ." ' He paused and peered closely at Delancey, who felt uncomfortable under his scrutiny. 'Thank you, Delancey, for what you said at dinner.'

What had been accomplished on board the *Caesar* was barely credible. The masts had been stepped and the ship was largely rigged. There was more still to do than was apparent, especially below decks, but Captain Brenton looked quietly satisfied. When the Admiral came on board towards sunset he saw a ship apparently ready, or almost ready, for sea. There was complete silence as he looked about him. When at last he spoke his words were brief and to the point.

'Captain Brenton, I shall be obliged if you will rehoist my flag when we sail tomorrow.'

There was a tremendous burst of cheering and the boatswain called for three cheers as Sir James left the ship, saying that he would return later. The work began again under frantic pressure, continuing all night without interruption. There was no instance in history of a ship being rerigged with such speed – so much Delancey could guess – but would the men be afterwards fit for battle? This was the question in everyone's mind, but what was the alternative? To leave the ship in harbour and take four ships out to fight the enemy's nine? That would be madness. Somehow or other the ship *must* be made ready for battle.

CHAPTER ELEVEN

Defeat into Victory

The enemy's sails were loosed at daybreak next day, Sunday, July 12th, but there was no actual movement until midday when the Franco-Spanish ships were forming line of battle off Cabrita Point, nor was this movement completed until after one o'clock. These were the hours during which the *Caesar* was receiving her provisions, powder and shot. Delancey played his part in supervising the stowage and it was two o'clock before he came on deck again, finding himself on the stage, as it were, of a theatre.

In brilliant sunshine with an easterly wind, the whole garrison and population of Gibraltar had turned out to watch the squadron sail. The ramparts were crowded from the dockyard to the ragged staff, there were folk on the quayside and right up to the pier-head. The enthusiasm was tremendous and the seamen were more thrilled than they would ever dare admit.

They had reason to be proud of their leaders. If the perfection of leadership is shown in the reaction to adversity, Sir James Saumarez had indeed survived the test, earning universal admiration by his calm and resolute behaviour. Captain Jahleel Brenton had achieved a miracle on board the flagship. Captain Richard Keats was said to be the best seaman of his day, Samuel Hood came of a famous naval family and others were hardly less distinguished. The Admiral's flag was hoisted as the *Caesar* was warped out of the harbour, the ship's band playing 'Cheer up my lads, 'tis to glory we steer!' Not to be outdone, the Governor had ordered a military band to the pier-head. where it responded by playing 'Britons, strike home!' There were deafening cheers as the flagship slid by and Delancey, watching from the quarterdeck, found that there were tears in his eyes. It was a scene that no one present was ever to forget. With the soldiers cheering and the girls waving, one ship after another made sail: the *Caesar*, *Venerable*, *Superb*, *Spencer* and *Audacious*, all of the line, the frigate *Thames* and the sloop *Calpé*.

Line of battle was formed off Europa Point and the moment was come to see what the enemy intended. It was not clear to begin with, whether the allied Admirals Moreno and Linois expected to fight at all. Had Saumarez been as decisively defeated as his opponent claimed, he would have been unable to encounter them again. Nor, in any event, should they have hesitated to fight with odds in their favour of nine to five. As a first step towards gaining their expected victory they should have tacked across the bay making the signal for closer action or general chase.

Far from doing that, they chose a defensive formation and sailed for Cadiz, their original plan revealing a determination, above all, to protect their trophy, the battered *Hannibal*. She was to have led the retreat followed by the three French ships in line abreast, these followed by the six Spanish ships, these again in line abreast. This was a rearguard formation.

But why should Linois, recently victorious (by his own account), have been retreating at all? As the evening wore on the allied squadron withdrew westward, their formation only modified by their Admiral's eventual decision to leave the damaged and jury-masted *Hannibal* behind at Algeciras. For the rest, their sole idea was to reach Cadiz and safety. With a following wind their flight was hampered only by the three French ships, crippled as they were by the damage they had sustained on the 6th.

Their consolation lay in the fact that the British squadron – with one significant exception – had been similarly damaged and might well be as slow. The exception was the *Superb*, which had not been present on the 6th, a relatively new ship built at Northfleet in 1798 and a sister ship to the *Pompée*, captured from the French in 1794. In the chase that was now to be expected, the pursuer and pursued being similarly slowed down by previous damage, the fastest ship was going to be the undamaged *Superb*, of French design, captained by the most brilliant seaman in either fleet. Some of the Spanish ships might have been theoretically as fast but their speed had to be that of their battered allies.

In battle the sailing master's chief responsibility was for navigation and Delancey took a series of bearings to establish the flagship's position on the chart. Forming thus a part of the captain's staff, he realised, first of all, that Saumarez had other Guernseymen aboard. In addition to the first lieutenant, Philip Dumaresq, it now appeared that the signal midshipman was called Brock, that a quartermaster was called Le Tissier, and that the cabin and wardroom stewards included a Le Poidevin and a Le Page. He also realised that the *Caesar*, even with the help of these islanders, was not going to make any very remarkable speed. The miracle had been to refit the ship in five days and he was as proud as anyone of what had been achieved. But the result was inevitably makeshift, an affair of wounded masts, fished yards and spliced cordage. When Captain Brenton wanted to make more sail, Delancey pointed out very respectfully that the additional stress would probably have the masts overboard. The east wind blew strongly through the Straits but the pursuers, as the light failed, were not visibly gaining on their prey. As against that, the *Superb* was gaining on the flagship. Seeing this, Sir James gave an order to Captain Brenton, who took the speaking-trumpet and hailed the *Superb*:

'*Superb*! The Admiral requests Captain Keats to make all sail and engage the enemy ship nearest to the Spanish coast! Shall I repeat that?'

'Orders understood,' came the reply and the *Superb*, with topgallants and stunsails set, came surging past and went ahead. She was soon lost in the gathering darkness, the enemy ships being already invisible, and the *Venerable*, next astern of the flagship, was losing distance and would soon be equally lost to sight. Delancey began to worry about navigational problems, submitting to Captain Brenton that the enemy must be presumed to be making for Cadiz but that there were shallows north of Cape Trafalgar which would make the pursuit difficult. The result was a conference in the Admiral's cabin – Sir James, Captain Brenton, Delancey and Dumaresq, with the chart before them.

With the decks cleared for action, the Admiral's cabin was no more than a space marked off with a strip of canvas, with a barrel as table and another for the Admiral to sit on, the scene badly lit by a couple of battle lanterns. The faces which ringed the chart, half-seen as the lantern swung, were all of them strained and tired.

'Having lost sight of the enemy,' said the Admiral, 'my intention is to reach Cadiz ahead of them and so catch them in the harbour mouth or near vicinity. Can we hope to do that?'

'Why, yes, Sir James,' replied Brenton confidently, 'the enemy must have shortened sail after dark.'

'I submit', said Delancey, 'that you have to weigh the dangers before setting the course. If we steer close to the land we may put the ship aground – the Spanish know this coast better than we do. If we keep well away from the shore the Spanish may well outdistance us. Finally, reaching Cadiz and sighting the enemy, we may find ourselves alone, having lost touch with the squadron.'

'Do you know exactly where we are now?' asked Dumaresq.

'Only by dead reckoning,' Delancey admitted. 'I last established our position by a bearing on Tarifa. It has been too overcast to take any observation since. Doing eight knots, we should be *here*.' He pointed to the pencilled cross he had made on the chart.

'You have allowed for the current?' asked Brenton.

'Yes, sir.'

'What course, then, should we steer for Cadiz?'

'I have marked it, sir. I wouldn't dare take the responsibility for heading any further east.'

'You are a cautious navigator, Delancey!'

'Isn't that my function, sir? As sailing master, I point out the dangers. Were I captain I might scorn them.'

'Too nice a distinction!' Brenton growled.

'Gentlemen!' said the Admiral, 'Delancey has fairly done his duty. It is I who have to decide, with God's help, and it will be my fault if we end on a sandbank with one ship to the enemy's nine. I shall keep further to starboard than Delancey approves and further to port than Captain Brenton will like.'

'One other point,' said Delancey, 'we have a stiff breeze now but we can't depend upon it after leaving the Straits. It could be fitful further north at this time of year and could die away to nothing.'

'It's our pursuit of the enemy that is dying away to nothing!' The remark came out almost as an insult.

'Steady, captain!' said Sir James. 'For all we know, the *Superb* may be in sight of them. I might add that I have more at stake than you have. Delancey told me yesterday that we won a victory on the 6th. He will add, I suspect, that the enemy's behaviour today is the proof of it. At the Admiralty they have a simpler way of reckoning. I fought an action on the 6th and lost the *Hannibal*. I had a long chase today and lost the enemy. It only remains for me to lose my command.'

Brenton came back handsomely after his previous outburst, 'What you will never lose, Sir James, is the respect of your officers and men!'

'Thank you, captain. It may be all I have left. But my trust is in God and the battle is not yet finished. What we need, I suggest, is a glass of brandy. . . . Steward!'

The brandy was appreciated but no further discussion led to any further conclusion. The basic weakness in any plan anyone could propose was that the squadron had dispersed. Contact with the *Venerable* might have been maintained by shortening sail but that would have left the *Superb* unsupported. As things were the ships were at least on the same course and might be within sight of each other at daybreak. To shape a course now for Cadiz might make it impossible to concentrate the squadron again. It was going to be a difficult decision but Delancey, in his own mind, had already decided. If it lay with him (which it did not) he would not alter course until daylight.

At half-past eleven the situation changed abruptly. From somewhere ahead came the sound of gunfire. It was at once clear that the *Superb* had overtaken the enemy and was heavily engaged. Flashes could be seen and the *Caesar* now steered towards them. *Superb* would have shortened sail before opening fire and the distance now quickly diminished between her and the flagship. A blue flare from the *Caesar* was intended to assure Keats that help was at hand but there was an unexpected response from the *Venerable*, only a few miles astern. Things looked more hopeful and every night-glass in the *Caesar* was trained on the *Superb* and her opponents, both sides using flares to illuminate their target.

To Delancey it was immediately apparent that the Spanish ships were still in line abreast, a feat of discipline which did them credit. Third and fourth from the left, obvious from their size, and level with each other were the two huge three-decked ships of 112 guns; the *Real-Carlos* and the *San-Hermenegilde*. Second from the left and ahead of the three-deckers was a French two-decked ship with a Commodore's pennant; probably the *Saint-Antoine*.

The two ships on the right of the line were more distant, which explained why the *Superb* was closing on those more within reach. For her to steer between two 112-gun ships seemed tantamount to suicide but that was evidently Keats' intention. He could count, admittedly, on the Spaniards' lack of experience (especially at night) but the disproportion in weight of metal was terrifying. Sternmost of all the enemy ships was one on the extreme left, possibly the *San-Augustin*, and she might have been the first target, at long range, of the *Superb*'s port broadside.

'A bold attack!' said Brenton to the Admiral.

'But an unequal combat,' replied Sir James. 'If he must attack three-decked ships, why can't he fight them one at a time?'

'I should never fight both batteries if I could help it,' muttered Dumaresq, '– not even with a crew up to strength.'

'You may be doing just that', said Brenton, 'before the night is over.'

Delancey said nothing but was careful to make a note of events, as material for the Master's Log. 'At 11.20 p.m. *Superb* seemed to shorten sail.' As the crash was heard of the *Superb*'s two broadsides, he inserted '11.35 *Superb* seen in action with two Spanish three-decked ships' and so continued with his record for the rest of the action. Under fire from her big opponents on either side, the *Superb* was seen to fire two more broadsides. It was evident, however, that she was drawing ahead of the Spaniards. Her hull was invisible in the smoke of gunfire but her topsails seemed now to be beyond the three-deckers, both very much in action.

'Good God!' exclaimed Delancey. 'Those Spanish ships are firing at each other!' What had happened was obvious. The smoke of the combined broadsides, three from the *Superb*, two from each of the Spanish ships, had filled the space which the British seventy-four had now vacated. Each three-decker was firing into the smoke, from which an unseen enemy was replying with vigour, and each new broadside added to the obscurity which prevented them from recognising each other. Their guns were now firing independently, the noise was continuous and Delancey was awestruck at the mere weight of shot being fired between two three-deckers at a range of less than three hundred yards.

'What an astounding spectacle!' said the Admiral. 'Leave them to it, captain, and pass them to starboard. The day is ours!'

'Aye, aye, sir.'

As the *Caesar* drew level with the Spaniards, Delancey observed that the further one, the *Real-Carlos* was on fire. He noted the fact and the hour, thinking to himself that he had just seen a perfect demonstration of the dangers inherent in the line abreast. He had been told about it as a midshipman and so had everyone else, but it made a difference to have actually seen it. In line ahead you were safe at least from one type of disaster.

Somewhere ahead of the flagship the *Superb* was now in action with the *Saint-Antoine* – or was she the *San Antonio*? – and the *Caesar*, followed by the *Venerable* and *Spencer*, was coming up on the other side of the same opponent. Delancey felt the ship reel under him as the starboard broadside fired, then heard the same noise from the following ships. He discovered afterwards that the wretched *Saint-Antoine* had already struck her colours.

Sail was now made after the other enemy ships but Delancey, looking back, saw that the burning *Real-Carlos* was drifting towards the *San-Hermenegilde*. Noting this, he was able to add, a little later, that they had collided and that both were on fire. They afterwards drifted apart, both of them doomed, the fire starting no doubt on the gun decks, spreading to the tattered rigging and so to the sails, which then fell on the decks again.

'God, what a terrible sight!' said Brenton to Delancey.

'Appalling, sir. It doesn't look as if they can ever bring the fire under control.'

'Not now. You have to stop it before it begins, and even with a well-trained crew you can still fail. Look what happened to the *Queen Charlotte*, and that began with no more than some hay for the livestock! The officers did their best and even managed to flood the lower deck. What they didn't manage to flood was the magazine. . . . The wretched Spaniards will be mostly untrained. They will have unused cartridges beside every gun, lighted matches for each gun captain, no water bucket at hand and no habit of instantly obeying orders. As for their boats, the *Superb* probably smashed the lot with her first treble-shotted broadside. I could wish it were over quickly.'

Looking aft at the two burning ships Delancey echoed the wish. They were among the finest ships afloat, and were probably the biggest and most well designed, built and equipped; but battles are not won by ship-wrights. They are won by disciplined bodies of men, by rules and safety precautions, by habituation to an exact drill, by doing everything quickly but correctly, by remembering what you have been taught and doing what you are told.

In the opposite direction, Delancey saw that the other enemy ships had disappeared into the darkness. They might outnumber their opponents – no, they were merely on equal terms now – but their one idea was to escape. Or was that unfair? They were under orders. Delancey added to his notes: 'Midnight, other enemy ships out of sight.'

In the immediate area there was light enough to see and the Admiral used it to make some signals; first to the *Superb* and *Calpé* to remain with the prize, *Saint-Antoine*: second, to the remainder of the Squadron, to make sail after the flagship. 'We'll aim to intercept them,' said Sir James, 'before they can reach Cadiz.' Delancey knew that the plan could not succeed. Cadiz might be no more than thirty miles away; even with a fitful wind the enemy should be nearing harbour by daybreak. The battle was over.

There was a dazzling flash, as of lightning, and then a deafening crack of thunder. Delancey covered his eyes for an instant, opening them in time to see the *Real-Carlos* blown apart. There was a mushroom effect as spars and ropes were thrown upwards in a cloud of smoke. Her sides bulged outwards, her guns crashing through her ports. A minute later she was gone, save for some debris in the water, and Delancey suspected that any survivors would have been killed by the concussion; a few, he thought, might have escaped earlier, perhaps to the *Saint-Antoine*.

'Poor devils!' exclaimed Philip Dumaresq. He was not looking towards where the *Real-Carlos* had been. He was staring at the *San-Hermenegilde*, and he was evidently feeling sick. Nearly a thousand men had just died but another thousand had yet to go, still fighting the fire and knowing by now exactly what their fate was to be. By the light of the flames he could see that a few men had jumped overboard and were swimming towards the wreckage of the *Real-Carlos*. They had perhaps the best chance of any provided they were good swimmers, but what when their ship blew up? There were no boats near them and how could there be?

Turning once more to his notes, Delancey added: 'At fifteen minutes past midnight the *Real-Carlos* blew up and sank.' He wondered for a moment whether she had flown an Admiral's flag? He thought not. Then he remembered that Spanish flag-officers always moved to a frigate when in presence of the enemy. The idea was that a battle could be more easily controlled by someone not actually involved in it; a reasonable notion except in so far as it meant sacrificing the force of example. Anyway, it was the Spanish custom. Vice-Admiral Moreno would not, therefore, have been on board. He would be half-way to Cadiz by now in the *Sabrina*, if that was the ship's name, and thinking himself lucky to be alive.

Reflecting on the enemy's losses, it struck him that the flagship had sustained no losses at all and had not so far been under fire. There was always something fantastic about war, the odd way in which some people were killed, the strange way in which others escaped. He tried to think of past instances of men knocked down by the wind of a shot, of his own appearance in a duel. . . . Never had he known the minutes pass so slowly. . . .

At last it came. There was another dazzling flash, another tremendous crack of thunder, and the *San-Hermenegilde* was gone in her turn. This time Delancey noticed the effect of the blast on the *Caesar* herself – a thump on the ship's hull, as if she had been hit by a giant hammer. The previous explosion must have had the same effect but he couldn't think why he had hardly noticed it. There was a difference this time, though, in that the flash was followed by darkness. There was no other burning ship to throw light on the scene where another thousand men had died. Now there would be boats from the *Superb* and the *Saint-Antoine* but he doubted whether there was much they could do. As for himself, his only response was to add a laconic note to his rough log: 'At half an hour after midnight the *San-Hermenegilde* blew up and sank.'

By the 13th Sir James Saumarez was on his way back to Gibraltar and to a hero's welcome. That day Delancey dined in the wardroom of the *Caesar* and was interested to compare notes with the other officers. It was the first formal dinner he had attended since joining the flagship. The bulkheads had been replaced, the table recovered from the hold, a clean tablecloth laid, the servants were all smartly dressed and the officers had all slept and washed and shaved.

'Last night', said the second lieutenant, 'was my first real sleep for about a week. I was never so tired in my life!'

'Never mind,' replied the captain of marines. 'You have now been in a naval battle and may be regarded as a hero for ever.'

'But isn't it absurd?' exclaimed Dumaresq, 'I've been in a dozen minor actions, being lucky to have come out alive. They count for nothing, however, beside a general engagement. We have won a victory and our Admiral will be made a Knight of the Bath, an honour he has earned ten times over. There may be other promotions –' (he coloured a little in saying this) 'and we shall be told what fine fellows we are. But what have we done? Our total service has been to fire two broadsides into a wretched ship which did not reply for the good reason that she had already struck. We did not fire or receive another shot, let alone suffer any damage or loss. We have been as safe as if we had been at Spithead!'

'Our achievement was not in fighting,' said the purser, 'but in having the ship ready for battle. We were nearly dead from fatigue before we left harbour.'

'All you say is true,' Delancey admitted, looking at Dumaresq, 'but it applies to the squadron as a whole. All the fighting was done by two ships, the *Superb* and the *Venerable*. The *Superb*'s chief effort was in capturing the *Saint-Antoine*, which took about thirty minutes. By sheer luck she induced those two Spanish three-deckers to destroy each other, an almost unbelievable business which took place before our eyes! And there you have the whole of our victory, the work of one seventy-four. As for the *Venerable*, she was fairly beaten by her opponent. But for our presence she might have been taken.'

'She left the *Formidable* in poor shape, though,' objected the second lieutenant.

'Of course she did, but the fact remains that our victory was gained by one ship.'

'The French will claim the victory for themselves,' complained the captain of marines. 'They'll describe the *Venerable* as wrecked, a fair equivalent for the *Saint-Antoine* and explain that the two Spanish ships were lost following a collision with each other.'

'They can say what they like,' said Delancey. 'The fact

remains that they did not offer to fight us. With a vastly superior force they still made their run to Cadiz. That is why I judge that they were really defeated on the 6th. After this subsequent affair that combined squadron is no longer fit for battle at all. Their morale is gone and each ally will be blaming the other. We can blockade Cadiz now with a couple of ships and I'll wager that they stay at anchor.'

'So perhaps we deserve a hero's welcome after all,' concluded Dumaresq. 'It is certainly what we are going to have!'

The setting of Gibraltar lends itself to drama, with galleries for the public and a place for the orchestra. When Sir James's squadron sailed into harbour on the 14th the ramparts were again lined with cheering spectators and the band on the pierhead was again playing 'Britons, strike home!' – or had it (as Midshipman Brock suggested) been playing that continuously since the day they sailed? Anyway, their return was triumphant and the *Saint-Antoine* was the trophy for display.

There was more than one opinion about that prize, Sir James describing her as a fine ship and likely to be fit for service in less than a fortnight and some others (Delancey among them) were convinced that she was good for nothing. It was a time for celebration, however, and not for argument. On the day after the squadron's return the royal standard was hoisted and the shore batteries fired a victory salute.

That night the fortress was illuminated – all this to annoy the Spaniards – and extra grog issued to all the seamen and marines. Next day the Governor gave a banquet and there were subsequent dinners given by each regiment with a certain rivalry apparent between the commanding officers' wives. As for Delancey, he said good-bye to his messmates on board the *Caesar* and was formally thanked by the Admiral.

'I am more than grateful for your help, Delancey, but you must forgive me if I do not mention you in my dispatch. If I reported that you had served on board as a volunteer you might be promoted but Dumaresq would not. As he more than deserves this recognition, I trust you will understand. I shall also ask for the promotion of the first lieutenants of the *Superb* and *Venerable*, both very worthy officers. You are deserving of promotion to post rank and I have said as much in a letter to Lord Keith.

'I am sending Dumaresq to England in the *Calpé*, bearing my dispatch to the Admiralty. Your promotion is recommended in a separate letter to their Lordships. I wish you to understand that you have a friend in the service and that I shall not forget the way you came to my help: as one Guernseyman helping another. You will have heard, no doubt, that there is talk of peace being made. Should this come about, I shall look forward to meeting you again in St Peter Port.'

Delancey was genuinely grateful for this offer of patronage. He knew by now that the automatic promotion of first lieutenants after a successful engagement was the end to many a naval career. The complimentary promotion meant an improvement in half-pay but carried with it no certainty of employment. Half those promoted after the Battle of Camperdown were still on the beach, or so he had been told, and likely to remain there, being men without interest or protection.

There was no reason to suppose that the first lieutenants of the *Superb* or *Venerable* would fare any better. What were their names, now? Samuel Jackson, he remembered, and James Lillicrap. What influence would there be behind someone called Jackson? What noble family was ever called Lillicrap? Such men were better off as lieutenants, secure of employment for as long as they were useful and not without some chance of making prize-money.

Dumaresq had better prospects, not because of his promotion but because he had the friendship of Sir James Saumarez. His own prospects were now almost on that level. He was not a follower in the sense that young Brock was a follower, someone for whose career the Admiral had assumed responsibility following a promise made to the boy's father, but he had been acknowledged as a neighbour and protégé. Saumarez was certainly going to be in high repute for the rest of the year. Any favour he asked of Lord St Vincent was likely to be granted. The only dark cloud on the horizon was this talk of peace. He could only hope that nothing would come of it.

Delancey returned to the *Merlin* with a sense of homecoming.

She was a fine little ship, well officered, well maintained and ready for anything. She was not a legend, as the *Speedy* had been before her recent capture, nor was her commander a lord: but she was nothing to be ashamed of.

He had met Lord Cochrane ashore and liked him better than he had at first, recognising at the same time that his liking might not be shared by more senior officers. Cochrane had a good opinion of himself, that was undeniable, but he had tremendous vitality and enthusiasm. He was not as conscious of social position as Dundas tended to be, possibly because his own was so assured, and he seemed to have forgotten Delancey's refusal to join with him in the hunt for *L'Espoir*. They had a glass of wine together and parted as friends.

Delancey realised, of course, that he himself would never be given the opportunities which Cochrane had demanded (or usurped) but he was conscious of having done well enough to deserve Lord Keith's favour. He had played his part in the fall of Malta and at the Battle of Algeciras and his name was no longer entirely unknown. Among those who congratulated him was Mrs Hardwick, who told him that Souraya had settled down very well in an English household and was well liked by everyone.

On the day after he resumed command of the *Merlin* Delancey was invited to a ball given by officers of the Royal Artillery. The notice was short and Delancey rather suspected that he was taking the place of some other officer whose plans had been changed. He accepted, however, taking no offence, and enjoyed the party. He was the predestined partner, he found, for a young lady called Marianne Wetherby, whose soldier husband was on duty during the early part of the evening. Marianne was young, vivacious and pretty, so much so that her husband deserted his post before the proper time, reclaimed her with a few curt words of thanks and left Delancey without a partner. His immediate problem – whether to go or stay – was solved for him by the belated arrival of Sir James Saumarez who greeted him in the hall.

'Glad to see you, Delancey. I hoped you would be here. I want you to meet my cousin, Colonel Saumarez, who has recently joined the Governor's staff.' The Colonel had evidently arrived after Sir James, who now made a little speech for his benefit.

'I know that you watched our first battle, Tom. After it had been joined you may have noticed a sloop going into action without any invitation from me. Well, here is the commander of that ship, an officer for whom I foresee a distinguished career.'

'Honoured to meet you,' said the Colonel. 'You played a gallant part, sir, in the recent engagement. Allow me to present you to my wife, Mrs Saumarez, and also to my younger daughter, Miss Julia Saumarez.'

Delancey bowed to the ladies and was received with unusual friendliness.

'I was myself a witness of your noble conduct!' cried Mrs Saumarez, 'and Julia was beside me. I remember how she clasped her hands and said "Well done!" '

'But I am a mercenary warrior and ask a reward,' replied Delancey with another bow. 'I ask Miss Saumarez to be my partner in the next dance.' This offer was accepted willingly with a smile from the mother and a little curtsey from the daughter. Delancey found himself re-entering the ballroom as one of the Admiral's party and one in high favour with the rest.

He had certainly wasted no time in exploiting the situation, which resulted from the Admiral's late arrival and which found the other officers already provided with partners. He made himself useful in fetching chairs and ordering refreshment and presently took the floor with Miss Julia, a lovely fair-haired young girl. She was very shy and he worked hard to interest or amuse her, being finally recompensed by a fleeting smile. She blushed enchantingly and her fair curls fell on the whitest shoulders. Her arms and figure were unbelievably delicate and her manner was at once friendly and restrained. He had never been in company with so pretty a girl and he was quick to ask for the privilege of taking her into supper. She assented shyly and he resigned her, temporarily, to a young Major Paget of the Second Regiment of Foot, who looked all too prosperous and eligible.

While she danced with other men he talked with Mrs Saumarez and expressed his admiration for the Admiral, whose victory must earn him still higher honours. As he talked he looked across the floor at Julia whose back was turned towards him while she listened to what was probably a funny story from a Captain of Engineers. He made at that moment a discovery which was unknown, he thought, to the rest of the world. A pretty girl is still pretty when her face is unseen. She betrays in every movement, in the slightest gesture, that she knows herself to be pretty, clinching the impression by the way she pats her hair into place.

Mrs Saumarez caught his look of admiration and told him how popular Julia had always been. 'She has no great fortune', she added in fairness, 'for ours is a poorer branch of the family, but I don't suppose she will be unmarried for long. We hesitated at first over bringing her to Gibraltar in time of war but all the talk is of peace.' That Delancey should take Julia into supper was warmly accepted by her mother who thus allowed the progress of a friendship. That the girl's parents should seem to encourage his suit seemed to Delancey too good to be true. It was all happening too quickly to be believed but Delancey had already fallen in love.

There was no way in which he could keep Julia to himself but Delancey could at least make it clear that he was not interested in any other girl. So he kept off the dance floor and presently found himself in conversation with a young diplomatist called Tarleton, who took a cynical view of the peace negotiations.

'What worries me', he explained, 'is that the victories of Lord Nelson, Lord Keith and now of Sir James Saumarez should lead to a peace treaty in which Malta may be lost to us.'

'Are you serious, sir?'

'Never more so. Nothing is yet agreed, you will understand, but the terms under discussion imply our returning the island to the Knights of Malta. There have been protests, of course, but my fear is that we shall lose in negotiation what we won in battle.'

'But that is absurd. The Knights are discredited and impoverished. The Order has had no useful function for at least a hundred years.'

'Just so. You know it. I know it. All the world must know it. But our Secretary of State knows something different. And what is our wisdom compared with his?'

'All this in the nineteenth century! This plan is fit for bedlam! It can't be carried out, however, because the Maltese won't accept it.'

'Exactly! And that is one reason for supposing that this peace will be of short duration. At least one of the British undertakings will be impossible to fulfil and this will give the First Consul every excuse to break all the other terms of the treaty.'

Delancey took some comfort from this conversation, although indignant to think that the Maltese should be cheated of what they had fought for and gained. They were surely entitled to British protection and a measure of independence. But an early renewal of war would change the whole situation and give them what they wanted. In the meanwhile, this coming peace would wreck his chances of promotion. It was odd, come to think of it, that Colonel and Mrs Saumarez should look with any favour on an officer of less than post rank.

Delancey was next in conversation again with the Admiral, who told him that the *Merlin* would soon be ordered home. 'It seems to me, however,' he added, 'that Guernsey will not be too far out of your way. As you know, I have a number of Guernseymen among my shipmates. Two of them were disabled at Algeciras but not so badly that they need want employment. When they are invalided I have a mind to send them home and tell them to report to Lady Saumarez. If they take passage in the *Merlin* you will be able to tell Lady Saumarez about the battle. You will also be entrusted with messages, I fancy, from Colonel and Mrs Saumarez to their friends on the island.'

Delancey quickly promised to perform any errand of this

sort. Looking across at Julia, he could not imagine disobeying a command from any of her family. He firmly told himself that he could not possibly marry the Admiral's niece, but the daydream persisted and he knew that it was not merely a matter of self-interest. It was the girl herself who was the attraction in this all but impossible prospect.

Before he could reach Julia, now with two other naval officers, Delancey was intercepted by Mrs Hardwick.

'I told you, did I not,' she said, 'that Souraya has settled down very well and that we are all very fond of her. She was upset, I must tell you, when she saw the *Merlin* going into action. The battle could be seen, you know, from the nursery window. We call her Catherine and she helps look after my two remaining children, Delia and Jimmy, who is called after the dear Admiral, a great favourite with them both. But she is older than you imagined; twelve, perhaps, or even thirteen, and quite forward for her age. She is beginning to know a few words of English and remembers two or three words of Italian. Some day she may be able to tell us where she comes from. I have taught her to say her prayers and I know that she prays for you each night.'

Delancey thanked Mrs Hardwick for her news and told her that he was glad to think that Souraya was so well cared for. Escaping from the lady with some difficulty, he secured Julia as a partner in the next dance and then led her on to the terrace, from which they could look down on the moonlit harbour. She had lost much of her shyness and came out with a sigh of happiness.

'I dreamed that life could be romantic', she confessed, 'and now I find that it is! There is everything here, the white columns, the scented shrubs, the naval uniforms and pretty gowns. And there are the great ships at anchor, overlooked by the frowning bastions from which the bugles sounded the last post.'

'A lovely scene,' Delancey agreed, with eyes only for the girl. 'But what is romance?'

'Romance is beauty, I think, and a background of authority and order, with love and laughter and a hint of danger.'

'Danger? Fear?'

'Yes. There must be the cannon and the sentinels, the gunfire heard across the bay. Will you point out for me the ship in which you fought?' Delancey indicated the flagship, well lit up for a party given by the wardroom officers.

'But how can that be, sir? You are the captain, surely, of another ship?'

'I served in the flagship as a volunteer on that occasion. My own ship is the *Merlin*. You can see her further to the left and close to the mole.'

'The *Merlin*? But I thought you were Captain Dundas?'

'He commands another sloop, the *Calpé*.'

'Dear me! And you are . . .?'

'I am Richard Delancey.'

'Good gracious!' (The name obviously meant nothing to her.) 'How very droll! Shall we go in? Mama will be wondering where we are.'

He escorted her back to Mrs Saumarez, who had heard of her mistake from another source since Colonel Saumarez had later met Captain Dundas himself. There was a sudden change in the atmosphere, not simply the result of mistaken identity. Mrs Saumarez had been talking, he guessed, with Mrs Hardwick and perhaps with Mr Slater. There was a story going round, he realised, and he must feature in it as the purchaser of a slave girl. Had he rescued her, sword in hand, the story might have been told to his advantage, but the mere mention of the slave market must be fatal. If he had ever had a chance of marrying Julia that chance was gone for good.

Having said good-bye and expressed his thanks to host and hostess, Delancey was on the point of leaving when he met Lord Cochrane in the entrance hall.

'Ah, Delancey, this war, it seems, is going to end too soon for either of us. There'll be no promotion now, least of all for an officer on parole, pending exchange.'

'Nor will an officer fare any better who served in the flagship as a volunteer and whose presence in action will not be mentioned in the dispatch.'

'I hope that you were luckier with prize-money. I can't

complain after that last cruise in the *Speedy*.'

'I was not as fortunate as your lordship.'

'But you may have shown greater skill in investment, as for example in Tetuan! Now don't take offence, man, no one thinks the worse of you – saving, perhaps, some old women of both sexes. A pity, however, that the *Santa Catarina* was in ballast. Her hull is not terribly valuable, I should suppose, and her sails and cordage look nearly worn out.'

'I may yet have a stroke of luck, my lord. The *Merlin* is ordered home, the war is not over and I might capture a prize or two at the last moment.'

'I have considered that possibility too. One might intercept a merchantman on the French coast, sailing without convoy in the belief that the war is already over. Or one might discover that war had indeed ended the day before, leaving one to face a costly action for damages.'

'Just so, my lord. For the next month or two we shall be cruising at our own risk. We might be lucky and then again we might be damned unfortunate.'

Back in his cabin aboard the *Merlin*, Delancey handed his cloak and sword to the faithful Teesdale, who asked whether the ball had been a success.

'Yes, there was something to celebrate. A pleasanter occasion than when you and I were running over the rooftops at Tetuan!'

'I often think of that night, sir, and say to myself that we were lucky to get away with it.'

'The story has been told on the lower deck?'

'Well, sir, it couldn't be secret, like.'

'No. So there is talk about Souraya?'

'Yes, sir, but the way the story goes she was a heathen princess, not the poor unwashed child I had the care of. Do you hear, sir, how she has fared?'

'Yes, Teesdale. She is nurserymaid to Mrs Hardwick, is happy and well liked and becoming a Christian.'

'I'm glad to hear that, sir. With respect, sir, may I say that no one thinks the worse of you for saving the girl?'

'Thank you, Teesdale. I still don't know what else I could

have done. Turn in now. I shall be on deck for a while.'

Delancey paced the quarterdeck for ten minutes and then paused, leaning on the gunwale and staring up at the Rock of Gibraltar. There were few lights now to be seen ashore or round the harbour but the night was starlit and he could just see the sentinel pacing the quayside. Two men on harbour watch were talking to each other quietly in the waist of the ship. The water lapped against the ship's side and a dog barked somewhere in the distance. How unlucky he had been over Julia . . . and yet he had been foolish to dream impossible dreams about a girl he had only just met. How could he have been so stupid, knowing that he had nothing to offer? There had been a perfection about her – that was it, and he had never met it before. He was awake now and the dream was over. There were the first signs of daybreak, a faint lightening of the sky, a first breath of wind from the sea. He realised, with wonder, that he would never see Julia again and that, whatever happened later, he would never forget her.

CHAPTER TWELVE

The Basque Roads

With an unusual sense of being on holiday, Delancey went shopping during what would probably be his last week in Gibraltar. Stirling was with him and Topley, each buying for his respective mess, and Teesdale came to carry what was bought for the captain's table. With the battle over and peace in prospect, the narrow streets of Gibraltar were crowded and business was brisk. There were colourful shops and market stalls with bargains in plenty offered by dark-faced old women in black dresses. People chanted or screeched the news of what they had to offer and customers flatly refused to believe that such outrageous prices could be asked for such inferior stuff.

Among the local people of mixed origin the British seamen moved in twos and threes, some the worse for liquor, others gaping at the monkeys and parrots which were offered for sale. It was a question whether an officer's uniform should be seen in the shopping street and Delancey, having bought what he needed, was about to send Teesdale back to the *Merlin* when he suddenly decided, very much on impulse, to send a present to Souraya, a parting gift to show that he was as much her friend as a gossiping world would allow. But what should it be? Cloth for a dress seemed the obvious answer and Delancey plunged into all the difficulties of texture and pattern, length and price.

It was a dark shop he had entered despite the dazzling sun outside and he was fairly surrounded by rolls and rolls of muslin and linen, cotton and silk. The scene was further complicated by the fact that he was not the only customer in the shop, with a babel of sound coming from the far side of a stack of merchandise. As a bachelor, his ideas were unusually vague and he failed to distinguish between stuff for curtains and stuff for clothing. At last, however, he saw what he regarded as the perfect material but buried, unluckily, under a pile of other goods.

Teesdale came to his rescue but with excessive vigour, the result being to overturn the whole display. Bolts of cloth rained on an unseen customer who called out 'Stand from under! The mast's been shot away and we're buried under the mizen staysail! Give us a hand, mate!' Something in the tone of voice was vaguely familiar and Delancey, making a short circuit, was quick to offer his apologies. From among the tumbled goods there emerged, of all people, Sam Carter, his smuggler friend; the man to whom he owed his escape from Spain back in 1796.

'Sam, you old rascal!' he exclaimed, 'what brings you to Gibraltar, and since when did you do business in satin and velvet?'

'Richard! Give me your hand! What a surprise to meet with you again after all these years!'

Sam Carter did not seem to have changed at all, being the same polite and cunning character, a good shipmate but as lawless as ever.

'Sam,' said Richard, 'I want a dress length for a girl – we'll call her a niece – aged twelve or fifteen. Tell me what to buy!' Sam Carter glanced round, chose some sprigged muslin and said, 'Buy five yards of that!' Ten minutes later the bargain had been struck, the stuff measured and paid for, and Teesdale given directions to call at Mrs Hardwick's on his way back to the harbour. Stirling went on to other shops, with Topley for company, and Delancey steered Sam into a tavern where they could talk over a glass of wine.

'Now,' said Delancey, 'tell me the news. Where, to begin with, have you hidden the *Dove*? She is not in the harbour. I hope she isn't lost?'

'No, the *Dove* is at Tangier but almost unmanned. Most of my men were impressed by one of your frigates. I came over here by ferry, having a little business to do.'

'But how will you reach home again, Sam?'

'Oh, I shall find some sort of crew. They'll not be real

seamen, though, not fit to go aloft in a gale of wind.'

'But fit for a passage to Guernsey?'

'It's not as simple as that, Richard. I must make the voyage pay. I shall have to visit the French coast.'

'And what is the cargo to be?'

'Brandy, I reckon. The better brands come from Bordeaux, La Rochelle, Orleans or Nantes but the best of all is cognac, distilled at a town of that name in the Charente. It comes down the river in boats.'

'To be shipped at Rochefort?'

'Yes, for regular shipment. But not all of it reaches Rochefort. Some boats unload at a point higher up and the barrels are shipped at places further south.'

'Behind the Ile d'Oleron in fact?'

'There or thereabouts, at places less public.'

'But why the secrecy, Sam? It doesn't matter to the French where the cognac is sold.'

'Nor it does, at that. But they can't allow a British craft into Rochefort, not in time of war; no, not even the *Dove*.'

'I suppose not. So you are familiar with that part of the coast?'

'I have been there and have friends there. But all those shifting sandbanks make it difficult and I would rather not attempt it with the crew I shall have. But I've no choice, d'ye see? I must have a cargo and cognac is best of any.'

'Could you discover, from hearsay, what men-of-war the French have at Rochefort?'

'Reckon I might. Does it matter now – with the war so nearly finished?'

'I don't know that it does. But your gaining some intelligence would give me the excuse to escort you.'

'Don't put temptation in my way, Richard. You mean it kindly, I know that and I thank you. But it won't do. You can't sail from Gibraltar in company with a known smuggler and I daren't appear on the French coast in company with a British sloop. That way would get us both into trouble and that's for sure. No, Richard, I'll do this on my own, pray for good weather and trust to luck.'

'Tell me, Sam, where do you go here for supper? Where do the masters of merchantmen meet?'

'At the General Elliott – you must have seen it.'

'I know the place. Could you join me there for supper this evening?'

'Gladly, Richard – or how would you word it among your service friends – "With pleasure, sir"?'

A time was arranged and Delancey, going on board the *Merlin*, changed presently into civilian clothes, an old brown coat with buff waistcoat, breeches and beaver hat. When he went ashore again he looked like a respectable tradesman, passably dressed for an evening at the tavern. He felt for the moment as if he had turned his back on more fashionable society and was master again of a revenue cutter or privateer. Sam was well known among the regular customers at the rather shabby inn and introduced Delancey to the others as his friend 'Dick Delancey, of Guernsey'. Then they supped together, faring quite well, and talked of old times.

'Whatever you do, Richard, even though you live to command in battle, you will always be remembered in St Peter Port as the man who captured the *Bonne Citoyenne*!'

'Those were the days, Sam! I made money, too, which is more than I have done recently. Yes, the *Bonne Citoyenne* out of Rochefort, laden with brandy and I forget what else . . . she had a sister ship, come to think of it – the *Libération*, later called the *Bonaparte*. Does she still make the same voyage, Rochefort to Cherbourg and back again in ballast?'

'I reckon so. Are you interested?'

'I should like to know her date of sailing from Rochefort.'

'That shouldn't be too difficult. But remember that she is heavily armed and you can't repeat the tactics you used against the *Bonne Citoyenne*.'

'True enough, Sam. But you forget that I command a King's ship now. I don't have to account to my owners for the damage!'

'And that's the truth! I had forgot for a moment that you had quit privateering. Yes, that makes all the difference between profit and loss. With the King to pay for the damage and three-eighths of the value going to you – yes, that would be worth your trouble! I'll ask around when ashore in France.'

The evening passed pleasantly and Delancey promised to look out for the *Dove* on the French coast. He would sail a day or two later than Sam and tell his men to watch out for the lugger. With a weak crew and on a treacherous coast, she might need help. He and Sam parted that night with great warmth, the smuggler promising to obtain news of the *Bonaparte* and Delancey promising to rescue the *Dove* if the need arose. Sam would signal for assistance if need be, a white flag by day or a blue flare at night. Whether they would actually meet on the French coast seemed doubtful but Sam had explained his plans in detail and Delancey at least knew where to look.

Three or four days later Delancey called at the Admiral's office for his final orders.

'Here they are,' said the flag-lieutenant. 'You go to Plymouth, sir, and I wish I were sailing with you. There was some idea of your visiting Guernsey but Sir James seems to have changed his mind about that.'

All this was said chattily, the flag-lieutenant unaware of the blow this would be to Delancey, who showed no sign of emotion. 'It has been decided instead that you should give passage to some convalescent men from the hospital – fifteen petty officers and seamen and twenty-two soldiers. These are men fit to walk, you'll understand, but not fit for active duty. They will be supernumeraries and the seamen will be due for discharge at Plymouth. There are some separate orders for the soldiers, but where the hell are they? My clerk will know. Maxwell!'

There was a hunt for the missing document and Delancey gazed unseeingly across the harbour. Sir James had not even wanted to see him! A single damaging story about his acquiring a slave girl at Tetuan had circulated among the wives ashore and this had been enough to lose him the Admiral's good opinion. Half the flag-officers in the List would have laughed and thought none the worse of him but Sir James was deeply religious, as he knew. In time, he supposed, the story would be forgotten and his services remembered. Or would they be remembered? The war was practically over and he would presently be ashore and on half-pay, unemployed for years and quite possibly for good.

The wording of his orders began 'You are hereby required and directed . . .' Should the sentence have ended 'to go ashore and stay there'? He pictured himself an old man in St Peter Port, still mumbling about the Battle of Algeciras. . . . He had been gazing absently at the *Merlin* but he now focused and took in the detail – the slim spars, the neat rigging, the fresh paintwork and the ship's reflection in the still waters of the harbour. He had made her a crack ship. She had come to be noticed and known. Now she would be laid up and so would he.

'Ah, here we are, sir,' said the flag-lieutenant, 'here is an order from the Adjutant at the Queen's Barracks. It lists the men, with rank and unit. This is your authority for giving them a passage . . .'

Other formalities followed, with receipts signed and lists initialled, and then he found himself in the street. Pausing to look over the harbour again, he saw the *Dove* under sail, having put in from Tangier the night before. She was too far distant for him to see the men on board but there was something amiss about the way she was handled. He could picture Sam Carter's exasperation with his scratch crew, with men unable even to understand what he wanted. She was actually in irons for a minute, then slowly paid off and headed for the Atlantic.

How hard it was to know where one's duty lay! With the war all but over, his last chance of action centred upon a single passage from Gibraltar to Plymouth. How far dared he diverge from the known track on the chart? He could go to the rescue of a British merchantman in distress – and the *Dove* could be described, at a pinch, as a merchantman. He could capture any French ships he encountered but might not go far out of his way in search of them. But how far was too far? As he watched, the *Dove* was fading into the distance and was now no more than a speck on the ocean. In the last resort, rather than take a King's ship into needless danger, he might have to take the most difficult decision of all and leave Sam to his fate.

Back on board the *Merlin*, Delancey gave orders for receiving the convalescent men, ordering young Mr Stock to take charge of them. With the ship to sail next day, as ordered, there was work for everyone. He nevertheless took the opportunity to invite his officers to dinner that day, midshipmen and all, being able to provide a better meal for them while the ship was in port.

Looking round the table, Delancey realised how fortunate he had been. There was Mather, so competent and dependable, the ideal first lieutenant who knew the capabilities (and limitations) of every man on board. There was Stirling, almost as competent but with some special gifts of his own, one being that extra ferocity on occasion, that actual love of battle.

Langford, the master's mate, was almost ready for promotion to commissioned rank. He had done very well, showing great resolution and disregard of danger, though he had only a moderate intelligence. He contrasted in appearance and character with Northmore, who was tall and fair while Langford was short and dark. Where Northmore could fail was in the routine work, the day-to-day drill in which Langford excelled. Where Langford was deficient was in initiative.

Left on his own in a difficult situation, Northmore, by contrast, came into his own. He had done well on board the *San-Felipe*, prize, in a situation which would have been beyond many another youngster. He was a promising young officer with a possibly distinguished career ahead of him. In his leisure hours Northmore was trying to play the flute but the mournful sounds he produced were unpopular with the others and especially with Langford.

As for Topley, he had come on well under Mather's tuition. He was still a little wild and still uncertain of his navigation but he had some budding gift for leadership. Topley was the humorist and could be quite amusing, as when he imitated Stirling's Scottish accent and persisted in his belief that Stirling had fought as a Jacobite at the Battle of Culloden.

David Stock, a mere child at first, was immersed in seamanship, in studying the sails and tying knots, but was responding to his new responsibilities as officer in charge of supernumerary seamen. Stock was sometimes invited to play chess with Mather, by whom he was always defeated, and would sometimes console himself by playing against Helliwell, the gunner, who could never win. They were all good friends and no one of them was useless or idle. As for their work, there was no smarter ship in harbour, of that he was certain.

After the loyal toast, Delancey proposed a toast to the *Merlin*, thinking that the commission was nearly over and that she might soon be laid up in ordinary. He could see that the others felt about her as he did and quickly added a word of consolation:

'We are not yet on the beach, gentlemen, and who knows what adventure we may have between here and Plymouth? There is time yet to make a name or make a fortune.'

'Allow me to suggest, sir,' said Mather, 'that you have made a name already? This is a sloop which fought in the Battle of Algeciras!'

'Not the only sloop, as we have to admit –' added Stirling.

'But who', asked Topley, 'will remember a sloop with a silly name like *Calpé*?'

It was a pleasant occasion but with work to follow for the ship had to be made ready for sea. As the activity and bustle died away at sunset Delancey looked fixedly at the evening sky. Tattered clouds had been swept away and there was a pale orange light which picked out the *Merlin*'s spars and rigging. Studying the sky, Delancey remarked to Stirling that the west wind was likely to stiffen before morning. As he fell asleep the *Merlin* was rocking gently at her mooring. They were plainly going to have a rough passage.

It was blowing a stiff breeze when the *Merlin* put to sea and the sloop shuddered under the impact of the waves.

'Away aloft!' shouted Mather and the seamen raced up the shrouds. 'Lay out!' was the next order and the topmen spread out along the swaying yards. 'Man the topsail sheets!' was the prelude to 'Let fall – sheet home!' The lower canvas filled and the ship heeled over, the spray flying over the forecastle as the stem crashed through the waves. The water foamed and bubbled alongside as the ship gathered speed. 'Man the topsail halliards – haul taut!' was followed by 'Hoist topsails!' Mather was about to call 'Man topgallant sheets and halliards' but looked first towards Delancey, who answered his unspoken query by shaking his head. The sloop was carrying canvas enough and there was dirt to windward. It would be blowing half a gale by midday. Gibraltar slowly fell astern and was soon blotted out by a rain cloud. The *Merlin* was alone on a waste of tumbling water.

Delancey went below to consult *Le Petit Neptune Français* or French Coasting Pilot. He had a difficult decision to make. With this wind his proper course, on a passage to Plymouth, would be well to the westward, but that would minimise his chance of intercepting any French merchantman. Then there was the *Dove*, a possible source of intelligence and certain to be near the French coast. Sam Carter had mentioned a place called Marennes as his port of shipment and Delancey began a more careful study of the chart. He found, first of all, a passage called the Pertuis Maumusson, which leads into the strait behind the Ile d'Oleron. Soundings within this passage ran to ten or fifteen feet at low water, which would be just enough, presumably, for the *Dove*. The passage was split by the Barat shoal and there were further sandbanks, behind which was the village of Marennes. Turning to the sailing directions, Delancey read as follows:

> To go to Seudre, or to pass through Maumusson it is necessary to have the country pilot; for these channels are not very steady and particularly that of Maumusson. They change very often, and are besides very winding and narrow, with a multitude of banks and rocks, which cannot well be described.

There was little comfort in that description but it was clear from the chart that Marennes could be reached by an alternative route, the Pertuis d'Antioche. This was complex too but better sheltered, the drawback being that it led into the French fleet anchorage off the Ile d'Aix. Studying the chart, Delancey did not like what he saw. For him to go anywhere near Marennes would bring the *Merlin* all too near Matelier shoal. The wind, admittedly, might die away over the next few days. But would it? Autumn seemed to be early this year with a hint of cold even now in September. He must not risk his ship among the sandbanks, least of all on a lee shore, whether for Sam or anyone else.

In fact the breeze almost died away off Finistere, then freshened a little as the *Merlin* crossed the Bay of Biscay. There was only a moderate south-westerly breeze when he first glimpsed the French coast. Keeping well clear of the Matelier shoal, the *Merlin* came in before the wind, aiming in daylight at a point just north of the Point de la Coubre. In late afternoon he was off Point d'Alvert and hoping to catch sight of the *Dove*. There was no sign of her and he concluded that she was either still at Marennes or had loaded her cargo there and gone.

On the whole, he suspected that Sam was still there, hampered by his inexperienced crew. He decided to remain off Point d'Alvert during the night, hoping that news of his presence would reach Marennes and that the *Dove* would appear in the morning. Next day, soon after daybreak, a small fishing boat came out from the Pertuis Maumusson and headed straight for the *Merlin*. When first sighted the boat was being rowed but she hoisted a sail when clear of the channel, dropping it again as she came alongside. There were four men aboard, evidently local fishermen, and the eldest of them brought a letter addressed to Captain Delancey, Royal Navy. It read as follows:

> I am here with the *Dove* at Marennes and five of my crew have deserted, gone ashore. I don't have men enough or goods enough to make the Pertuis Maumusson, which is impossible anyway in a westerly wind. For the Pertuis d'Antioche at night I should need a local pilot and there is none dare offer. It is dangerous here because news of the *Dove* may reach the French Navy. Could you lend me some hands to bring the *Dove* out? Sorry to give trouble. Sam

Delancey's response was to bring two of the fishermen

aboard and give them some brandy. The elder, who owned the boat, was the skipper; the other spoke a French which was easier to understand. They were far from successful, between them, in describing the *Dove*'s predicament. It seemed to Delancey that Sam Carter, who could persuade these fishermen to deliver his message, might as easily have persuaded them to man the *Dove* for her passage through the Pertuis Maumusson. The difficulty was in making the fishermen understand his question. So far as he could make out, they were afraid of someone called Delmotte of Brouage, but it never emerged who he was, whether a local official or a rival fisherman.

The conversation ground to a standstill and Delancey had to make up his mind. Providing his guests with some more brandy, he went on deck to check the wind direction. As he had rather expected, the wind was veering westwards and freshening. This decided him finally against giving Sam the help he wanted. It would have been a question anyway, whether he should risk half a dozen men in as dubious a cause, but the wind clinched the matter. The *Dove* could neither stay where she was (apparently) nor come out by the Pertuis Maumusson.

So it was the Pertuis d'Antioche or nothing and for this Sam needed a pilot, whom Delancey could not supply. His instinct was to join Sam, using the fishing boat, and tell him to hold a pilot at pistol-point. But that was against all regulations and would leave the *Merlin* without her proper commander. He was no more entitled to risk a lieutenant in this service. Dare he, in fact, send anyone? He considered and rejected Langford and Northmore. David Stock was hardly more than a child.

What about Topley? He was growing up but was a little too frivolous, a little too inclined to see the funny side of things. Would such a mission as this make a man of him? Or would it break him? Delancey made a final decision and shouted 'Pass the word for Mr Topley.' When the youngster arrived, Delancey told him the situation and showed him the route by which the *Dove* must escape. Then he turned from the chart and gave his orders:

'These fishermen will take you to a lugger called the *Dove*, at anchor off Marennes. Her master has valuable information for us about the French fleet. He cannot come out by the Pertuis Maumusson, not with the wind in this quarter. He cannot attempt the Pertuis d'Antioche without a pilot. He has asked me for a party of seamen to help bring his lugger out. I have to refuse that request. All I can spare him is one man – you.

This is a dangerous mission, Mr Topley, and you will be risking your life. This is what we all have to do while we are in the King's service. Your task is to help bring the *Dove* out and assure Mr Carter that I shall meet him outside the Pertuis d'Antioche and do what I can to baffle the persuit. You will go well armed, with at least two loaded pistols. You will be as ruthless as necessary and you will assist Mr Carter as far as St Peter Port, Guernsey, where this ship will call to pick you up. Is all that clear? Very well then. You will leave in five minutes' time, taking this bottle of brandy with you to inspire your boat's crew. I wish you luck!'

Turning away, Delancey shouted 'Pass the word for Mr Mather!' and told that officer that he was losing the services of Mr Topley and would have Mr Stock as replacement. They watched as the fishing boat headed back for the land. 'A boy today,' said Delancey, 'and a man tomorrow – or possibly dead. . . . What do you think of the weather?'

'There will be half a gale by morning, sir.'

The wind was rising and the *Merlin* had begun to pitch. Dark clouds were gathering to the westward and, in the other direction, a fishing boat was racing into the Pertuis Maumusson under a scrap of canvas. It began to rain as Delancey went to breakfast and he thought that Mather had understated the case. In his own opinion it was going to blow a gale.

During the rest of that day the *Merlin* was heading, close-hauled, into the Atlantic. With each hour she encountered a stronger wind and a heavier sea. Under shortened canvas, the ship pitched and rolled. Topgallant masts and stunsail booms had been sent down, staysails furled and topsails reefed. Below decks everything had been lashed into place with double breechings on the guns and every chest or table secured to a ring-bolt. Merely to move about the ship was an effort in itself, and there were a few minor mishaps resulting in cuts and bruises.

Dinner was served with difficulty and without the pea-soup there should have been. Delancey decided to wear ship before dark, while the men could still see what they were doing. With careful timing the ship was brought on her new course. There was an awful moment when it looked as if she might be caught by a wave on the beam but she paid off in time and now had the wind on the starboard quarter. Canvas was still further reduced before nightfall and then the watch below turned in. For those on deck there were moments when a crescent moon could be glimpsed between tattered, racing clouds. Every part of the ship was creaking and groaning with the strain of her pitching and rolling. The noise of the wind through the rigging was a constant moan rising to a shriek when a harder gust than usual tried, as it seemed, to tear the ship apart.

On deck, Delancey looked back on mounting rollers in sinister pursuit and thought of the constant care that had been spent on the rigging, none of it too slack or too taut. The ship and her crew were being tested now and it was in such weather as this that a past mistake or instance of neglect could turn into present disaster. All was so far well but he knew that the worst was still to come.

And what would happen to the *Dove*? She would be driving now through the Pertuis d'Antioche, with sandbanks on either side and somewhere ahead a French squadron riding at anchor in the Aix Roads. Sam Carter would have this advantage that the anchor watch on each man-of-war would have something else to think about. But the channel was narrow and all must depend on somebody knowing each twist and turn. How was Topley shaping up to the situation? Sam would have thought the boy a poor reinforcement but his presence would give his skipper another officer, another man on whose loyalty he could count. It might make all the difference and Delancey believed that it probably would.

At first light the French coast was a dark line ahead of

them, seen through clouds of spray. Studying the land, Delancey could see that his navigation had not been at fault. The *Merlin* had Les Sables d'Olonne on her starboard bow. He took Stirling into his day-cabin to study the chart. They had both to hold on to the table as they talked.

'If all has gone well, we should sight the *Dove* within the next hour. We shall soon afterwards sight a frigate coming through the Pertuis Breton.'

'May I ask, sir, why you think that?'

'Well, Mr Stirling, the enemy must do something. If the *Dove* went through the Basque Roads during the small hours, there might have been gunfire, there should at least have been a report. So the French Admiral will order a pursuit.'

'But in what direction? How is he to know?'

'He won't know. That is why he will send out two frigates, one through the Pertuis d'Antioche with orders to patrol as far as the Gironde estuary; the other through the Pertuis Breton with orders to patrol as far as the Ile d'Yeu.'

The ship lurched heavily and both officers clung to the table. A book which Delancey had been reading slid across the deck and rapped against the ship's side. The lantern swung violently and there came sound, from the steward's pantry, of broken crockery. It was now blowing a full gale and men were already exhausted by the mere effort of holding on.

'Do you think the *Dove* will be taken, sir?'

'It will depend upon whether she was damaged during the night. If she is not crippled, Sam Carter will take her into shoal water where a frigate cannot follow.'

Delancey's prediction was, as Stirling thought, uncannily accurate. As it grew light Les Sables d'Olonne were on the *Merlin*'s starboard beam. The look-outs then reported, almost at the same time, a sail to the south, which would be the French frigate, and a tiny scrap of sail to the north, evidently the *Dove*. Delancey's telescope swept a waste of stormy water under a leaden sky. The gale was blowing now from the south-west. There were these two patches of canvas and no other sail to be seen.

'We are faster, I think, than the *Dove*,' Delancey concluded, 'and the frigate is a little faster than we are . . . '

'God, sir, look at that!' Mather, who had relieved Stirling, pointed aft.

A mountainous wave, bigger than any they had yet seen, was overtaking them. It was a green-grey mass of water flecked with foam, intricately seamed and furrowed, lightened at its crest by the sunrise, darkened below by the shadow of the preceding wave. It came on quite slowly and Delancey found himself estimating their chance of survival. Had it been breaking, they would all have been dead in a matter of minutes. But the mountain ridge was sharp-edged, hardly beginning to curl inwards. It came nearer – and nearer – and then, sickeningly, the stern of the *Merlin* began to sink like a stone.

Down, down it went and Delancey, clinging to the mizen shrouds, had the feeling that his body was weightless, his feet merely touching the deck, no longer resting upon it. Would the fall never end? Looking aft, the moving mountain was now, seemingly, twice the height. It blotted out the sky, filled the world with its threatening immensity. Would the *Merlin* slide stern-foremost into the giant wave, never recovering from its present fall? But, no, the fall had been checked. It seemed, for an instant, as if the ship were at the bottom of a well.

Then, with frightful speed and force, the ship's stern was tossed upwards. It felt now as if a giant were trying to push Delancey through the quarterdeck planking. The weight on his feet was increasing and as he looked forward, he could see the forecastle far below him, poised as if about to disappear beneath the surface. The stern was nearly at the summit and he had a glimpse of the sunrise.

There was a sudden crash as the tip of the wave came over the stern and washed down the ship like a waterfall. He was nearly torn from the mizen shrouds by the weight of the water and, gripping convulsively, saw with wonder that the helmsmen were still at their post. The crest of the great wave was now ahead of the ship, a retreating mountain on its way to make its final collision with the rocky coast.

Now the ship's stern was sinking again, almost as sickeningly as before, but the next wave, as Delancey could see, was no such monster as the one that had passed. He had a feeling that the worst of the storm was over and that the gale would lessen in the course of the morning. Soaked to the skin and desperately tired, he wondered to find that he was still alive.

On deck again after a change of clothes and an attempt at breakfast, Delancey found that the situation had somewhat changed. The day was brighter, the wind lessening, but that damned frigate had gained perhaps a mile. The *Dove*, by contrast, was losing ground. He could see no damage to her rigging but she might, of course, be leaking as the result of having gone aground.

'Where are we, Mr Mather?'

'Opposite Noirmoutier, sir. The Ile d'Yeu is on our starboard quarter, Belle Ile somewhere ahead of us.'

'And what course is the lugger steering?'

'She is heading eastward of Belle Ile, sir.'

'It seems to me that she is doing more than that.'

'Sir?'

'As she is heading, she will pass east of Les Cardinaux and so into Quiberon Bay.'

'But then she'll be trapped. I should guess, sir, that she is damaged and that her master means to put her ashore before she sinks.'

'Sam Carter? Not he. I think it's time, however, that we gave that frigate a choice. We'll head west of Belle Ile and see which prey she chooses to follow.'

'Aye, aye, sir. She'll follow us, surely, as more worth capturing.'

'I wonder.'

Over the next three hours the chase continued, the pursuing frigate closing the distance but clearly following the lugger rather than the sloop.

'I can't make it out, sir,' said Mather. 'The lugger is passing east of Hedic and Houat. She will be trapped in the Bay.'

Delancey closed his telescope and turned to Mather with a smile.

'So the frigate pursues the smaller prey – the craft that cannot escape!'

'Is Mr Carter doing this in order to save us, sir?'

'Not exactly, Mr Mather. North of Houat there is a passage through the reef which the *Dove* can pass and a frigate can't. So Mr Carter has led the frigate on, letting her gain on him. I'll lay ten guineas that the *Dove* is undamaged but has been towing an old sail astern. Now he will slip through the channel – one he knows about and I know about – and will leave the frigate trapped in Quiberon Bay, far to leeward of the *Dove* and further to leeward of the *Merlin*.

'By the time the frigate has tacked out of the bay, which will take hours, and rounded Les Cardinaux, there will be no other damned vessel in sight. We and the lugger will both be over the horizon and out of the picture. So the French captain will give it up and head for Rochefort. "Citoyen Admiral," he will report, "two British frigates tried to reconnoitre the Basque Roads but I chased them off!" This will gain him the ribbon of the Legion of Honour and he is welcome to it. We shall be safely at anchor off St Peter Port.'

'Guernsey, sir? I supposed that we were bound for Plymouth.'

'But, surely, Mr Mather, we have no alternative? I must recover the young officer I lent to a British merchantman in distress.'

Later that day Mather repeated this conversation to Stirling, adding with some hesitation that the captain had almost winked at him. 'I couldn't swear to it, mind you, but his eyelid did seem to close for an instant.'

'A bit of spray, I expect,' said Stirling, 'But I do wonder, sometimes, what he is up to, especially when he looks most innocent. He has made himself this chance to visit Guernsey – his own home, after all.'

'We were lucky to shake off that damned frigate. I feared at one time we should be brought to action.'

'But he never gave it a thought. Do you realise, sir, that we manoeuvred for hours in the presence of the enemy and never so much as cleared for action?'

'And that's true enough. But the captain would have played some other trick even if the lugger had not been there. No French frigate could catch this sloop in a hundred years!'

CHAPTER THIRTEEN

The Last Chance

Winds were light and variable during the latter part of the night and it was broad daylight when the *Merlin* came slowly into the anchorage off St Peter Port. There was the harbour in the foreground, with red-roofed houses huddled beside it and straggling up the hillside. There was a faint haze of smoke from the chimneys and the cry of the gulls as they circled round the fishing craft. Among the houses facing the harbour was the one where Richard Delancey had been born. Although strangers lived there now, he still had the sense of homecoming.

With conditions so ideal for the purpose, he could not resist the temptation to show off a little, performing a trick which is just possible for the well-trained crew of a crack ship in what was almost a dead calm. As the sloop drifted into the anchorage her guns saluted Castle Cornet, the boom of each gun echoing off the cliffs. For a space of perhaps three to four minutes the *Merlin* was hidden in a cloud of smoke. When the smoke finally cleared, she was seen to be at anchor, her sails neatly furled, with a boat alongside in the water, looking for all the world as if she had been there for a week.

There were appreciative comments along the waterfront and exclamations from women on their way to market. The trick had been worth watching and one or two seamen ventured a guess as to who the sloop's commander must be. The man who had no need to guess was old Captain Savage, who had last seen the *Merlin* in Grand Harbour, Valletta. He was on the jetty when the gig pulled into the steps and called for three cheers from the longshoremen and idlers who were assembled there. 'And three more cheers for Sir James and the victors of Algeciras!'

Delancey stepped ashore while the boat's crew tossed their oars and was greeted by Savage at the top of the steps. 'Welcome home!' cried the old man, and Delancey, with Northmore and Stock at heel, stepped ashore amidst raised hats and shouts of welcome. He had not counted on making any such triumphant entry – he had planned, indeed, to be there at daylight – but it came, as he had to admit, as a pleasant surprise. Moving up High Street, he was greeted all the way, pausing here and there to shake hands with old privateersmen and schoolfellows.

After calling on the Governor, who was not at home, he went on to call at the Saumarez town house. Lady Saumarez received him and welcomed him home to Guernsey. In return, he gave her his own account of her husband's victory, adding his assurance that Sir James was unhurt and in good health. If he had no specific message it was because his visit to Guernsey had not been planned. So kind was his reception that he asked for a word in private, leaving his aides-de-camp to talk with the other members of the household. He then told Lady Saumarez about the slave market at Tetuan.

'She was a mere child,' he explained, 'and I couldn't leave her to be sold into a life of suffering and shame.'

'But of course you couldn't!' exclaimed Lady Saumarez. 'Your action does you credit.'

Then Delancey explained that what he did was easy to misunderstand. 'The stories told in Gibraltar were greatly to my disadvantage,' he went on, 'and the Admiral himself thought the worse of me.'

He hoped that Lady Saumarez would some day let the Admiral know the truth. She readily agreed to do him justice and guessed that her husband would himself have had second thoughts about it. She made it clear that Delancey would always be welcome at her home. He left with the feeling that this was true and that his career might prosper accordingly.

He met Captain Savage by previous arrangement and they dined together at the Golden Lion. During dinner the landlord brought them news that the *Dove* was entering harbour. A message was sent down to the harbour with the result that

Sam Carter and young Topley came to join them in a glass of wine.

'Well, Sam,' said Delancey, 'we managed to give that frigate the slip!'

'So we did, Richard, but I owe my escape to Mr Topley here!'

'Tell me what happened.'

'Well, things looked bad. Five of my men deserted and there was none I could depend on save my mate and boatswain. Then these two Frenchmen came aboard, a man called Delmotte and another called Guichard and they had four of their men behind them. Their idea was that I should sell them the *Dove* for a quarter of her value, otherwise they would betray me to the police. Yes, things looked bad. I didn't know what to do.

'But then there was a lamp alongside and the sound of voices and into the cabin comes your Mr Topley. The mere sight of his uniform put new heart into me. He didn't say much but I told him in a few words what was happening. It is odd, come to think of it, that Delmotte allowed me to explain: I suppose he thought Mr Topley a mere boy.

'Anyway, Mr Topley asked just one question, "Which of these two men is the better local pilot?" I replied, "Guichard," and pointed to him, knowing that he lived there, although Delmotte was the leader in this affair. A moment later Mr Topley drew his pistols, shot Delmotte through the heart and pointed the other at Guichard. "Disarm him" was all he said.'

'What did their men do?'

'Nothing. With Delmotte dead, there was no fight left in them. We let them go, tied Guichard to the mizen-mast, cut the cable and hoisted sail.'

'It must have been a difficult passage.'

'You can call it that. But Mr Topley here told Guichard that he would have a bullet through his head the moment our keel touched bottom. He was a good pilot after that, attentive and careful.'

'So Delmotte thought Mr Topley a mere boy, did he? He

was wrong, Sam. Mr Topley is a man!'

'He is that, Richard; and thank you for the loan!'

All this time Topley was the picture of confusion, looking more like a child, but Delancey put him at his ease by saying 'Well done!' and sending him off with a message to the first lieutenant. Then he turned to Captain Savage: 'You see, sir, I had a difficult choice. Here was this smuggling craft held to ransom. Had she been a real merchantman under the British flag I might have sent her an officer and a party of seamen. But she was a smuggler and in a French port. Should I leave her to her fate? I couldn't do that either. So I decided to send her one man. But which man to send? I seem to have chosen the right one!'

'You did that – and Sam here was in luck.'

'That's true,' said Sam, 'but in years to come I shall wake up screaming in the belief that I am in the Pertuis d'Antioche in pitch darkness on an ebb tide. And now, Richard, I want to show you how grateful I am. I made some inquiries about that ship, the *Bonaparte*. I reckon she'll be off Cape La Hague in three days' time.'

'And the war not over?'

'There's no word of peace yet, although news is expected almost any day now.'

'So there's still a chance?'

'Yes, but I'll have another talk first with Citoyen Guichard, who is still aboard the *Dove*. Dine with me tomorrow, Richard – you, too, Captain Savage – by which time I may know more than I do now.'

Delancey and Savage accepted the invitation with pleasure and they went on together to buy some supplies for the inevitable parties which would mark the end of the commission: wine, rum and tobacco included. Then Delancey returned to the *Merlin* and heard the story from Topley of how the *Dove* made her escape. Topley was thanked and congratulated on a tricky piece of navigation. Thanks to him the French had been cheated of their prey.

That evening Delancey had Mather and Northmore to supper with him at the Golden Lion. Over their wine Mather expressed his sorrow that the *Merlin*'s commission was coming to an end.

'It takes so long to bring a crew up to our present state. Take that little display as we entered port this morning – we could never have done that a year ago and few other ships could do it at all. Week by week, month by month, we have promoted the good men, trained the unskilled, cured the idle of idleness and found simpler work for the stupid. We have worked at it, sir, and the result is the crew we have. We were lucky, though, in one way. We had no men who were actually disloyal.'

'That wasn't luck,' said Delancey, 'I got rid of those at the outset.'

'How did you do that, sir?'

'I sent them ashore under the command of young Topley – this was in the early stages of his career, before he had gained confidence – so they all deserted and poor Topley was mastheaded for neglect of duty.'

'I remember that, sir,' said Northmore, 'I wondered at the time why you should have sent Topley instead of me.'

'But you see what I mean,' Mather persisted, 'we have, at long last, an effective man-of-war and now she is to be paid off. It seems almost a waste of effort!'

'It is not a waste of effort,' Delancey replied, 'and that for two reasons. In the first place we have also trained ourselves. What we have done before we can do again but next time more quickly. In the second place this commission is not yet at an end. We may encounter and capture a French corvette between here and Plymouth. That is certainly not inevitable and may not even be likely, but bear the possibility in mind. The war is not ended yet.'

'Aye, aye, sir.'

The party ended pleasantly and Delancey sent Mather and Northmore on board again so as to relieve Stirling and Topley whose turn it would be to come ashore. These last two would meet Delancey on the quayside at eleven.

With a feeling of temporary freedom from other responsibilities, Delancey strolled around the town and looked in at another inn, one he knew to be a haunt of smugglers and privateersmen. Delancey was recognised at once by several of the inn's regular patrons, acquaintances he had made during the privateering period of his life. He was asked at once to join them. 'It's good to see you, captain,' said one of them, 'and the way you brought your ship into port was worth watching!' There was a chorus of agreement on this score and Delancey joined the party around the fireplace.

All present wanted to know about Sir James at Algeciras and some of them could name the other Guernseymen who had been serving in the flagship. Delancey told them the story, feeling at the same time that he was gaining stature by his association with the local hero. Then he led the conversation round to privateering and was told that business had declined of late. There had been too many British men-of-war in the Channel and too few French merchantmen. Delancey asked whether the talk of peace might not lure the French from their harbours.

'We've thought of that,' said Will Duquemin, 'but what if peace is made and we in Guernsey not the first to hear about it? We should be in court and accused of piracy, murder and heaven knows what.'

'Or accused at best of wrongful detention,' added Luke Tostevin. 'No Letter of Marque holds good after the war is ended. Any mistake the like of that could ruin captains and owners alike. Several of our regular privateers are laid up already and those at sea have mostly been sent letters of recall.'

'Things were better in the first few years of the war,' maintained Will, 'and people here still talk of the way you captured the *Bonne Citoyenne*. No cleverer capture was ever made, and no private man-of-war out of Guernsey has ever taken as big a prize with as small a loss. We used to talk in those days about Delancey of the *Nemesis*. No, sir, you have not been forgotten.'

'What has happened to that other ship which used to frequent Cherbourg? Do you hear of her these days?'

'Ah!' said Tostevin. 'You mean the *Libération*, sister ship to the *Bonne Citoyenne*, trading out of Rochefort. They have changed her name and she is now called the *Bonaparte*.'

'And has no one tried to capture her?'

'No.' Duquemin shook his head slowly. 'When you captured the *Bonne Citoyenne*, the other ship was given six more guns and another twenty men. She is too strong for us now even if she wasn't before. We have talked it over time and again – haven't we, Luke? – but we have agreed in the end to let her alone. She would outgun any privateer we have. She might be taken by any two of our ships but the result would be to wreck all three of them. As you know, captain, that sort of action is never worth while.'

Conversation became general and Delancey was glad to hear the local gossip. Then another group of men arrived and he was made to repeat the epic story of Algeciras for the newcomers' benefit. There was a chorus of approval for Sir James Saumarez, of whom Lord Nelson was regarded, in St Peter Port, as a poor imitation. Sir James was the man to beat the dagoes or the frogs. 'Did you ever hear about Sir James in the *Crescent*?'

The tales were told again, having lost nothing in the telling. A toast was drunk to the Hero of Algeciras and another to Captain Richard Delancey. The time had come, it was now generally agreed, for Paul Rouget to sing his song. In the midst of this performance, the verses being innumerable, Delancey quietly left the room and found himself in the deserted street. The town church clock struck eleven as he reached the quayside where Mr Stirling and young Topley were waiting.

As they were rowed out to the *Merlin*, Delancey asked Stirling what he thought of St Peter Port, which was looking very picturesque in the moonlight.

'A fine anchorage, sir, and pretty well sheltered, and there are some useful shipbuilding yards, all well covered by the guns of the castle. There are some good shops in the High Street and one, a little further to the north, has a sign painted with your name, sir. It is rather faded, though, as if it referred to some earlier corn chandler, not to the man who lives there now. There are plenty of wine merchants and I would guess that they sell wine more cheaply than the merchants of Southampton.'

'And what is your opinion, Mr Topley?'

'I suspect that there are two sides to St Peter Port. There are the town houses of the island gentry, all very elegant and neatly painted, placed in some respectable streets and close to some useful shops and counting houses. But down below, nearer to the harbour, there are dark lanes, narrow stairs, mysterious cellars and crooked entries. I can see that lower part as a scene for secret meetings, conspiracies and plots.'

'You have used your eyes, young man,' said Delancey with approval, thinking to himself that Topley was nearer the truth than he would ever know. 'But a black cellar is sometimes merely filled with coal.' He looked back at the dark waterfront with its few lighted windows still reflected in the water. Of the darkened windows, one (he could just identify it) had been his bedroom. How remote his boyhood now seemed! But he had slept there once or twice even when already a midshipman, of much the same age as Topley. What Topley had said about St Peter Port was perfectly true, as Delancey was in a good position to know.

But the two aspects of St Peter Port were less distinct than a chance visitor might suppose. Some stately houses in High Street had cellars which opened into alleyways off the quayside. There were fine ladies in the parlour and rats down below. Further south he could just make out the gable of the warehouse which the Prince of Bouillon had used as his headquarters. He could remember the time when the Prince had his spies in France, when the French aristocrats thronged the High Street, when Republican agents were plotting the invasion of Ireland. He had been a junior lieutenant in those days and had come to know of some of the plots and counterplots.

The British secret service was now based in Jersey – so much he knew – but there would still be French agents in St Peter Port and as active, maybe, as they had been in 1794. He hoped that no rumours could reach them of what he intended, with the result that an escort for the *Bonaparte* would be sent out from Cherbourg. But Sam, he knew, was not the man to divulge secrets, and there was little time left in which the French could take action.

Next day Delancey met Savage and Sam Carter at the Golden Lion and they dined together very pleasantly.

'I have made some inquiries', said Sam, 'and am fairly certain that the *Bonaparte* should be off Cape La Hague within the next few days. It would seem just possible that the French might delay her passage until after peace has been made. That would, in fact, be the sensible thing to do. But they may believe that the war is already over; and, for all we know, they could be right at that!'

'It is now October 9th,' said Delancey, 'I shall sail this evening and be in a position to intercept the *Bonaparte* tomorrow. I shall have to ensure somehow, that I am not seen from the French coast, which would give the game away.'

'For my part,' said Sam, 'I shall try to send you a message if we have news here of the war being ended. Where will you be?'

'This side of Alderney.'

'I'll sail that way when we have the news. When you catch sight of the *Dove* with ensign reversed, union down, you will know that the signal means "Cease Fire". '

'Thank you, Sam, for all your help, and I'll hope to God I don't glimpse that signal through the smoke when my wretched opponent is about to sink!'

'But look, Richard,' said Captain Savage, 'how are you going to capture this ship without great damage to either side? I think you told me that she actually mounts more guns than you do?'

'She is said to have twenty-four guns. The ideal plan would be to capture her by boarding.'

'What, in daylight?'

'It has to be in daylight. All my information leads me to expect her off Cape La Hague at daylight in two or three days' time. The voyage is timed to ensure this, so that she passes Jersey in the dark, for safety, and then has daylight for entry into Cherbourg.'

'So you mean to disguise the *Merlin* as a French merchantman?'

'There isn't time for that, sir. The most I could do would be to pass, at a distance, as a British privateer.'

'Would that serve any purpose?'

'It would encourage the French captain to fight rather than to try to escape.'

'But I know, Richard, what gives you the idea,' said Sam with a laugh. 'You captured the *Bonne Citoyenne* by disguising your privateer as a man-of-war. Now you want to capture her sister ship by disguising your man-of-war as a privateer. This is your artistic approach to life – your idea of – what do I mean?'

'Symmetry,' said Captain Savage. 'We know your weakness, Delancey! You want to make your battle a work of art.'

'There's something in that,' Delancey admitted, 'But I also need to make some money. I may be on half-pay for the next ten years and this may be my last chance to win an estate.'

'That reminds me,' said Savage, 'I want to see Anneville Manor the other day. You told me in Malta – do you remember? – that you were trying to rebuild that ruin, which once belonged to your mother's family. So I decided to visit the place on your behalf. I found your builder on the site.'

'Old Mr Renouf.'

'Yes, old Mr Renouf. He told me a long story about how difficult it is to find good workmen these days. There is so much building on the island, much of it by newcomers to the place, that folk are wondering where the real Guernseymen are to live. He asked me whether I had seen Hauteville lately. Anway I had a look at the building, which is not yet habitable. Mr Renouf wants to demolish the old chapel but I told him you would never agree to that. "It's not everybody's idea of a home," he said finally, "but the coach-house is good and so is the water supply." Completion of the work will take years, Delancey, and will cost hundreds of pounds. Your best plan would be to sell the old ruin and buy a modern cottage in St Sampson's. Come and stay with me while you are furnishing it.'

'How kind of you, sir, to make the offer! You will understand, however, that I have to decline. My plan is to live at Anneville in any part of the building that has a roof and so be able to stand over Renouf, see what he does and urge him on!'

'What it is to be a romantic!' cried Savage. 'I never before met anyone who went into action with half his mind on a gothic ruin. When you sight the enemy you will say "This should help pay the builder!" When you fire your first broadside you will think "This should earn me another cart-load of granite!" When you give the order to board the enemy ship you will somehow have to restrain yourself from shouting "On to victory, and on to pay for the carpentry!" When the Frenchman lowers his colours you will exclaim "That takes care of the drainage!" As for your men, I can imagine one of them whispering, as he dies, "Never mind – I have helped at least with the plasterwork and paint!" '

Delancey laughed with the others over this but with a horrid doubt in his mind as to whether there might not be some truth in the caricature. He also had to realise he would have only a share of the prize-money and would face ruin if he unwittingly captured a French ship after the peace treaty had been signed.

The *Merlin* sailed after dark that evening and without attracting attention, watched only by Captain Savage and by Sam Carter. There was a freshening breeze from the westward and the sloop gathered way as she went up the Russel. Lights ashore in Guernsey slid by and disappeared astern. Alone in his cabin, Delancey sketched out his plan of attack, listing the duties and allocating the role which each of his officers would play. He considered again the idea of disguise and thought of what was and was not practicable. Something might be done but he would be wrong, he concluded, to make too much of it.

It would be easy to fly the privateer's jack, the union with a broad red border, but what was the point? Of more use would be a foreign ensign, just enough to introduce an element of doubt. His object with the *Bonne Citoyenne* had been to frighten her into a small harbour. His object this time was the exact reverse, to give the French ship confidence and lure her into a very unequal battle. He made a diagram to illustrate his plan of attack and found himself absent-mindedly adding a little picture of the action as he saw it develop. Yes, he thought, old Savage had been right. He was a romantic, perhaps even a frustrated artist.

He tore up his pen-and-ink drawing and threw the fragments through the stern window. The time had come to be severely practical, a man of action and not a dreamer. He knew what had to be done. Could he now ensure that all would go as he had planned it? Going on deck he saw the ship clear of the Casquets and then hove to at a point west of Alderney. As she idled there, at slack water, Delancey sent for his officers, master's mate and midshipmen, down to and including young David Stock. To them he issued his orders for the expected action:

'I intend to intercept and capture a laden French merchantman bound from Rochefort to Cherbourg and likely to appear in these waters during the next few days. She is called the *Bonaparte* and mounts about twenty-four guns. She is well manned and will not easily surrender. She might, however, take refuge in the nearest French harbour if threatened by a more powerful opponent. I shall try to confuse her at first, giving this ship the appearance of a privateer.

'My aim is then to capture her with the least damage to either side. This means a capture by boarding. For this purpose we have, as it happens, some extra soldiers and seamen; not all fit for a desperate conflict but all useful in making a show of strength. Before the engagement I propose to lower our boats and tow them alongside on the side away from the enemy; that is, if the weather should be suitable. I shall then engage with the other, probably the starboard, broadside.

'Mr Langford, I shall place you in command of the three carronades on that side of the quarterdeck and your task will be to concentrate their fire on the enemy's wheel. Aim each weapon yourself and shoot only at the one target. The main battery will be under the command of Mr Mather and will fire into the enemy's gunports without injuring his masts and rigging. Mr Topley will be stationed on the forecastle, ready to make a threat of boarding. You will fire grapeshot from the starboard carronade as if to clear the way, and I shall place under your command the supernumeraries. You will not actually board the enemy ship, but will brandish cutlasses and cheer.

'With the enemy thus distracted, Mr Stirling and Mr Northmore will lead half the seamen and all the marines into our boats and so board the enemy on the further or disengaged side, passing just under our opponents' stern. It will be the special task of Mr Northmore to lower the enemy's colours, entering by a stern window should one be unguarded. Mr Stock will act as my aide-de-camp. We shall rehearse the operation tomorrow and again on the following day, should the *Bonaparte*'s tardy arrival give us the opportunity.

'My general purpose is to give the enemy confidence at first, suggesting to them that their opponent is merely a privateer, and then overwhelm them by a direct threat and an indirect assault. I cannot do much to disguise this ship but I might hoist the sort of ensign which a privateer might choose; Prussian, perhaps, or that of the Papal States. It is now your chance, gentlemen, to ask questions. It is important from the outset that every man should know exactly what he is to do.'

A number of questions were asked and several suggestions were accepted, but the point was soon reached when Delancey could say: 'Very well then, gentlemen. We all know the plan. It remains to detail off the various parties and then explain the plan to each.'

When the others had left the cabin Mather remained behind, very much at attention.

'With respect, sir, I have a protest to make.'

'Well?'

'Mr Stirling is to lead the main attack while I merely hold the enemy's attention. What credit there is will go to the junior officer.'

'Yes.'

'The war is nearly over, sir, and this may be my last chance of promotion.'

'Is that all the protest you have to make?'

'Yes, sir.'

'Very well then. I want you to sit down, at ease, and forget for a moment that you are under my orders. We are brother officers and – I hope – old friends and shipmates. You see me writing a gazette letter in which Stirling is mentioned as leading the boarding party. But no such letter will be published. We are merely capturing a merchantman. She happens to mount as many guns as we do but that will make no difference. She is not a man-of-war. There will be no credit, therefore, and no promotion for anybody.'

'I'm sorry, sir. I was misled, I think, by the care with which you planned the attack.'

'If it were merely a question of capturing the *Bonaparte*, no plan would be needed. My problem has been to make this capture without any notable damage to either ship.'

'I quite understand that, sir. Any damage must reduce the value of the prize.'

'But you *don't* understand, Mather. What if the war has ended and we none the wiser? I may have to hand this ship back to the French. I don't want to return them a leaking, dismasted and bloodstained wreck.'

'No – I suppose not.'

'And I don't want to bring *this* ship into Plymouth with her topmasts gone, her pumps working and twenty men wounded. I should be asked "What have you been doing?" My answer would be "I've been fighting a French merchantman". Do you think I should be promoted for *that*? Or you either?'

'No – I see what you mean.'

'But do you? The war is ending – may have ended. Do you think their Lordships of the Admiralty want to promote *anyone* at this moment? Or even confirm an acting rank? Not they. The peace, for all they know, may last for twenty years, at the end of which time we may be thought too old for active employment. By promoting us now they would increase our half-pay for a lifetime and gain nothing by it.'

'I see . . .'

'There's another thing you don't see. Suppose the *Bonaparte* turned out to be a national frigate and suppose we captured her, we should both be promoted because that is the rule. Suppose there is war within five years you would lack interest to gain a command. But as lieutenant you would be employed and might have a chance to distinguish yourself.'

'Yes, that is true. Forgive me, however, if I am still wondering why Stirling is to lead the boarding party.'

'I'll tell you why. I have tried to give each man the role in which I think he will do best. For keeping you on the *Merlin*'s gundeck I have three reasons. First, you are the best first lieutenant I am ever likely to have and I don't want to throw your life away. Second, I want you at hand to take my place if I should be killed or wounded. Third, for the actual boarding, I think that Stirling is the better man, with fewer brains but more natural ferocity. He is not, I think, your equal in directing, as opposed to leading, an attack.

'That does not mean, however, that you are fitted now to command a man-of-war. You will some day deserve promotion but you are not as yet fit for it. The proof of that lies in all that I have just told you. Had you been fit for promotion you would have known all that already.

'The one thing you must realise is that we have all worked together, trained together, fought together and come to know something of each other's qualities. It is possible that we are all going to be tested again in action. You will see then whether I have chosen the right man for each task. If I am proved wrong, take careful note of my failure. Remember that, some other time, it may be for you to make the choice.'

Then the exercises began in earnest. Delancey had difficulty at first with the invalid soldiers and convalescent seamen. They found it hard to grasp the idea of a feint attack. To board a French ship seemed reasonable to them but to go through the motions without actually doing it was something outside their experience.

The soldiers and seamen under Topley's command had been provided with muskets and bayonets – weapons the real boarding party were better without – and Delancey had finally to compromise by allowing them to fire volleys as if to clear the enemy decks before launching their attack. They were to begin the action hidden in the forecastle and they practised a spectacular movement in which the soldiers swept up to the bulwarks and the seamen came after them in a second wave, led by Topley, and carrying a makeshift gangplank. The signal would be made by Delancey and the feint attack would be further dramatised by a bugle call and by beat of drum. Stirling's men were armed only with cutlass and pistol, leaving them free to scramble on board the Frenchman through the gunports.

Langford's gunners were told what they had to do and why. 'To shoot away the enemy's wheel is to cripple her for the time being but without serious damage to the prize.' Mather's gunners were told what the signal would be to open fire – the firing of the quarterdeck carronades – and also the signal to cease fire; the sound of the boatswain's pipe, sounding 'Belay'. When all arrangements had been made and checked the *Merlin* settled down to patrol the approaches to Cherbourg.

After various false alarms the expected French merchantman was sighted on the sunny morning of the 13th, the wind southerly and the sea moderate. The *Merlin*, with a Prussian ensign, stood slowly across her bows with boats already lowered on the side further from the enemy. So far from avoiding battle the *Bonaparte* shortened sail before heading for the French coast, thus presenting her broadside to the privateer.

The two ships converged under easy sail, the *Merlin* slightly the faster and ready to accept the leeward position. When the sloop's bowsprit was overlapping the French ship's stern, Delancey told a boy to haul down the Prussian ensign and hoist the British. He then drew his sword and ordered Langford to be ready to open fire. Beside him on the quarterdeck he had the boatswain, young Stock and two boys to act as messengers. The minutes passed slowly and Delancey found himself watching a rather similar group near the Frenchman's wheel. Seen in the sunlight, with the blue sea as background, the *Bonaparte* looked a fine ship, and sat deep in the water with what was evidently a full cargo. All her guns were run out on what would be her engaged side, thirteen in all and of much the same calibre as those of her opponent.

At last the moment had come . . . Delancey pointed his sword towards Langford and shouted 'Fire!' The bang of the carronade was almost instantly followed by the crash of the broadside and the enemy's reply. The battle was fairly joined and the smoke billowed between the two antagonists, blowing back across the *Merlin*'s deck. Walking over to the lee side of the quarterdeck, Delancey could see that the boarders were scrambling into the boats alongside, directed by Stirling from the entry port.

There came the crash of the second broadside and another smoke cloud. Langford was aiming each carronade in turn but had not yet hit his target. The sloop was still overhauling her opponent, however, and the two quarterdecks were not yet opposite each other. Round shot were flying overhead and one of them had already splintered the spanker boom. Making less noise were the musket-balls, fired from the French ship's gangway and thudding into the woodwork.

Then came a crash and confused noise forward and Delancey could see that the *Merlin*'s foretopsail had come down. He jumped at once to the wheel and told the quartermaster to put the helm hard over. The *Merlin*'s bow swung towards the French ship, her bowsprit being entangled with her opponent's mainmast shrouds. This was not a manoeuvre which Delancey had planned but there was no alternative. The *Merlin* would otherwise have dropped astern and, with both ships still very much under way, the boats could not have attacked. The impact of the collision and the fall of the *Merlin*'s foretopsail, had now brought both ships to a virtual standstill. The bow cannon on either side were now engaging at very close range, those further aft being more distant from each other. As guns began to fire independently the din and smoke became more continuous.

Leaning over the lee bulwarks near the break of the quarterdeck and using his speaking-trumpet, Delancey shouted down to the boats 'Carry on, Mr Stirling!' Only when he had seen them push off did he turn back and call 'Away boarders!' in the direction of the forecastle. There came a bugle call in reply and the measured beat of the drum. A minute passed and then the soldiers poured out of the forecastle and lined up as if to attack. They had no means, in fact, of reaching the enemy but their menacing appearance was very much as planned and rehearsed. Under the orders of a corporal they presented muskets and fired a volley.

There was a pause while they reloaded and then the bugle sounded again, to be followed once more by the drum beat. A wave of seamen, also armed with muskets, came up on the soldiers' right and presented their muskets.

As their volley crashed in turn, Delancey sent the boatswain to take some sail trimmers and shift the foretopsail from where it buried the forecastle carronades. Once that had been pulled away it might have been just possible for the seamen to board the enemy ship by means of the bowsprit and covered by the soldiers' fire. To underline this threat he ran forward, waving his sword as if to urge on the boarding party.

Looking across at the *Bonaparte* he could see, between clouds of drifting smoke, that the French crew had been assembled to repel boarders. All the men not at the guns were grouped forward, with boarding pikes and cutlasses. Delancey longed to look astern and see whether his boats were disappearing, as they should be, round the French ship's stern. He knew, however, that he must not so much as glance in that direction. He must have every Frenchman watching for the rush across the bowsprit.

To make doubly sure of that he joined the party on the forecastle, shouting through his speaking-trumpet, now towards the boatswain and now towards Mr Topley. 'Come on, men!' he yelled, pointing his sword towards the enemy ship.

He was answered by another bugle call, by beat of drum and a further volley from the soldiers. Then he called for three cheers, which were given with enthusiasm. It would take a very level-headed Frenchman to realise that all this noise was unaccompanied by a single move in his direction.

While the smoke billowed from the cannon fire Delancey

ran aft again and saw that his boats were safely out of sight. Swearing when he realised that he had lost the boatswain, Delancey sent young Stock to request Mr Mather to cease fire and one of his boy messengers to ask Mr Bailey to pipe 'Belay'. Then he looked across to see whether the tricolour was still flying. To his annoyance it still was.

But Langford's fire had cleared the enemy's quarterdeck. Without smashing the wheel, which seemed to be intact, his fire had driven away both officers and helmsmen. 'Shall I shift to another target, sir?' asked Langford. 'No, cease fire altogether,' replied Delancey.

As he watched he saw Stirling and his men pour from the *Bonaparte*'s main hatch and sweep forward to where the Frenchmen were still facing the threat posed by Topley and his men. Taken thus unexpectedly from behind, the enemy had no chance at all. There was some feeble resistance but most of them dropped their arms and called for quarter. The men who manned the battery that had been in action had surrendered more easily still, being caught unarmed.

The action was virtually over but Delancey was able to watch another scene, all the more clearly visible now the smoke had all but dispersed. From the hatch on the French ship's quarterdeck there emerged young Northmore, cutlass in hand. He walked straight to the ensign halliards and pulled down the tricolour from the mizen peak. He rolled it up carefully and walked back to the hatch. A minute later he had gone below, leaving the quarterdeck again deserted. Watching this scene with a smile, Delancey wondered for a moment what had happened to the French captain. Perhaps he had gone below and had been secured in his cabin.

Going forward, Delancey shouted across the gap between the two ships to Stirling to free the *Merlin*'s bowsprit, cutting away the Frenchman's rigging as necessary. Then he told Langford to pass a line over to the prize, attach a rope and then haul the two ships alongside each other. As this was done he told young Topley to go and find the captain of the French ship and bring him on board the *Merlin*. 'Should he retain his sword, sir?' asked the midshipman, to which Delancey replied

'He won't have one. Be off with you.'

Then Delancey went down to the main deck to learn from Mather what the casualties had been. 'Four seamen slightly wounded,' was the answer. 'The French fire was mostly ineffective.' 'And damage?' 'Nothing much, sir.' Delancey paid a quick visit to the sick-bay and was told that there were five wounded altogether, all from wood splinters. He had a word with the bandaged men and told them that the French had surrendered.

He then went to see whether the carpenter was examining the bowsprit. He was. He knew already that the well had been sounded and that the ship was not leaking. He came to the conclusion that his tactics had succeeded and that casualties and damage on board the *Merlin* were negligible. The foreyard was gone – broken in three places (hence the failure of the slings) and so was the spritsail yard, but there was nothing else beyond repair.

The *Bonaparte*, he realised, would not have escaped so lightly but she was not dismasted and could make harbour without difficulty. It remained to detail the prize crew and set a course for Plymouth. In the circumstances he did not expect to be questioned too closely about the capture he had made. The two ships were now lashed together, the French crew battened down under guard and sentries placed over the *Bonaparte*'s spirit room, arms racks and officers' quarters. The officers of the *Merlin* had done or were doing all that had to be done and Delancey, as captain, had little else, seemingly, to worry about.

Mr Midshipman Topley could now be seen on his way back from the prize, crossing by the improvised gangway and heading for the quarterdeck.

'Well,' said Delancey, 'where is the French captain? Was he killed or wounded?'

'No, sir,' replied the youngster, white-faced. 'He is in his ship's powder magazine. His gunner is with him. So far as I can understand their language, sir, I think they mean to blow us all up in ten minutes.'

CHAPTER FOURTEEN

Touch and Go

For an instant Delancey's vision was blurred. He was shaken as one might be shaken by an earthquake. In a moment of easy triumph he was suddenly faced with defeat and death. With an effort he pulled himself together.

'I see. Did you see them?'

'No, sir. They are *inside* the magazine. The doorway is covered by a blanket with a slit in it through which to pass out the cartridges – very much the same as we have. The magazine is lighted like ours, too, from the light-room next to it. I could hear what they said but could not see them or see to aim.'

'Where are the other French officers?'

'In the great cabin, sir, under guard.'

'Right. We'll go there first and you'll lead me to the magazine afterwards.'

It was an occasion for thinking fast. Delancey's first instinct was to discover, if he could, whether the French captain would do as he threatened. When he entered the *Bonaparte*'s great cabin, with Topley still at his heels, he asked for the first mate. Of the four men present, one stepped forward and introduced himself as Michel Varignon, second captain.

'Are you ready to die for the First Consul?' asked Delancey.

'For him, for the flag, for the glory of France.'

'Good. You will die in about five minutes. Your captain means to blow up the powder magazine.'

'Incredible! He must be mad!'

'But is he mad enought to do it?'

Varignon looked at the other officers, met their eyes and shrugged.

'Yes, he could do it. Captain Charbonnier is a patriot, you

understand, a fanatic and – perhaps – in some ways – mad.'

'In that case I can only say – good-bye.'

Approaching the magazine, Delancey sent Topley ahead of him to tell the French captain who he was.

'Halt!' said a voice from within the magazine. 'Come no nearer or I fire this pistol into the nearest barrel.'

'Very well,' Delancey replied, 'I have halted. What are your terms, captain?'

'First, I want the two ships tied together so that the one explosion will destroy both.'

'They are tied together, captain.'

'Keep them so. Then take them into Cherbourg with the tricolour hoisted over the British ensign, surrendering your corvette to the first French man-of-war you see. You know the alternative. I shall shout "Vive la France" and fire.'

'But of course. Nothing more natural. But tell me, captain, how will you know down here what is happening on deck? How can you tell whether we are in Cherbourg or Portsmouth? You had best come on deck and see for yourself.'

'Do you take me for a madman? I stay here with my finger on the trigger.'

'Why not leave your gunner here? He can hold a pistol as well as you.'

'No. I shall stay where I am. He will go on deck, holding his pistol. If you separate the two ships, if you do not make for Cherbourg, if you threaten him in any way, he will fire a shot; and that will be the signal to me.'

'Very well then. What is his name?'

'Jean-Pierre Grobert.'

'Right. We are under his orders.'

'Go on deck then. He will soon join you. Should he not return to me every quarter of an hour I shall fire, destroying both ships and all on board.'

'Agreed.'

As Delancey withdrew he heard urgent whispering inside the magazine. Jean-Pierre Grobert was being briefed on his part. Once on the main deck Delancey told young Topley to explain the situation to all the other officers. All weapons to be uncocked and all captured weapons unloaded. 'Tell them that one shot will be enough to kill us all.' He himself went back to the *Bonaparte*'s great cabin and explained the position to Varignon while the others listened.

'What sort of man is Grobert?' he asked. 'Is he another fanatic and as eager to die?'

'No, no,' replied Varignon. 'The captain is a bachelor, you will understand, disappointed in love, disappointed at being refused rank in the Navy, disappointed again in business; a man with little to live for. Grobert is married with a wife at Nantes –'

'And three children,' added the purser.

'He also has the promise of promotion to a bigger ship,' said Varignon, clinching the matter.

'But he will obey the captain's orders?' asked Delancey.

'Unquestionably,' said the second mate. 'Grobert is not the sort of man to have ideas of his own.'

'I see. Well, Grobert is coming on deck. If you will all give me your parole, I will leave you free to talk with him. I suggest that you raise the question with each other, in his hearing, whether Captain Charbonnier is or is not insane. I need not remind you that all our lives are at stake.'

The parole was given and Delancey led the party to where the gunner had placed himself near the main hatch. From where he was, Grobert could see what was happening and the sound of his pistol would certainly be heard in the magazine. To Delancey's relief, Grobert appeared to be a red faced rather plump little man whose normally cheerful expression was clouded by the current situation. Pistol in hand, he looked the picture of misery.

Going near him, Delancey called out 'We are about to make sail. You can tell your captain that the two ships are still together and that our course is to the north. I have brought your friends on deck and you will perhaps like to talk with them.' Walking off, he gave orders for the *Merlin* to get under way. 'Make sail – main and mizen topsails, forecourse and fore t' gallant.'

He did nothing with the *Bonaparte*'s sails as that ship's

running rigging had still to be knotted and spliced. There was infinite difficulty in steering but the *Merlin* and prize began their slow passage northward.

The worried gunner of the *Bonaparte* went below to report progress, returning presently to say that the captain had merely said 'Vive la France.' Grobert was accosted by the other French officers, who joined with him in anxious conclave. Going over to them, Delancey said casually: 'Nice weather for one's last day on earth, don't you think?' As he strolled away again, Virignon hurried after him: 'But we are heading, surely, for Cherbourg?' Delancey shook his head. 'I am under orders to take my ship into Plymouth and this I shall do.'

'But that puts us all under sentence of death.'

'Exactly.'

'But is there no other way?'

'There is indeed. Persuade Grobert that his captain is a lunatic.'

'But how would that save us?'

'He could tell your captain that we are entering Cherbourg when we are actually coming into St Peter Port.'

'He would expect French officers to come on board and congratulate him.'

'If you can think of a better plan I shall listen to you with the closest attention.'

'I can think of no better plan but what you propose is impossible. Grobert listens to us and then says that he must obey his captain. Nothing we say can shake his determination to do what he has been told to do. He is inconceivably stupid!'

Moving slowly north of Alderney, Delancey was coming to a point at which he had to head east or west and do so while Grobert watched. The man might be stupid but not to the point of confusing the points of the compass. He would know at once whether the *Merlin* was heading for Cherbourg or not. All Delancey had gained so far was time. His only plan now would be to overpower Grobert and send someone below to impersonate him. That would almost certainly fail. On second thoughts, he would have to do it himself and try to shoot

Captain Charbonnier through the blanket, with odds against him of about a hundred to one. His hand, for one thing, would be too unsteady to aim. . . . He was sweating now and hoped that nobody would notice. Perhaps, however, they were all sweating themselves . . .

There came a hail from the *Merlin*'s mast-head: 'Sail on the starboard quarter.' He looked round for a telescope and then realised he was in the wrong ship. He shouted across to Mather 'What vessel is that?' and received the answer 'A lugger, sir, heading this way under all sail.' For a moment he thought that the incident was irrelevant. Then he remembered Sam Carter's promise. This would be the *Dove*, almost certainly, and with the worst possible news. Worst possible? Well, it might prove his immediate salvation. The lunatic in the magazine would hardly want to blow up both ships in time of peace. He decided to heave to.

'Mr Mather,' he shouted, 'back the main topsail!' While the yard was being braced round, he turned to Grobert and pointed to the approaching lugger.

'You can tell Captain Charbonnier that a craft is approaching which may have important news. Then return on deck. I want you to be present when the news is received.' As Grobert went below Delancey repeated much the same words to Varignon and the others. 'If you hear the news when I do you will know that there has been no trick, that the lugger's captain will not be saying what I have asked him to say. If you have a telescope, I should be glad to have the use of it for a few minutes.'

The third mate produced an old spyglass and Delancey studied the lugger. It was the *Dove* beyond question and – yes – she was flying her ensign with the union downwards! So peace had been made and the *Bonaparte* was no lawful prize. He could be sued by the French owners for wrongful detention, for damage and for compensating the wounded. He would have to sell Anneville and realise on all he possessed. He would be left penniless and in debt. He should be grateful, he supposed, if he were left alive but it was, from his own angle, a grim conclusion to the war and a disastrous beginning to the period of peace that was to follow.

The *Dove* hove to near the *Merlin*, striking her reversed ensign and lowering a boat. Ten minutes later Sam Carter reached the *Bonaparte*'s deck and was greeted there by Delancey, who said at once 'Sam, I want these gentlemen to hear the news from you, one of them (he indicated the purser) will interpret if you speak slowly.' Sam looked slightly bewildered but did as he was asked.

'Captain Delancey, gentlemen, news has just reached Guernsey that preliminary articles of peace were signed on October 1st. For some reason there was delay in sending confirmation of this to the Lieutenant-Governor of Guernsey. Peace had in fact been made before the *Merlin* sailed from St Peter Port.'

When the interpreter conveyed the sense of this to Varignon, Grobert and the others, Delancey thanked Sam warmly for bringing the news and then turned to Varignon:

'Please be good enough to tell Captain Charbonnier that the war is over, that you yourself heard the news directly and that there is now no point in making any further sacrifice, whether of ships or men. Take Grobert with you and send him in first.' To the others he said 'I think the moment has come for a glass of wine, to celebrate the fact that we are at peace. Mr Topley, send my steward over with two bottles of champagne. I hope that we shall find the glasses we need in the great cabin.' An informal party was held, Delancey proposing a toast to the First Consul and *Bonaparte*'s purser proposing a toast to George III. They had reached that point when Grobert and Varignon returned.

'Captain Charbonnier will not quit the magazine until both ships have entered Cherbourg.'

'And I am still under orders to go to Plymouth,' said Delancey. 'Gentlemen, forgive me for a moment. I must have a word in private with your gunner.' Outside the cabin he spoke urgently to Grobert.

'We are dealing with a madman. He has to be disarmed. Don't you agree?' Prey as he was to conflicting emotions, Grobert finally nodded.

'Very well then. Return to Captain Charbonnier and tell him that we are bound for Cherbourg and that you have brought him wine with which to celebrate. Has he one pistol or two?'

'He has one in his hand, the other tucked into his belt.'

'That being so, you must take two glasses of wine, one for yourself. Push the blanket aside and enter the magazine with a full glass in each hand. Throw the wine quickly over each pistol to wet the priming. Then step aside. I shall be just behind you. Is that clear?' Grobert nodded and Delancey pocketed two glasses and an opened bottle, half full. They went down to the magazine once more. Delancey picking up a belaying pin on the way. When near the magazine, Delancey took off his shoes, poured the two glasses of wine and handed them to Grobert, telling him by gesture to enter the magazine. Delancey followed him silently and heard him identify himself.

'It's Grobert here, captain. We are under way for Cherbourg with a fine breeze. The war is over and we are celebrating. We have all been drinking your health as a hero but we feel that you should drink too. I have brought you a glass of wine.'

'Thank you, Grobert,' he heard Charbonnier say. 'A glass of wine would be welcome.'

Grobert pushed the curtain aside and there was a scream of rage – the single word 'Assassin!' Springing forward, Delancey brought the belaying pin down with all his force. There was a satisfying thud and the unconscious man fell to the deck. Delancey hauled him out of the magazine, disarmed him, closed the door and locked it, pocketing the key.

'And now,' he said to Grobert, 'we'll join our friends in the great cabin. Perhaps we have earned a drink ourselves.'

The *Merlin* was entering the anchorage opposite St Peter Port with her prize astern and the *Dove* in company. It was an almost windless evening and the sea was glassy calm. Slowly the *Merlin* glided in under all sail, reflected as if in a mirror. 'Boom!' went the first gun of her salute and the smoke billowed, hiding her from view as successive guns fired. When the smoke cleared she was to be seen once more at anchor, sails furled and a boat lowered. The *Bonaparte* dropped anchor at the same time but with less of a flourish. The ship would have to be restored to her owners and it was only a question of how and when. Mr Stirling could at least find consolation in the fact that her captain in the meanwhile was in irons. The *Merlin*'s boat was now approaching the steps near the town church and Delancey in the sternsheets could see that Captain Savage was among those on the quayside. The bystanders raised a cheer as Delancey stepped ashore and Savage met him at the top of the steps.

'Well done, Delancey!'

'But peace was made before the capture. She will not be condemned and I may be liable for damages.'

'Fiddlesticks! The preliminary articles have been signed but peace does not become effective in the Channel until twelve days afterwards. As from the 14th, tomorrow, all prizes must then be restored to the owners. Your prize of today belongs to the captors and three-eighths of its value belong to you; a pretty useful sum if the ship and cargo are as valuable as they look. A capture made after midnight would have landed you in trouble but a capture this morning was perfectly legal. It was touch and go, Delancey, but you are home and dry.'

MAPS

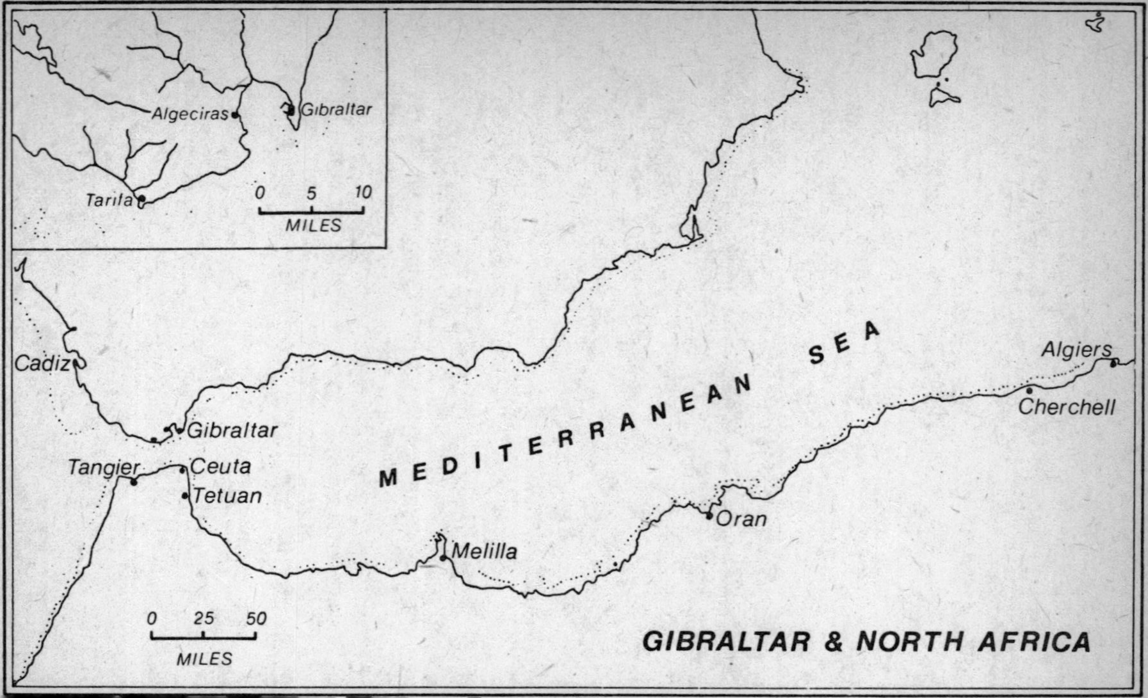
Algeciras
Gibraltar
Tarifa
0 5 10
MILES
Cadiz
Gibraltar
Tangier
Ceuta
Tetuan
MEDITERRANEAN SEA
Melilla
Oran
Algiers
Cherchell
0 25 50
MILES
GIBRALTAR & NORTH AFRICA

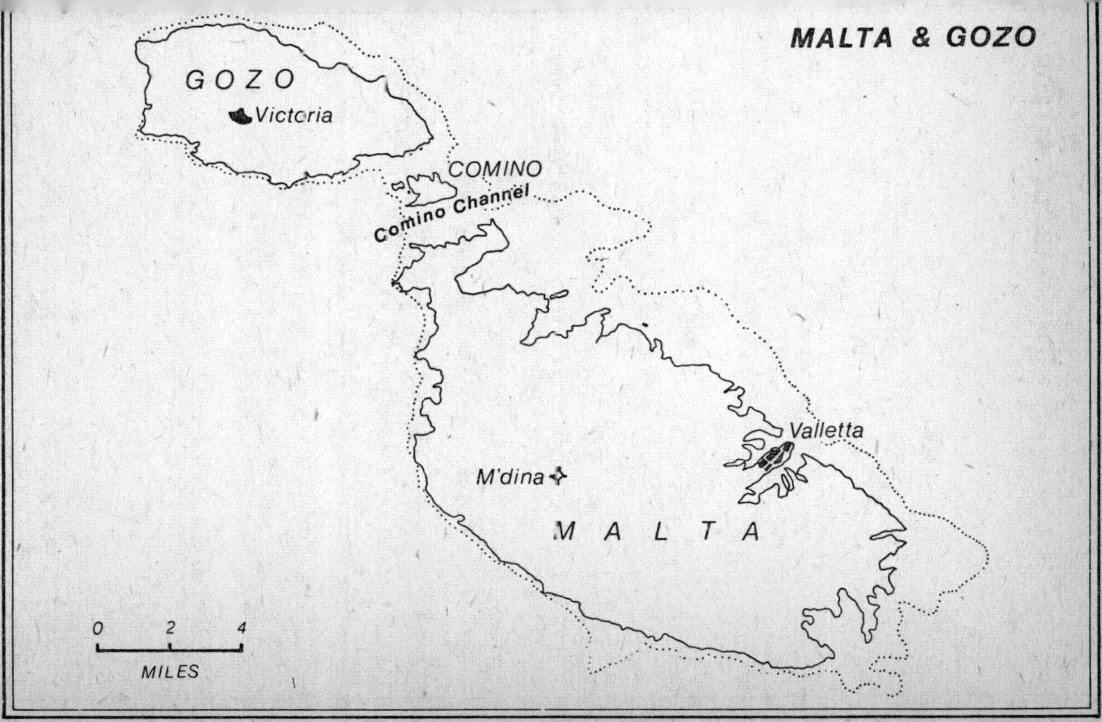
MALTA & GOZO
GOZO
Victoria
COMINO
Comino Channel
Valletta
M'dina
MALTA
0
2
4
MILES

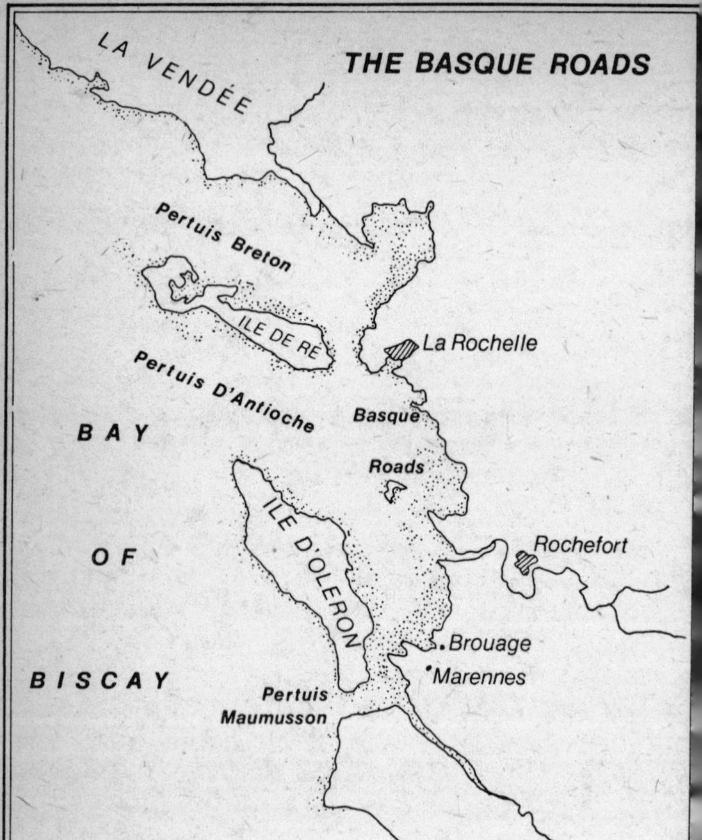
THE BASQUE ROADS
LA VENDÉE
Pertuis Breton
ILE DE RE
Pertuis D'Antioche
La Rochelle
Basque
Roads
BAY
OF
BISCAY
ILE D'OLERON
Rochefort
Brouage
Marennes
Pertuis
Maumusson
0
5
10
MILES

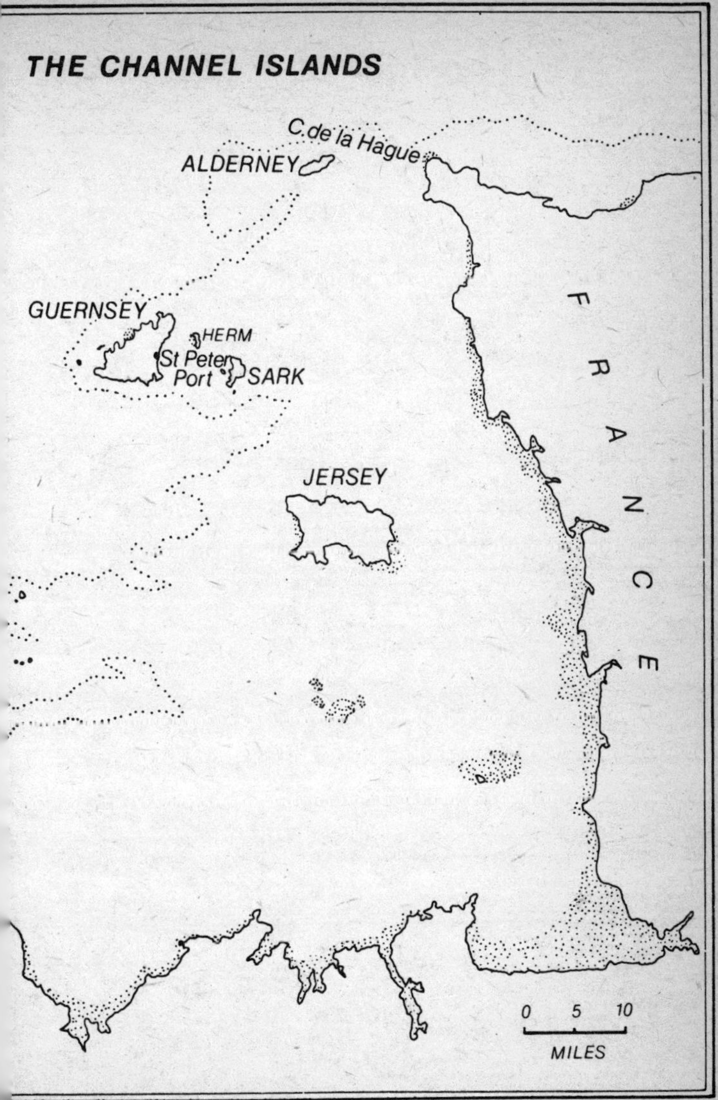
THE CHANNEL ISLANDS
C. de la Hague
ALDERNEY
GUERNSEY
HERM
St Peter Port
SARK
JERSEY
FRANCE
0 5 10
MILES

Also Available From Magnum Books

C. NORTHCOTE PARKINSON

Devil to Pay

This is the first of C. Northcote Parkinson's naval sagas set in the period of the Napoleonic Wars, introducing Richard Delancey, dreamer and man of action, sensitive and tough, a real man of the sea.

By a quirk of fate Dalancey is denied his wish to see action on a ship of the line, and finds himself sent on a dangerous mission to the French coast. His apparent success turns sour, and still without a posting he becomes a revenue man, later graduating to command a privateer. His exploits in the English Channel soon become legendary. But a new turn of events presents him with a chance to redeem himself and return to His Majesty's service – a chance which could cost him his life.

The Fireship

The second novel by C. Northcote Parkinson featuring Richard Delancey.

Having obtained a position on the *Glatton*, a converted East Indiaman with an unusually heavy and devastating fire power, Delancey is soon to see action under Admiral Duncan in the Battle of Camperdown. But the events of the Nore and Spithead mutinies intervene to upset the course of his career; finding himself acting for the defence at the court martial of one of his fellow officers, he acquits himself well, but falls foul of the naval establishment. It is then that he is given command of a curiously antiquated vessel – a fireship.

BEN HEALEY

Captain Havoc

Wrongly convicted of witchcraft and condemned to a living death on a slave galley, the mysterious Englishman called Sir John Havoc could present no further threat to his powerful enemies at the court of Louis XIV, The Sun King. But out of nowhere come his rescuers – a haughty Knight of Malta, an Arab magician neither man nor woman, and a beautiful and seductive Hungarian princess. Then, from the scented harems and pirate-infested coast of North Africa, through the turbulence of plague-stricken Italy begins a thrilling chase in a desperate bid to preserve a 300-year-old secret from the powers of evil . . .

RONALD LOCKLEY

Seal Woman

Cut off by a high rampart of cliffs, the forgotten shoreline of Kilcalla Bay is filled with all the wild beauties of untouched nature. There a young stranger meets and falls in love with Shian, the seal girl, whose past is strangely interwoven with age-old legends about human ties with the inhabitants of the deep. As their relationship develops he decides he will accompany her when she swims with the seals to their refuge far out on the western horizon.

CLARISSA ROSS

417 0257	Moscow Mists	£1.25

J. I. M. STEWART

413 3677	The Gaudy	85p
413 3687	Young Pattullo	85p
417 0189	A Memorial Service	85p

ALAN WHITE

417 0232	The Long Summer	70p
417 0233	The Long Silence	70p

SANDRA WILSON

417 0229	Alice	70p
417 0250	Wife to the Kingmaker	80p

These and other Magnum Books are available at your bookshop or newsagent. In case of difficulties orders may be sent to:

Magnum Books
Cash Sales Department
PO Box 11
Falmouth
Cornwall TR10 109EN

Please send cheque or postal order, no currency, for purchase price quoted and allow the following for postage and packing:

UK	19p for the first book plus 9p per copy for each additional book ordered, to a maximum of 73p.
BFPO & Eire	19p for the first book plus 9p per copy for the next 6 books, thereafter 3p per book.
Overseas customers	20p for the first book and 10p per copy for each additional book.

While every effort is made to keep prices low, it is sometimes necessary to increase prices at short notice. Magnum Books reserve the right to show new retail prices on covers which may differ from those previously advertised in the text or elsewhere.